"How did she die?" Corinne asked in a hollow voice.

"I don't know."

"Shot, like Simard?" Coffen suggested.

"I hadn't the nerve to examine her," Prance said, and went forward tentatively to take a closer look.

He touched her stiff shoulder but could not bring himself to raise her head. When Coffen moved closer to do so, Corinne reached instinctively for Luten's hand. His fingers tightened on hers, but he was looking at Mary as Coffen lifted her head. She saw the pain in his eyes and felt a warm rush of love. It always surprised her that this lofty lord held such deep and true feelings for life's unfortunates. . . .

By Joan Smith
Published by Fawcett Books:

THE SAVAGE LORD GRIFFIN
GATHER YE ROSEBUDS
AUTUMN LOVES: An Anthology
THE GREAT CHRISTMAS BALL
NO PLACE FOR A LADY
NEVER LET ME GO
REGENCY MASQUERADE
THE KISSING BOUGH
A REGENCY CHRISTMAS: An Anthology
DAMSEL IN DISTRESS
BEHOLD, A MYSTERY!
A KISS IN THE DARK
THE VIRGIN AND THE UNICORN
A TALL DARK STRANGER
TEA AND SCANDAL
A CHRISTMAS GAMBOL
AN INFAMOUS PROPOSAL
PETTICOAT REBELLION
BLOSSOM TIME
MURDER WILL SPEAK
MURDER AND MISDEEDS
MURDER WHILE I SMILE
MURDER COMES TO MIND

MURDER COMES TO MIND

Joan Smith

FAWCETT CREST • NEW YORK

A Fawcett Crest Book
Published by The Ballantine Publishing Group
Copyright © 1998 by Joan Smith

http://www.randomhouse.com

Library of Congress Catalog Card Number: 97-94399

ISBN 0-449-00287-X

Manufactured in the United States of America

First Edition: April 1998

10 9 8 7 6 5 4 3 2 1

Chapter One

Coffen Pattle watched as the postman in his jaunty red jacket went whistling into the house next door, carrying a small, cylindrical package, the twin of which Coffen's butler had just handed to him. He returned to the breakfast table for another cup of coffee and opened the package, before ambling across the grass to the house next door to discuss it.

He found Lady deCoventry sitting on a striped sofa in her elegant saloon on Berkeley Square, frowning at a letter printed in black ink on fine vellum paper. The missive had come not folded but in a scroll, like an official proclamation. It was so elegant it belonged under glass. Coffen's scroll, already stained with coffee and smeared with jam, was no longer suitable for framing.

"I see you got one, too," he said, peering at Corinne from bright blue eyes.

He looked, as usual, as if he had just tumbled out of bed. His mud-colored hair was tousled. A sprigged waistcoat stretched taut over his stout upper body, and his blue jacket was rumpled.

"Yes, from Reggie," she replied. "I expect Luten got one as well."

Her fiancé, the Marquess of Luten, lived directly across the street. The letter writer, Sir Reginald Prance, Bart., lived two houses up from him. The four together were known in London society as the Berkeley Brigade, a set of young Whig aristocrats who led the ton in matters of style.

"Did Prance invite you to Granmaison?" Coffen asked.

Prance, mourning a tragic love affair (his mistress had been murdered), had retired to his estate in east Sussex. His excuse

1

was that he was recuperating from a bout of lingering melancholia, but the reason, they suspected, was a fit of pique. He did not approve of Corinne's decision to have a small, private wedding. He had assumed the arrangements for her wedding to Lord Luten would be left in his capable hands. After all, a marquess and a countess—even if she was a widow—deserved a lavish do.

"Yes," she replied, "and I must say I am tempted, but I doubt Luten would leave London at this time."

"You ain't seeing much of him these days. Where you ought to be going is on your honeymoon."

"We decided to wait until Prance is back before making any plans," she said. "Luten is very much involved with this maritime war with America. We have already lost some of our best cruisers. And with Napoleon in trouble in Moscow, the government wants to profit from the situation," she said vaguely. Luten was a member of the Whig shadow cabinet that kept an eye on the Tory ministry. "They keep him very busy at Whitehall."

Despite the exculpating words, Coffen noticed that she was nursing a fit of pique. He nodded at the familiar refrain and reverted to the matter at hand. "Granmaison is only thirty-five miles away. In Luten's rig and with a team of four, you would be there in half a day. Or if he took his curricle, a couple of hours. I'm going anyhow. I miss Prance. I hate him, but I miss him."

Corinne smiled fondly. This good-natured fellow was incapable of hating anyone. "You don't hate him."

"P'raps not. The thing is, he makes me feel worthless. He's too neat. He knows too much. Languages, art, books. He is always up to some new rig, tahrsome fellow." He glanced at his scroll. "What do you make of these hieroglyphics?"

Corinne frowned at the roll of vellum. "He says he has had a 'gorgeous notion,' and we must come at once to discuss it with him. I daresay this scroll and funny square printing are clues. The writing looks Japanese."

"If he's turned into a Hindoo, I'm through with him."

2

"It is the Indians who are Hindus, Coffen. The Japanese are . . . er, Buddhists or some such thing."

"They ain't Christians in any case." Anyone else, in his view, was part devil.

"I doubt it's that. Reg is not religious."

The door knocker sounded in an imperious way that left little doubt as to the caller. "Luten," Coffen murmured.

Within half a minute, a tall, elegant gentleman appeared in the doorway. From his disdainful fingers dangled the familiar scroll. The inherited authority of generations could be read on his aristocratic face. Corinne could never quite believe that she had caught Luten. His jetty hair, casually brushed forward à la Titus, grew in a widow's peak. Finely drawn eyebrows arched over a pair of smoky gray eyes. A strong nose and square jaw lent authority to his lean face. Over his broad shoulders a blue jacket of Bath cloth sat like a second skin. The immaculate cravat at his throat was arranged with simple elegance.

His sharp eyes made a quick tour of his fiancée. As he advanced toward her, his sardonic expression softened to a spontaneous smile. She sat in a shaft of sunlight that lent radiance to her beauty. The contrast of her pale, finely carved face and raven-black hair suggested a cameo, to which a pair of dancing green eyes lent vivacity. Her tall figure was not on display, but he was familiar with every inch of it. He knew it by heart.

He glided forward and placed a light kiss on her uplifted cheek. "*Ravissante,* as usual," he said in a burred drawl that did not quite conceal his infatuation. He nodded at Coffen and said to them both, "I see Prance has summoned you as well."

"Yes, we have been discussing the visit," Corinne replied, trying to read his intention.

A sharp frown drew Luten's eyebrows together. "He can't expect us to go darting off into the wilds for one of his absurd fancies. He might at least have given us a hint as to the nature of this 'gorgeous notion.' Is it fish, flesh, or fowl?"

Coffen's eyes glowed with interest. "You figure it's food?"

"No. Prance don't eat," he said categorically.

"He nibbles a bit of bread," Coffen pointed out. "Mean to

3

say, he's thin as a chicken bone, but even Prance has to eat something or he'd die."

"Prance does not live by bread alone, unfortunately," Luten said. "He requires a deal of attention as well."

"We were just saying how much we missed him," Corinne said. "Coffen is going."

"I thought I would dart down," Coffen said. "It ain't far. Only three hours as the crow flies." Without Prance to correct this assault on logic, Coffen escaped uncorrected.

Corinne looked hopefully at Luten. His bright eyes regarded her blandly. They revealed none of the jealousy he felt. Prance had always had a *tendre* for Corinne. Was this some scheme to lure her away from him? "And you? Are you going?" he asked.

"I would like to. London is quiet at this time of year."

"There is Lady Jersey's ball this week," he said, hoping to entice her to stay, without actually asking her to. There was a peculiar reluctance on both their parts to admit their infatuation. Three years before, Corinne had rejected his offer of marriage. She had been young, just recovering from the death of her husband, and had not realized Luten's eligibility. Luten had taken a pique over the refusal. On her part, she could not quite believe she had finally brought him to the sticking point again.

"It will be only a small do, in autumn."

"Sussex will be blustery this time of year, with winter coming on," he mentioned.

"It is only early October! And a particularly fine autumn, too, if you ever got your nose out the door to enjoy it."

"Prance gets the ocean breeze at Granmaison."

"It is miles from the ocean!" Her shoulders drooped. "You aren't coming," she said, trying to conceal her annoyance.

"I couldn't possibly get away before the weekend." As it was only Monday, this meant the better part of a week away from each other if she went. "But if you wish to go, don't let me stop you," he added with an air of indifference. He even went on to add, "It will leave me free to work without interference."

"I didn't realize I was interfering, as I seldom see you before ten o'clock at night!" she shot back.

"Then you might as well come with me," Coffen said to

4

Corinne, oblivious of Luten's damping scowl. "Glad for the company. We'll leave Luten here to look after England. Carry on the good work, Luten."

She looked at Luten. She would have stayed in London had he asked her. He glanced out the window, with still that air of indifference his pride demanded. "Will you come on the week-end?" she asked.

There were grave matters afoot at Whitehall. The French general Malet was conspiring to end the war and reinstate Louis XVIII while Bonaparte was away in Russia, but he dare not breathe a word of this to mere unparliamentary mortals.

"I'll try to get away early and go down Friday. We cannot let Mouldy and Company run amok." Mouldy and Company was the Whigs' derogatory name for the reigning Tories. "When will you leave?" he asked.

"Today," Coffen said. "We could get away right after lunch, eh, Corinne?"

Again Corinne looked at Luten. He glanced at his fingers, then brushed his nails against his jacket. "I can be ready by then," she said to Coffen.

"You'll take Mrs. Ballard with you?" Luten asked, rather imperiously. It was more a command than a question. He looked at her then, with an angry scowl growing on his brow. Mrs. Ballard was Corinne's companion. He disliked to see his fiancée visiting Prance unchaperoned.

"If she cares to come. Prance's aunt Phoebe is there, so it is not really necessary."

Luten placed very little reliance on Prance's unconventional aunt Phoebe. "Mrs. Ballard would enjoy the little holiday," he said, sensing her rising anger.

"I'll invite her, but she won't want to miss her whist game tomorrow evening. It is the highlight of her week."

"I don't see why you must oblige Prance by catering to his whim. He is only sulking." He had a lowering feeling he was sulking himself and vowed to say no more.

He drew out his watch. Ten-thirty already! He had a meeting with his party's leaders, Grey and Grenville, at eleven. He glanced at Coffen, hoping he would leave and give him a moment's privacy with Corinne to say good-bye or talk her into staying in London. He was angry with her for going, and also felt guilty for not going with her, but would feel worse if he forsook his colleagues in the House. Coffen sat on, scratching at a spot of egg yolk on his trousers.

"I might as well go," she snapped. "There is nothing to do here."

"Well, if you consider a ball nothing. I shall give your regards to Lady Jersey."

"Oh, you will be going without me?"

"Do you object? I shall be here all alone."

"Of course not. Do as you like," she said with a toss of her curls. "I am sure Prance will have some entertainment planned," she added, to retaliate.

Her green eyes flashed angrily. Luten's gray eyes had turned to ice. "No doubt. Then I shall see you on Friday if I can get away." He hesitated a moment, then leaned forward and dropped a cool kiss on her fevered cheek and left.

Coffen rose and stretched. "I'll be getting on home then. About lunch—"

"Do join me. We'll have a bite early and get away by twelve." Before she changed her mind and stayed at home.

Coffen agreed eagerly. It was no secret that his cook could not cook. His coachman could not read a map, and his valet was as unkempt as his master. Coffen had a knack for choosing poor servants, whose minimal abilities deteriorated even further under his lax hand.

Corinne went abovestairs and Mrs. Ballard came to help her pack. A mousy little ecclesiastical widow, Mrs. Ballard discussed at length whether she ought to go with her mistress, before being talked out of it. She didn't want to go and Corinne didn't want her to, but the show of mutual dependence had to be kept up. The lady was the late Lord deCoventry's cousin.

"Who will help you dress, milady, if I don't go?"

"I managed to dress myself for the first seventeen years of my life. And Reggie has plenty of servants. I shall manage."

Corinne had grown up in genteel poverty in Ireland. It was there that her first husband, Lord deCoventry, three times her

6

age, had discovered her and bought her from her papa for five thousand pounds. The four years of their marriage had been unfruitful but otherwise satisfactory. The three years since his death, however, had been more enjoyable for the young widow.

"Well, if you're sure you don't need me. I did want to take care of the linen this afternoon. Will you be wanting to pack your green *peau de soie*?"

"Yes, and the bronze taffeta. Reggie's dinners are strictly formal."

"I'll put paper between the skirts to lessen the wrinkles."

Coffen's packing was less complicated. His valet, Raven, tossed half a dozen shirts and a nightgown into a small trunk, threw in stockings and smallclothes, and folded his evening suit carelessly on top. He forgot to pack evening slippers.

Within the hour, Coffen was back at Corinne's for luncheon.

"I've spent the last hour going over the map to Prance's place with Fitz, but there's no relying on him," he said. "We must keep our eyes open to see he gets us there safe and sound. We continue on the main road as far as Lewes, but not quite. Just t'other side of Heath. At least it's broad daylight. No need to hide our blunt and jewels, eh? Not much chance of the highwaymen getting at us."

This was always a problem for Coffen. He was frequently attacked. Mrs. Ballard *tsk*ed and ate her soup. Corinne toyed with her food. She hardly knew whether she was angry with Luten or herself. She only knew that Luten would be at Lady Jersey's ball without her. The ladies would be throwing their bonnets at him. And in his present mood, he might just decide to catch one of those bonnets.

Shortly after noon Coffen's carriage and team of four clattered out of London, with two small trunks stored on top. Fitz, his coachman, made only two wrong turns, and in both cases, Coffen caught him. No highwayman came to molest them as they traveled the miles through the autumnal countryside, past harvested meadows where cows grazed on the stubble. Fields of grayish sheep dotted the hillsides. An occasional orchard varied the landscape. The trees were fading to yellow and brown. It was an overcast day. Between the lackluster view and the absence of Luten, Corinne was in a sad mood.

Coffen sensed it, and tried to cheer her up by conjecturing what Prance's surprise could be. "Not writing another dashed poem, I hope. His *Rondeaux* were wretched. I never could finish them, though I read most of some of them."

"The vellum paper and black ink are a clue. Perhaps he's having a Japanese-style party. That would be different."

"We won't have to wear long dressing gowns, will we? I wager Raven didn't pack mine."

"Certainly we will. Reg does not do things by halves."

"They don't eat with them twigs like the Chinamen, I hope?"

She shrugged. "Reggie will know."

"Aye, he will. He knows everything and insists on telling a fellow, no matter how often you yawn. He's as bad as a school-master, only worse. I wish I knew as much about one single subject as he knows about them all. Ah, there is Granmaison! At least he hasn't turned it into a Hindoo temple."

In the distance, an arrangement of turrets and peaks suggesting an ancient castle pierced the skyline, like an illustration from a book of fairy tales. This fantastic building seemed the proper abode for Sir Reginald Prance.

8

Chapter Two

As the carriage bowled up the winding drive, enticing glimpses of stone and windows and roofline appeared between the swaying branches of elm and oak. When they rounded the last bend, Granmaison rose before them like a phantasmagoria from a green stretch of lawn. It was a rough old stone bastion below with narrow windows and an oaken door six inches thick, studded with square-headed black nails. The upper stories had been modified over the years at the whim of its various owners to a hodgepodge of styles. There were poinard turret tops, swelling bartizans bulging out at the upper corners, and at the far end a round fortlike tower with a crenellated top and slits in lieu of windows, which looked as if it were an afterthought, but was, in fact, the most ancient part of the whole. The mélange was more curious than beautiful, yet, like its present owner, it had a certain charm greater than the sum of its parts.

As they alit at the front door, a tall, slender gentleman they scarcely recognized as their old friend Prance came walking stiffly forward from around the corner of the house to greet them. He had combed his hair straight back and plastered it to his head with some oil that darkened his brown hair to black. His eyebrows were arranged in peaks at the center, and his usually cynical expression was smoothed away until his face looked like a mask. Even this was not the greatest change. His usual blue jacket, waistcoat, and buckskins had been replaced by a blue and white dressing gown with wide, sweeping sleeves and a broad band around the waist. On his dainty feet in lieu of top boots, he wore black felt slippers. His arms were

9

crossed, with his hands tucked into the ends of the sleeves. He did not shake their hands, but bowed ceremoniously from the waist and said, "Welcome to my poor abode, my excellent friends."

Corinne and Coffen exchanged a startled look.

"Is that you Prance? What the devil ails you?" Coffen demanded, staring in consternation.

"I enjoy perfect health, thank you, Pattle. Corinne, you are looking a trifle peakish. Luten is not coming?"

"He'll try to join us on Friday. Business at the House."

"Still harping on minor quotidian cares, I see, but never mind. Come along the *roji* to the teahouse for refreshment."

Coffen frowned. "Eh?"

"The dewy path, Pattle."

"What teahouse? Have you opened up a tea parlor? If your pockets are to let, you should have told us. There must be some better way to make a living than peddling cups of tea."

"There is no charge, and my pockets are not to let. I have turned my gazebo into a teahouse. *C'est tout.* This is the dewy path," he said, withdrawing one hand from his sleeve and gesturing to the perfectly dry way in front of him, where rudimentary flat stones had been placed in an irregular path along the side of the house. "I have had it constructed along the lines formulated by the great Sen Rikyu. It is to remind one of a trail through meadows to a sylvan retreat."

"It reminds me of the perfectly good cobblestone path you used to have here. Who is this Senricky?" Coffen asked suspiciously. "Do you have a new neighbor?"

"Alas, no. Sen Rikyu is an ancient Japanese tea master. I shall introduce you to the ritual of *chanoyu*." He led them along the path for what seemed a long distance.

"I knew there'd be some Japanese tomfoolery at the bottom of your 'gorgeous notion,' " Coffen grumbled. "I'll remind you I ain't ancient yet. I'd prefer a glass of wine."

Prance, who could usually be relied on for a good argument, just smiled tolerantly. He drew to a stop in front of a wooden gate and said, "We shall linger a moment here, in the outer garden, to contemplate nature."

"What garden?" Prance asked, looking about in vain for a flower.

Prance gestured to a few small yews and a hawthorn that had been tortured into strange shapes. "It is, perhaps, hyperbole to call it a garden yet, but in time . . . The stone lantern can be lit at dusk," he said, pointing to a plinth two feet tall, atop which sat a lantern. "Breathe in the pure country air," he said, and took a deep breath.

Coffen inhaled deeply. "It still smells like the stables at least," he said approvingly.

"What is the gate for, Reg?" Corinne asked, as she noticed it was not attached to a fence.

"It is to separate the outer garden from the inner," he explained. "You will find the mood becomes increasingly restful as we proceed to the inner garden." As his guests were displaying no sign of appreciating his handiwork, he opened the gate and ushered them into the inner garden without further contemplation.

"What sort of flowers do you plan to put in the garden?" Corinne asked, in a civil way.

He shook his head as if she were a moonling. "No flowers, dear. Just the peaceful mosses, ferns, and that little juniper you see there, hugging the ground, while one wayward branch reaches a tentative finger to the sky."

"I see," she said, with a speaking glance to Coffen, who furrowed his brow in confusion.

"I hope you ain't turning Hindoo on us, Prance. Dash it, this ain't a garden, and no amount of hyperboling makes it one. You could teach that Senricky fellow a thing or two about gardens."

Softened by the implied compliment, Prance said, "You'll feel better when you've had your tea. Come along to the teahouse."

They continued over a few more stepping-stones to the teahouse, né gazebo. The marble, domed structure had been built in the last century by Prance's papa in emulation of Prince George's Brighton pavilion. Prance had had the gracious entranceway lowered to form an ugly and inconvenient crawl-in door. He bent his head and entered. Corinne and a grumbling Pattle followed him into the tearoom. A servant outfitted in a plain blue dressing gown was preparing the tea at a table at the side of the room. Coals were arranged in some sort of metal box with a grated top. Those tantalizing aromas of yeasty breads, mutton or ham, and an apple tart were noticeably lacking, as was any evidence of their presence in the gazebo.

"What have you done to the seats?" Pattle demanded. "What are we supposed to sit on?"

Prance gestured to a low wooden table, with pillows placed around it on the floor. One yellow chrysanthemum with its stem removed floated in a bowl in the center of the table. The servant placed a rough earthenware teapot and three small, handleless cups in front of Prance.

"The point is to keep it simple, to add to the serenity," he explained. "The accoutrements are of the most humble, to keep us humble. I have spurned the gaudy display of a bouquet, but allowed us the indulgence of one perfect blossom." He explained that they really ought to share one communal teacup, but as Corinne and Pattle were new to *chanoyu*—and as he drew the line at drinking out of someone else's cup—he had provided them each with one. He showed Corinne to her cushion, then knelt gracefully on one beside her, lowered his derriere onto his heels, and with a dramatic swoop of his flowing sleeves, lifted the teapot.

After a deal of grumbling and a damping frown from Corinne, Pattle sat on the cushion with his knees jackknifed out at either side. "Hold on. There's something in my cup," he said as Prance poured the tea.

"That is a chrysanthemum petal, Pattle, to remind us of the approach of autumn."

"We don't need reminding. It's perishing cold out here." He stuck in his finger and drew out the offending petal. His eyes scoured the table. "Is there any milk and sugar?"

"One does not use milk and sugar!"

"I hope this ain't your idea of a 'gorgeous notion,' a cold cup of tea in a chilly old gazebo with no chairs to sit on."

Prance smiled tolerantly. "This is only the overture. After tea, I shall take you to the *nina*."

Coffen narrowed his eyes. "Who?"

"Not who, what. The *nina* is the garden. Thus far you have seen only the suburbs of the real *nina*."

"Why didn't you say so? I hope there's flowers in it."

"It is still under construction. I wanted to hear your ideas— after I have initiated you into Tachibana Toshitsuna's *Sakuteiki*, of course."

The strange syllables flowed smoothly from his lips, or as smoothly as the alien sounds permitted after long practice.

"You ain't initiating me into anything of the sort," Pattle said firmly. "What the devil are you talking about anyway?"

"Literally, *Sakuteiki* means *Notes on How to Make a Garden*. The elegant simplicity of the title! Only a Toshitsuna could have come up with it. Nature reduced to its most basic elements—rock, water, sand, a few simple plants. I came upon a copy of the book, translated into English, in the library the day I arrived. I was seeking solace in Shakespeare. You know how I dote on William." Prance was on a first-name basis with all the literary greats. "My discovery of *Sakuteiki* was the hand of providence, the very thing I needed to lift me out of that dreadful melancholia after Yvonne's death." He lowered his head a moment and drew a long, shuddering sigh in remembrance of his beloved, whom he had known for scarcely a week.

Corinne did not laugh, but let Prance enjoy his fit of histrionics. She wished Luten were here to enjoy it with her.

"You hardly knew the woman," Coffen reminded him.

"Ah, but I knew her so intimately. Two hearts beating as one in wildly abandoned passion."

"Is that why you invited us here, Reg? To help you design the garden?" Corinne asked, feeling she had been duped.

He overcame his grief and said playfully, "That is only part of the reason. I have already drawn up an outline of the *nina*, or if I become ambitious, I shall make it a *kaiyushiki*—a stroll garden. It is to be built behind the apple orchard, in any case. The little mound of earth there will be my *shumisen*, and of course, we shall want water. You must help me decide between *ito-ochi*, *nuno-ochi*, and *tsutai-ochi*. I am inclined to *nuno-ochi*. Water falling in a broad sheet will be more effective with my bridge of Wu."

His listeners turned blank faces to him. He might as well have been speaking Greek. It was precisely the reaction Prance had anticipated. It gave him an excuse to ride his new hobbyhorse.

"One of those high-arched bridges one sees in Japanese artworks. The *shumisen* is a sort of minimountain. In the Buddhist cosmology it symbolizes the hub of the universe. I shall have difficulty finding an *ishitate-so* in England."

Coffen reamed out his ear with the end of his finger. "Eh?"

"A priest who arranges the stones. I am not referring to an English priest, of course."

Coffen struggled to his feet. "That's it! I've heard enough. I ain't turning Hindoo, and that's the top and bottom of it. Rubbish, dragging us miles to sit on a cold floor, drinking cold tea, to see a garden with no flowers. You've turned loony, Prance. You ought to see a doctor—or a clergyman. And furthermore, you shouldn't have greeted Corinne in your nightshirt."

Prance rose to his feet and bridled. "Are you referring to my *kirimon*?"

"How the deuce should I know? I don't talk Japanese."

"I had this especially made, with my *mon* on the back." He turned to display the back of his *kirimon*, where three lions passant, his family crest, had been stylized to have an Oriental look.

"You said the garden was only part of the reason," Corinne said. "What is the rest of the reason you invited us, Reg?"

He sniffed. "If you share Pattle's disinterest in the finer things of life, then no doubt you will disagree with me, but *I* thought the *nina* would make a fine venue for your wedding."

"Venue!" Coffen cried. "Ain't that where they try criminals?"

"It has that connotation in legal parlance," Prance admitted. "More generally, it means a place where an action or event occurs. What do you think of the idea, Corinne?"

She was appalled. To be married in a field in late autumn,

14

away from either London or Ireland, was not at all her notion of a nice wedding. "Would it not be rather chilly?" she said.

"I had planned to erect a screen against the north wind. Since my neighbor stole those ten acres of prime oak forest from me and chopped down the trees, there is a stiff breeze there, where I am building my *nina*. Or we could wait until spring for the wedding, as Luten seems in no hurry," he suggested mischievously.

"I'm afraid we would not like to wait that long," she replied.

Pattle just shook his head. "This is the worst idea you've ever had, Prance, and that's saying a good deal. Go and put on your trousers and let us sit on a sofa. Do you have any wine, or have you emptied your bottles and put in cold tea?"

"The austerity does take a little getting used to, but I am convinced that you will eventually come to appreciate the refinement of Oriental culture. How it has simplified my life! I am through with vain, lavish desires. I shall introduce you into the Zen philosophy."

He allowed himself the Western privilege of taking Corinne's elbow to lead her back along the *roji*, through the gate, and thence to his saloon, where Coffen finally got his chubby bottom onto a comfortable chair, and was handed a glass of wine.

He looked all around the sybaritic splendor of Prance's saloon, where no refinement had been spared to create a room fit for a hedonist. Prance's Zen hand had not yet invaded this space. There were fine European paintings on the silk-hung walls. The chairs were as soft as eiderdown; mahogany furnishings gleamed from regular applications of beeswax and turpentine. Only the carpet was from the East, and it was Persia, not Japan, that had created the masterpiece. Coffen thrust his stumpy legs toward the blazing grate and drew a deep sigh of contentment.

"Where is your aunt Phoebe?" Corinne asked. Prance's maternal aunt, Phoebe Dauntry, kept house for him. She was a spinster of a certain age.

"Tante P—my little Gallic play on words; *Tant pis*, French

15

you know—nipped down to visit Lord Simard, my neighbor. I wonder what can be keeping her. She knew you were coming."

"That would be her now," Coffen said, as the front door opened.

They all looked to the doorway as Miss Dauntry came in. She was familiar to them from former visits. They were accustomed to seeing a lively if slightly hagged dame with rouged cheeks, flashing dark eyes, and Titian hair that owed its vivid tint to chemistry. One of her main preoccupations was to present a dramatic appearance. They found themselves staring at a wild-eyed lady whose gown was mussed and bore traces of dust and nettles. Her elaborate Titian curls were falling about her ears, and round circles of rouge stood out on her pale cheeks.

When she placed her hand against the doorjamb to steady herself, Corinne noticed her fingers were soiled. There was earth beneath her fingernails.

Phoebe said in a shaking voice, "Lady deCoventry—and oh, it's Mr. Pattle, of course. How nice to see you. I quite forgot you were coming today. Such an incon— Oh dear. Welcome to Granmaison. And now if you will pardon me, I shall just nip abovestairs and—pardon me."

On this disjointed speech she turned and raced toward the staircase.

Coffen sniffed. "She's been having tea in the teahouse, I fancy."

"No, something is the matter," Prance said, and went flying after her.

Coffen said, "I wager Prance has been at her with his Zen and Senricky. I don't know about you, but I plan to dart back to London at first light tomorrow and warn Luten to stay away."

Corinne had a dreadful, sinking sensation that there was more than Zen the matter with Miss Dauntry. She looked like death, or as if she had just seen death at close hand.

Chapter Three

The quarter of an hour until the return of Prance and Miss Dauntry passed comfortably for Pattle, with the wine bottle at his elbow and the fire warming his toes. Corinne was less easy. Her Irish spirit had intuited the tragic death of Prance's lady, Yvonne, and she felt the same sense of dreadful foreboding now. Miss Dauntry usually greeted her with open arms. The two ladies were not at all like mother and daughter, more like a favorite aunt and niece. Miss Dauntry had shown Corinne that advancing years need not take the joy out of life—but something had taken the joy from her old friend's life now. Her agitation grew as she waited, listening to Coffen natter on about leaving at first light tomorrow.

Even when Prance led his aunt Phoebe into the saloon, her hair and gown now restored to their usual splendor, the feeling remained. Prance had also changed out of his *kirimon* and put on normal clothes. Phoebe's dark eyes glittered as she greeted the guests. The fingers that accepted a glass of wine trembled. Corinne noticed that, while she had washed her hands, traces of earth remained imbedded under her nails.

"What must you think of me, Lady deCoventry, making such a wretched entrance!" she said. "It was that hound of Simard's that caused it. Hannibal broke loose and chased after me. I went tearing into the meadow and tried to climb a tree— no easy accomplishment for one of my years and size. It made a shambles of my toilette."

"Simard ought to have the beast put down," Prance said, and *tsk*ed. "He took a bite out of the gardener last month. I carry my pistol when I go to call on Simard, and shouldn't hesitate to shoot if Hannibal attacks me. Why did you call on Simard, Tante P? Was it that business of Bertie's inheritance?"

Bertie was Miss Dauntry's nephew and Prance's cousin. His maternal parentage was seldom spoken of. Phoebe's young, unmarried sister, Cybill, had been ruined by the debauched Lord Simard when she was an innocent girl of sixteen. As Simard was married at the time, he could not marry the mother, nor had he shouldered his financial responsibilities as he ought. As a graduate of the infamous Hellfire Club, he would have required a kingly fortune to recompense all the women he had ruined. Cybill had been a lady, however, and he had at least been gentleman enough to pay for the mama's extended visit to Ireland for her accouchement, accompanied by Phoebe. There, Bertie had first seen the light of day, and his mama had seen the last. She had had the decency to die in childbirth. An imaginary Mr. Puitt had been invented, having been hastily married off to Cybill and dying like his wife before Phoebe brought the infant back to England, where she had raised him with all the love of a childless, lonesome woman.

When Simard had felt like it, he provided food, shelter, and some tutoring, though he had never sent the lad to one of the better schools. The meager dowries of Cybill and Phoebe, along with some contributions from Prance, had taken up the slack when Simard failed to provide. Upon Bertie's reaching his maturity five years ago, Simard had cut off all funds. He said it was time to let Puitt fend for himself. Bertie, a large, good-natured man who was half educated and half a gentleman, though not accepted by the best society, had been at loose ends.

Prance had come to the rescue. His own mama had recently died, so he brought Phoebe in as his housekeeper and made Bertie his steward. Bertie lived in the gatehouse but ran quite tame at Granmaison. It was understood that when Simard died, he would leave Bertie five thousand pounds. As Simard aged and became addicted to the bottle, his estate deteriorated. His temper, which had always been bad, worsened. That summer he had announced that he could not see his way to leaving Bertie anything. Phoebe had not had a minute's peace since.

By turns she tried badgering, haranguing, and coaxing Simard into fulfilling his obligations. Nothing fazed the wretch.

"Yes, of course, it was to do with Bertie's money," she replied. "It is the only thing that would convince me to visit the old satyr. I thought if I took him a bottle of my cherry liqueur, it might turn him up sweet."

Coffen smiled in memory of maraschino, his favorite drink. "Good stuff, masherino," he said.

"And did it work?" Prance inquired of Phoebe.

"No, it is a lost case. I fear Bertie must spend the rest of his life as your steward, Reggie. It is very kind of you. I don't know what would become of us were it not for your generosity."

"It is you and Bertie who do me a favor, Tante P. It is lovely to know you are here, looking after Granmaison for me. No one else would take such a keen interest in the estate as family does. There is none of that wondering if some stranger is picking your pocket during your absence. You and Bertie look after my poor belongings admirably. We must see if we can do something more for Bertie. Build an addition to the gatehouse when he marries, and increase his salary."

"So kind, Reggie, but even with all that, he can hardly hope to marry a lady."

"He's a good-looking fellow, though," Coffen mentioned. "And a sound man. I like him."

"Everyone likes him—except his papa," Miss Dauntry said grimly. "He is not wicked enough to appeal to Simard."

They were interrupted by the sound of feet running up the stairs from the kitchen. Blakeney, the butler, went darting down the hall to arrest the servant before he had the temerity to enter the saloon. There was a whispered colloquy in the hall, then Blakeney came to the door and said in an ominous voice to Prance, "A word in private, sir, if you please."

"What is it, Blakeney?" Prance said. "You can speak freely. These are my nearest and dearest friends."

Blakeney's flat, impassive face was calm, but his eyes sparkled. "There has been an accident at Atwood, sir."

"At Lord Simard's place?" Prance asked, with moderate interest. "What happened? Did that hound of his bite someone?"

"No, sir. His lordship was shot—fatally."

Prance leapt to his feet. "Good God! How did it happen?"

"It is unclear, sir. Mr. McAlbie, the justice of the peace, has been called to look into the matter. As it is Lord Simard, the servants did not think it fit to call the local constable. I felt you might like to know."

"Yes, of course. Thank you for telling me," Prance replied. "Is there anything I can do?"

Blakeney's eyes slid to Miss Dauntry and examined her with a close scrutiny. Corinne noticed it, and remembered her premonition of disaster. She also remembered Phoebe's distraught condition when she arrived home. Corinne looked at Phoebe and noticed the knuckles clutching the arms of her chair were bone-white, like her face.

"McAlbie seems to think Miss Dauntry might be of some help in his inquiries, as the servants informed him she was on the premises at the time of—or shortly before—the accident."

Prance laughed. "You didn't shoot him, did you, Tante P?"

"Of course not!" she cried, in a strangled voice.

"Well then," Prance said. "After all, it isn't a case of murder, is it?" he asked, in a rhetorical spirit.

"It seems it might be, sir," Blakeney replied.

Coffen bounced out of his chair with an unaccustomed vigor. "We'll just toddle on down to Atwood and look for clues," he said. He placed great faith in the efficacy of clues in solving murder cases. "It'll be something to pass the time."

"I'll go with you," Corinne said at once, rising to her feet.

Prance was not tardy to join them. "Will you come, Tante P?" he asked.

She said nothing, but just shook her head and staggered to her feet.

"If McAlbie wishes to see my aunt, then he can come here," Prance said. "She is unwell. Go have a lie-down, Tante Phoebe. I'll handle McAlbie."

She took a deep breath and said, "You run along, Reg. I'll join you later if I feel up to it."

"If you go, take the jig. Blakeney, fetch my pistol, in case Hannibal is still on the loose."

Blakeney bowed and left at a magisterial gait to fetch the pistol. By the time Corinne got on her bonnet and pelisse, the butler was holding the door for her and the gentlemen.

When they were outside, Prance said, "There's a shortcut to Atwood through the spinney."

He led them to the opposite side of the house from his Japanese garden, skirted the meadow, and continued through the spinney. Tall trees rustled around them as the north wind blew. An occasional bird clung to a branch, too dispirited to sing. The sky overhead was leaden, adding to the dismal atmosphere. Corinne thought of London. If she had stayed there, she would be attending some party with Luten this evening. And instead she was worrying about Phoebe, and what her involvement could be in Simard's death. Surely she had not murdered him?

As they were traveling at a fast pace, Coffen became short of breath and begged Prance to slow down.

"You don't suppose your aunt did it?" he asked Prance.

"Of course not, but I wouldn't blame her if she did. I expect it will be nothing more than a hunting or poaching accident. Simard's woods are full of poachers. He extracts such inordinate rents from his tenant farmers that they help themselves to his game. Otherwise they'd never have meat on their tables. He's a nasty piece of work."

"A rack-renter," Corinne said. "It sounds quite like how the absentee landlords go on in Ireland."

As they emerged from the spinney, the west elevation of Atwood rose before them, across a stretch of home garden. Its architecture was the antithesis of Prance's house. Where Granmaison was a small building, all frills and flourishes and turrets and towers, Atwood was a massive gray limestone rectangle that looked more like a public building than a house. A series of statues decorated the east front, but from this angle there was nothing to distract the eye save the long facade, punctuated at regular intervals with windows on three stories.

"Looks like a prison," Coffen said.

Prance gazed at the fortresslike walls. " 'Stone walls do not a prison make,' Pattle."

21

"They can be brick, of course."

"My meaning was that the interior is not lacking in creature comforts—though that was not Lovelace's meaning."

The truth of his statement was evident as soon as they entered. Prance led them to the main entrance on the east side. Dolman, the aged butler, admitted them into a vast expanse of Connemara marble hallway, with heavily embossed plaster walls and ceiling. The candles in the extravagant girandole overhead were not lit, but a shaft of sunlight from the doorway struck the hanging crystals and reflected dancing rainbows on the walls. The lands of Atwood might be in some disrepair, but all was well tended inside the house. No dust marred the surfaces. Fresh bouquets of flowers on various tables sent a pleasant whiff of perfume wafting through the hall, blending with the tantalizing aroma of roasting beef.

And who would eat it? Simard lived alone with only his servants in this vast house. He had no legal children. He was not the amiable sort to invite impoverished relatives to share his home. Any elderly aunt or cousin who might earn her keep by looking after his house would be reluctant to live with a man of such an evil reputation. The scent of brimstone lingered still over this superannuated graduate of the Hellfire Club.

"Mr. McAlbie is in his lordship's study," Dolman said portentously, and led them down the marble-floored hall, past walls inlaid in carved oak and hung with oil paintings.

The study door hung open. McAlbie came out to greet them. He was a typical country squire. Prance had once used him as the model for John Bull in a series of English characters he painted to illustrate a friend's book. McAlbie had not changed much in the three intervening years. He was still in his fifties, fat, gouty, wearing an ill-cut blue jacket and a head of graying hair that looked as if his housekeeper had shorn him with one hand while stirring a pot with the other.

"Where is Mrs. Dauntry?" he asked, looking from one to the other of the new arrivals.

"In a state of shock, McAlbie," Prance replied. "Unable to join us. Dreadful business." He introduced Lady deCoventry and Coffen. McAlbie smirked like a schoolboy at the lovely Lady deCoventry and seemed to forget the reason she was here. He offered her wine, which she declined.

Like Coffen, she was eager to get into the study and search for clues. Over McAlbie's shoulder she saw a large, oak-lined room with a French door on the far wall. A fire smoldered in the vast stone grate, with crossed swords hung on the wall above. A set of bronze statuettes of nude ladies in erotic poses prancing across the mantel was the only reminder of Simard's scarlet past.

As soon as she entered the room, she noticed the over-powering smell of brandy and soon discovered the cause. A decanter had been thrown or dropped on the stone apron of the fireplace. The brandy had seeped into the stone and run onto the floor beyond. She noticed it in a passing glance before she spotted the body slumped over the desk.

She had seen death before and wondered if she was be-coming inured to it. This time it did not seem so bad. Whether it was because the other victims had been younger women, or because Lord Simard was so universally unpopular, or because his manner of death was less gruesome, she could not say. Her other encounters with death involved a seamstress who had been strangled, and Prance's friend Lady Chamaude, who had been brutally stabbed. Lord Simard had been shot through the heart, but this was not noticeable at a glance. His pose suggested he had nodded off to sleep with his head resting on the desk blotter.

It was only when McAlbie lifted the late Lord Simard's head and shoulders that she saw the dark stain spreading over his striped waistcoat onto the lapels of his blue jacket. She just glanced at the face, and thought it did not look much different from the last time she had seen it, except that his eyes were closed, and the silver at his temples was more pronounced against the sable hair around it.

He had been a handsome older gentleman when she first met him five years ago and must have been an Adonis in his youth. Dark hair, flashing black eyes, pale skin, regular features, and

23

good teeth, the whole spoiled by an air of dissipation. Had those eyes and lips smiled in pleasure instead of leering in priapic invitation, she could have liked him.

She felt a nudge at her elbow. Coffen leaned toward her ear and whispered, "Believe I've found a clue."

Chapter Four

While McAlbie pointed out details of the scene to Prance, Coffen drew Corinne aside. He narrowed his eyes to slits and tossed his head toward the desk, where two used brandy glasses sat side by side.

"Seems he had a caller, eh?" he said in a low voice. "He wouldn't use two separate glasses himself."

"Good work, Coffen!"

"And another thing, I don't see any signs of that masherino Phoebe says she brought him. I wouldn't mind having a gargle of it."

"Maraschino," she corrected automatically.

"That's the stuff. It ain't here. The servants may have taken it away. Pity. Before I can find out what's wrong, I've got to discover what's right. Mean to say, for a thing to be a clue, it's got to be different from normal. I'll have a chat with some of the servants. Women for choice. They're better talkers. Old Dolman looks as if he wouldn't squeal if he was stuck. You see what you can get out of McAlbie. He's sweet on you, to judge by his smirks."

He wandered into the hallway. Corinne scanned the room for clues, and found it odd the French window into the garden was open in October, when the breeze was strong enough to require a fire in the grate. McAlbie, who kept darting admiring glances at her, soon joined her.

"The French door was open when Betsy—she's the parlor maid—discovered Lord Simard's body," he said, "P'raps he took a stroll in the garden. The roses are still pretty—like your cheeks, milady." He went to close the door.

"Dolman says Simard had no callers except Aunt Phoebe," Prance explained to Corinne. "Perhaps she left the door open when she left."

"Or he had another caller," Corinne said. "Your aunt Phoebe doesn't drink brandy, does she? There are two glasses on his desk."

"Now, isn't that a caution!" McAlbie exclaimed, back and still smiling. "I never noticed that. This lady is sharp as a bodkin, Sir Reg. She will solve the little mystery in no time. Not that there is much mystery. You'll notice that stand of cedars on the little mound there, right in line with the window and the desk. Someone was taking a shot at a rabbit and missed. There'll be no finding the culprit. His bullet went straight through the window into poor Simard's ticker. Dead in a second, and not a bad way to go. Dead as a doornail. What ought one to do? Bury him, I daresay."

"Has Malton been notified?" Prance asked.

"Now, there is something I could be doing. The heir—oh my yes, I must notify Malton."

"Have you called a doctor?"

"Dolman did it. Spadger ought to be along any moment. He was attending a birthing this morning. I heard it as I came from the village on my way here. Poor Mrs. Olsen always has a long struggle of it—and then presents her husband with another gel. Five of them in a row. I would give up if I were Olsen. Well, I'll be off, then, to speak to Malton. A happy day for him! He never thought he would be Lord Simard so soon. Simard was only in his sixties and healthy as a horse, despite the way he lived. Drinking, whoring, dear me! And with all his efforts, he never produced a son. A legitimate one, I mean. Plenty of the other sort, I shouldn't wonder."

"I'll keep an eye on things here until you return, McAlbie," Prance said.

"I appreciate it. Not the thing to leave a body alone. Look around, see if there's anything I forgot to do. Ought I to throw a blanket over Simard, do you think?"

"I'll do it."

26

"I'll have a word with your aunt after I call on Malton. No need for her to leave Granmaison if she's feeling poorly."

After he had left, Corinne went into the hall to join Coffen. She found him chatting to the downstairs maid, whom he introduced as Betsy. She was a thin, severe-looking woman of thirty-odd years, with her thick brown hair pulled under a cap.

"Betsy says she heard two shots," Coffen said. The glow of suspicion lit his blue eyes. He was on the trail of clues. "Lord Simard was only shot once. The first shot must have missed."

"McAlbie thinks it was poachers. There's no poachers this close to the house," Betsy said firmly. "In the woods from time to time, but not as close as the shots I heard. I was dusting in the hallway. I heard a shot from that mound of cedars. I thought it might be Mr. Puitt out shooting rabbits. He does that for his lordship from time to time, when they get too plentiful and invade the home garden. This close to the house, it could only be Puitt."

"And the other shot?" Corinne asked.

Betsy drew her lips into a prim line and considered a moment before speaking, as if determined to tell the truth, the whole truth, and nothing but the truth. "I'm not sure it was a shot. I heard a loud crack from his lordship's study or maybe just outside the window. It was hard to tell. It sounded like a shot, but when I went to the door, Miss Dauntry told me his lordship had dropped the brandy decanter. She told me there was no hurry to clean it up, for it landed on the stone apron and could do no harm. She said she was having a private talk with his lordship, and they didn't want to be interrupted in the middle of it. It would be about Mr. Puitt," she added knowingly.

Corinne deduced there were no secrets in this house.

Betsy's brown eyes narrowed and she said with an air of self-righteousness, "Mind you, I didn't see his lordship when I went to the door. Miss Dauntry just opened it a crack and stood in the opening, almost as if she wanted to hide something. I heard her chatting on after I closed the door, but I didn't hear him speaking. I told Mr. McAlbie. He didn't make nothing of it. Pretty odd, I thought."

"Are you suggesting Lord Simard was already dead?"

27

Corinne asked bluntly. It was fear that lent the harsh edge to her words and sent Betsy scampering to defend herself.

"I'm just saying I didn't see his lordship alive after that shot, milady. Or hear him, just Miss Dauntry talking a blue streak. Nervous, like."

"But you are not certain it was a shot? It might have been the decanter falling?"

"It could of been," Betsy admitted. "Odd she didn't want me to clean it up."

As they talked, a pretty young female servant appeared at the end of the hallway. She came darting forward, twittering in excitement. Glossy chestnut curls bounced out from under her cap. A pair of dancing brown eyes were aglow. Her white apron was pulled taut across a generous expanse of chest.

"Did they find out who did it, Betsy?" she asked.

"This is Mary, the upstairs maid," Betsy said, by way of introduction. "McAlbie says it was an accident." She sniffed.

"I wager it was. I saw a man in that stand of cedars this very afternoon."

"Who?" Coffen barked.

The pretty young servant cast an arch smile at him. "I don't know, sir. It was too far away for me to tell. I just saw the shoulder of a blue jacket. He was wearing a curled beaver and riding a brown hack. A real gent."

"When? What time?" he asked.

"I haven't got a watch, have I?"

"And would have no use for one, since you can't tell time," Betsy added spitefully. "Was it around the time you heard the shot, Mary?"

"I didn't hear no shot," Mary said, "but it was ten or fifteen minutes before Dolman told Tom his lordship was dead."

"That would be about the time I heard the noise," Betsy said. "As close to three o'clock as makes no difference."

"How long after you heard the decanter break did Miss Dauntry leave?" Coffen asked Betsy.

"I didn't see her go, nor did Dolman. She must of left by the French door in his study, the way she came in."

"How long before Simard's body was discovered, and who discovered it?"

" 'Twas Dolman. He went to remind his lordship he'd asked for an early dinner, since he had a meeting of the Parish Council tonight. That was about ten minutes after I spoke to Miss Dauntry. Dolman told me first, then Tom. Tom was there, trimming the lamps in the hall."

Mary, who had been listening with her ears stretched, spotted a young footman at the end of the hall. He was handsome, in a cocky sort of way, with a wave of dark hair and a good build. Mary curtsied and ran off to join him.

"That's Mary's fellow, Tom," Betsy said, with an air of injury. Then she added slyly, "Tom is one who won't be sorry at this death."

"Lord Simard was fond of Mary, was he?" Corinne asked.

"That's one word for it," Betsy said. "If there's nothing else, ma'am, I have my work to tend to."

"That'll do for now," Coffen said. When she had left, he said to Corinne, "A spiteful chit and homely, too. Jealous of Mary's looks, I shouldn't wonder. She has hair like a thatched roof. An affliction I'm familiar with. It can turn a person sour. But if Tom was jealous of Simard, he might have slipped downstairs, waited until Simard was alone, and shot him after Phoebe left."

"No, that would be three shots, or two and the decanter falling. Let us go back to the study and see if Prance has discovered anything."

"Yes, let's. One thing no one has mentioned, it might have been suicide. For all we know, Simard might have been head over ears in debt or dying of some fatal disease. We'll see if there's a pistol on the floor. There was none in his hand. It might have fallen."

"Don't suicides usually shoot themselves in the head?"

"It ain't a rule. There's a *Code Duello*, but no *Code Suicido*. Let us see if there's a note hidden under his body."

When they returned to the study, Prance stood in front of the grate, looking at the broken decanter and spilt brandy. He looked up and said, "Any clues, Pattle?"

"We're still looking. Help me heave the body up and have a look for the suicide note."

"You think it was suicide?" Prance asked, brightening.

"If there's a gun."

With this incentive, Prance braced himself for the unwelcome task of touching a corpse. The two men carefully lifted the inert body from the desk. There was no note, only a blotter with a large quantity of blood soaked into it.

"He kept a gun in the right-hand drawer," Prance said, wiping his hands on a clean handkerchief. "He showed it to me once. Said he never meant to be caught off guard if a distraught husband called on him."

"Perhaps one did," Coffen said.

Corinne drew out the top right-hand drawer. When she saw no gun but only a welter of papers, she tried the two drawers beneath it. They were tidier. The papers were in folders, but there was no gun. Coffen repeated the performance on the left side. He found a bottle of brandy in the bottom drawer, but no gun. They also raised the head and shoulders again and looked in the small middle drawer, still without luck.

"There's no gun. It wasn't suicide," Prance said.

"Wait! He might have dropped it. Let me check the floor," Corinne said, and looked beneath the desk. She had again that dreadful foreboding that it was murder, and Phoebe was involved. When she got up, she said, "No gun. He's wearing knitted slippers. That is odd."

"Not really. I do it myself. Bunions," Coffen said, and knelt down to examine the slippers for clues. "Hole in the toe. It don't look as if he was expecting company, or he would have put on better slippers. Another thing, he hadn't been outside. No earth on the bottom, just a bit of dust. No brandy splashed on him either. You'd think it would have, if he dropped it. I wonder who called on him after Phoebe left. Betsy said he had no callers." He rose. "Let us see if there's any clues by the French door."

The days were short in October. Twilight was already falling. He lit a lamp and took it to the French door. The flagged patio beyond the door was not amenable to footprints.

No suspicious trail of dusty prints invaded the study. "If anyone came in this way, we'll never know it."

"Phoebe might have dropped the brandy," Prance suggested. "She was here."

"Aye, she was, but Phoebe told Betsy that Simard dropped it. We'll ask your aunt, but she didn't bring him any bottle of masherino, Prance. I asked Betsy. Nobody took one out of this room, and there ain't one here now. Funny Phoebe'd lie about that."

"That was an excuse for the visit," Prance explained. "She didn't plan to discuss Bertie's money troubles in front of you, until I asked her. That was gauche of me."

"I'm not suggesting she killed him, Reg," Corinne said, "but you must have noticed how distracted she was when she came home."

"Who wouldn't be, when they'd been chased by a mad dog?"

"That's true," Coffen said, nodding. "And there's that second used brandy glass on the desk. I wager he had a caller. Maybe one of them distraught husbands you mentioned. Or maybe Tom had a glass after he shot Simard."

They discussed what Coffen had learned from Betsy about Phoebe's visit and the broken decanter. "Made quite a point of saying she hadn't actually seen Simard alive after that noise that Phoebe said was the decanter breaking, but Betsy hinted could have been a bullet."

"She's a spiteful hussy," Prance said, "but sharp. Not much gets past Betsy."

"Any chance she might be lying?" Coffen asked. "Does she have a grudge against your aunt?"

"She has a grudge against the world. She's the sort who would put the worst possible slant on things, but not tell an outright lie. She's chock-full of religiosity. Loves the notion of hell—for other people. That sort of a religious fanatic."

"It seems we'd best have a chat with your aunt Phoebe," Coffen said. "And we'd best send for Luten, too."

Prance pokered up and said, "We can solve this little mystery without Luten's assistance. He did not choose to come when I invited him. He has more weighty problems than a mere murder."

"Very likely, but he'll be sore as a gumboil to miss out on this if it's murder."

"What do you think, Corinne?" Prance asked.

Like Prance, her feelings had been hurt, and she was much of a mind not to beg him to come, though she wished he would. "He is much too busy," she said.

Prance drew a weary sigh. "This is not the sort of visit I had envisaged," he said. "I see work on my *nina* grinding to a halt if we become mired in another case."

Coffen scowled at him. "Don't blame us. She's your aunt."

Chapter Five

Corinne lay in bed, wide-awake at three o'clock in the morning, mentally reviewing the events of the strange day just past. The sound of Phoebe snoring in the room next door had kept her awake for an hour, until eventually she became accustomed to the racket and dozed off. Phoebe was not snoring now, but it was still Phoebe who kept her awake. Surely poor, attention-loving Phoebe was not a murderess. She was a kindly soul and more a mother to Prance than his own mama had ever been.

Suddenly, Corinne heard sounds of movement in Phoebe's room, then the door open. She decided to follow her and try to discover what had really happened at Atwood. McAlbie had taken Phoebe's being asleep with good grace when he came to call, but she would have to tell the truth sooner or later.

By the time Corinne lit her bedside lamp, threw a negligee over her nightgown, found her slippers, and went into the hall, she was just in time to see a drift of white dressing gown disappearing around the bottom of the stairs. Phoebe was carrying a lamp. Corinne had left hers behind. As the darkness closed in around her, she wished she had brought it with her. She ran swiftly and silently down the stairs. Again, she arrived just as Phoebe was making a turn. Phoebe did not head for the stairs down to the kitchen as expected. She chose the other route, to the conservatory that was attached to the side of the house by a glassed-in passage where Prance wintered a dozen palm trees. The trees were there now, forming an allée along the length of the passage, and casting swaying shadows on the floor as the moonlight struck them.

Was Phoebe meeting someone? Corinne peered down the passage and saw the lamp flame flicker. It darted to and fro through the moving plants in the conservatory, like a giant firefly flitting about in the darkness. There was plenty of cover to allow Corinne to slip in behind her, undetected. She concealed herself behind a life-size reproduction of a statue of Hebe, wine server to the gods, whose wine jug had been turned into a planter to hold a billow of jasmine. The fronds brushed against her cheek and shoulders as she stood peering through the shadows.

The warm, moist air of the conservatory was sweet with the perfume of flowers in bloom. The warmth was welcome after the dart through the chilly house, but it did not completely stop the shivering. What was Phoebe doing? She didn't look around as if she were expecting to meet someone, but went directly to the gardener's worktable in the corner and picked up a small object. She worked her way through the potted plants to the farthest corner. Corinne edged closer behind her to watch.

Phoebe held a little hand spade. She dug into the earth of a lemon tree growing in an enormous earthenware pot in that far corner. When she had a hole of the proper size, she took a dark object from her pocket and put it in the hole. Then she shoveled the earth back in, turned, looked all around, put the hand spade back on the worktable, and sped the length of the conservatory, out along the glassed passage, and disappeared into the house. She had buried something under the lemon tree, and Corinne had a pretty good idea what that something was. The size was right.

The moving branches in the conservatory suddenly seemed menacing. Corinne's instinct was to run like a hare out of the place, but curiosity overcame fear. The corner was not so very far away, and the moonlight slanting through the window wall gave plenty of illumination. She took herself by the scruff of the neck and went forward swiftly, ignoring the fronds of palm and fern that grazed her cheeks and shoulders with ghostly fingers. And when she got there, she realized she didn't have anything to dig with. The worktable was in a far, dark corner, but she could see where the earth in the pot had been disturbed.

She dug her fingers into the soft, moist soil and felt the cold, hard touch of metal. She dug a little deeper and pulled out a pistol.

It was a fancy piece, the barrel done in chased silver that had been allowed to tarnish. The stock was plain ivory. Perhaps a dueling pistol. Luten had told her the bucks spurned silver mounts as they reflected the light and made the duelist vulnerable.

The next question was, what should she do with it? If she took it, and Phoebe came back here looking for it— Should she hide it? She didn't intend to give it to McAlbie. If Phoebe had killed Simard, it was likely an accident. Even if it wasn't, she no doubt had a good reason. She would tell Prance and let him decide. After all, Phoebe was his aunt. She wished with all her heart that Luten were there. A warm glow engulfed her to think of Luten, who always seemed to know exactly what to do and had the courage to do it, even when it involved breaking the law, so long as the end justified the means. A mixture of Solomon and Machiavelli, Prance had called him.

She should have let Coffen send him a note telling him of the murder. She'd do it tomorrow. Surely he would come when he realized she was quite possibly prey to a murderer on the loose. In any case, the gun was safe here and could be recovered when and if necessary.

As she stood with the gun in her fingers, she thought she heard a sound at the entrance to the conservatory. She froze, listening. Was that a footfall? A mouse? No, only the branches of trees swaying in the breeze, touching the various statues Prance had sprinkled here and there amid the plants. She stuffed the gun back into the hole, covered it, and patted the earth into place, while still listening. No more sounds came to turn her skin to gooseflesh.

She brushed off her hands, dreading the passage back, with all the clinging leaves and vine tendrils brushing her face. She would make a quick run for it, not stopping until she was safely in the house. She took a breath, lifted up the tails of her negligee, and began the dash out of the conservatory.

It was just as the doorway loomed ahead of her, with the

moonlight glancing in the windows, painting the row of palms a ghastly silver, that it happened. One strong hand grabbed her wrist. Another clamped over her lips, muffling the scream that rose in her throat. The hand holding her wrist moved; she felt a strong arm pinioning her against a man's hard chest. Her heart slammed against her ribs, and her throat was suddenly dry as a bone and aching.

The man's head leaned menacingly over her shoulder. His chin brushed her cheek. "Not a sound," he said. Then she heard a gasp of breath, and simultaneously recognized the voice. "Corinne? What the devil are you doing here?"

She turned to face him. He loosened his grip, but still held her in the circle of his arms. Shadows lent a touch of danger to the familiar lineaments of his face. "Luten! You frightened me to death!" she scolded, but she fell into his arms, trembling with relief and joy.

He had hurried through his work at Whitehall and invented a family emergency to explain his sudden trip. Done it all to be with her. And when he gazed down on that face he prized above life itself, he could not be angry with her. Only happy that he had come—and she seemed equally happy to see him. Everything was all right between them.

His arms tightened around her, then he lowered his head to kiss her. He felt the quick quiver of response shiver through her as their lips touched. It was always that way with them. Their verbal communication was lacking, but their bodies knew what they felt and wanted. The conservatory seemed suddenly a garden of love. The miasma of exotic perfumes was heady, lending another charm to the encounter.

The kiss was escalating to passion when he felt her mood change. He could sense the heat cooling and kissed her harder, tightening his arms around her while she tried to withdraw. What was happening? Didn't she love him anymore? What notions had Prance put in her head?

She pushed him away with both hands and stared at him. In the shadows, her green eyes looked black. There, where he expected to see love, he saw what looked dreadfully like suspicion.

36

"Coffen summoned you, didn't he?" she asked. "I told him not to. You didn't come to see me. You only wanted to help solve the murder."

His muscles tensed at the word. "What murder?" he asked in a hard voice.

"Don't you really know?"

"Would I be asking if I knew?" he shot back.

She read his anger, and regretted her suspicious question. "Old Simard was murdered this afternoon," she said. "Shot to death in his study."

"Good God! Why didn't you let me know?"

She peered up through her eyelashes and said, "I didn't want to interrupt your work, Luten."

His frown deepened at this blatant hypocrisy. Only a few hours ago she had been trying to tempt him into coming. Then he thought of the danger around her and his grip on her tightened insensibly until his fingers bit into her arms. "Why are you running around alone at night in your nightshirt when there is a murderer on the loose?" he demanded gruffly.

"I found the gun that killed Simard. Phoebe buried it under the lemon tree. I thought Coffen must have written you. He said he would. If he didn't—if you really didn't know—why are you here?"

Luten did not say the obvious thing, which was the truth and would have pleased her. He was here because he regretted their argument and could not work with it nagging at him. Theirs was a strange sort of love affair. While they were madly in love, both were uncertain of each other, and unwilling to demonstrate the depth of their feelings.

Corinne was a widow and from a modest family. She could hardly believe the illustrious Marquess of Luten, who could have had his pick of heiresses, really loved her. Luten's uncertainty was of a different origin. He was fully aware of his eminence on the Marriage Mart. Yet despite it, Corinne had rejected him the first time he offered for her, shortly after her husband's death. Not only rejected him, but in a nervous fit of surprise, had laughed at him. The memory of it still caused a spurt of anger and a strange ringing in his ears.

"I managed to finish up my business in the House. Curiosity to learn Prance's 'gorgeous notion' brought me."

"Oh." He watched as a shadow of disappointment moved across that pale, beautiful face he loved. "That, and of course, eagerness to see you," he added stiffly.

She tossed her shoulders. "How flattering. Well, you have stumbled straight into a murder case, Luten. You must hurry up and solve it, for you will want to be getting back to the House soon. And pray, why were you lurking in the conservatory like a sneak thief?"

"I was trying to find an unlocked door to get in without rousing the house. I know Prance keeps the front and back doors locked. I thought the gardener might have left the conservatory door open. He did. I had no sooner entered than I heard someone coming. She—I thought it was a he at first—seemed to be moving stealthily. Always suspecting the worst, I thought I was about to capture a thief. Then Phoebe streaked by, looking like death. I decided not to add to her fear by leaping out at her. Then I heard you coming. I thought it was you who had frightened Phoebe, so I stopped you."

"I see. Well, I expect you want to know all about the murder."

"Indeed I do. I have a feeling this may be a long story. Shall we go into the saloon and be comfortable?"

He took her arm and led her down the glassed-in passage to the saloon.

Chapter Six

Corinne sat on the sofa, Luten in a chair opposite, while she outlined the details of the case thus far. She was annoyed that he didn't sit beside her; he knew she would be, but did it anyway to show his annoyance at not having been called to help solve the murder. Also, he wanted to understand exactly what was going on and he knew that if he sat beside her, he would reach out and touch her, and from there, anything could happen. He only touched her with his eyes. She looked especially fetching in a lacy white negligee that suggested the softly feminine curves it covered. A cloud of jet-black curls, tousled from sleep, framed her delicate face. He found it hard to concentrate on what she was saying. In the end he stopped looking at her and stared at the Fragonard on the far wall instead.

Corinne gave a brief, businesslike account of the day's doings. She was miffed with Luten. He gave no indication of paying attention to anything but the murder.

"So there you have it," she said, when she was finished.

He was silent a moment, thinking. "Were it not for Phoebe's burying that gun, I would think it was an accident," he said. "I know she has loathed Simard forever, since that business with her sister, Cybill. He is not much loss to the world."

This sounded as if Luten didn't plan to take a hand in the crime. "He will be a loss if Phoebe ends up in the dock. We must do something, Luten!" she declared. "The party can spare you for a few days. You have been working day and night."

"I planned to stay a few days, but I hoped we would have better things to do than chase after a murderer."

"Well, you were mistaken," she said bluntly. "What you

would be doing if it were not for Simard's death is have your poor ears lambasted with Prance's 'gorgeous notion,' which is to turn Japanese and study Buddhism and build a stupid garden with no flowers."

"Ah, taken up religion, has he?"

"Yes, and he wants us to be married in his rocky old garden in the dead of winter, wearing dressing gowns, which he calls *kirimons* or some such thing."

He felt a rush of tenderness as he gazed at her angry little face, with her green eyes flashing. "It will pass, love," he said tenderly, and rose to join her on the sofa. "It's our wedding, not Prance's. We'll do it the way we choose."

"If we bother to do it at all," she snapped. "You already treat me like a wife—ignoring me."

"Do I hear an echo of Prance's philosophy in that speech?"

"It's true, isn't it?" she parried. Luten drew a weary sigh.

"Of course it's true. Why else did I travel all these miles, but to ignore you?"

The longcase clock in the corner emitted four tinny chimes. "You should get to bed, Luten. You must be dog-tired," she said, gazing at him. At this hour the incipient stubble of whiskers was showing on Luten's usually impeccably shaved face. She found that suggestion of masculinity exciting.

"And we must be up with the fowl in the morning, to begin solving this case, but first . . ." He drew her into his arms for a long kiss. As her soft body melted into his, he felt a fierce rush of love and longing.

Corinne's Irish temperament, swift to wrath, was equally swift to forgive, and be cajoled into love. That whisper of whiskers on his lower face was excitingly rough, lending a new sensation to the embrace.

When her response left no doubt as to her feelings, he said, "This is really why I came."

She smiled sweetly and said, "Liar," in a caressing voice.

Despite his late night, Luten was at the table at eight the next morning. Coffen and Corinne were there, tucking into gammon and eggs, which Coffen had arranged with the chef the night before.

"You want to grab some of this meat," Coffen said, after greeting Luten. "Prance is on a fish and rice diet. Did Corinne tell you he's turning Hindoo?"

"I heard he's taken up religion."

"You haven't seen him. He's slicked his hair back and taken to wearing dressing gowns and felt slippers in the daytime. I fear he's slipped a cog this time. You want to have a word with him. He'll listen to you. Making a dashed cake of himself, tahrsome fellow."

When word of Luten's arrival was taken abovestairs to Prance, however, he decided against donning his *kirimon* and felt slippers. They were not suitable for the sort of investigations the day would no doubt hold. He was suitably attired in a blue jacket of Bath cloth, a striped waistcoat, fawn trousers, and gleaming top boots when he entered the breakfast parlor. Only an echo of the hairdo and rearranged eyebrows remained to hint at his new passion.

"Luten, welcome!" he cried, pouncing forward to shake his hand as if Luten had come from the New World, instead of only thirty-odd miles away. "No doubt Corinne has informed you of what is going on here."

"I have heard."

"I intuited you would come when you received my message. You must have ridden *ventre à terre*."

Corinne's ears perked up at this news. She didn't know Prance had written to Luten. Her eyes narrowed at Luten.

He said, "Message? I didn't receive any message. When did you send it?"

"I sent a footman off on my fastest steed last night to summon you. At Coffen's insistence."

"I must have left London already. I left at eleven."

"Ah, then you passed my lad on the road. I sent him off around ten."

Luten quirked an eyebrow at Corinne and smiled, as if to say, "So there!"

Prance went to the sideboard to fill his plate and returned to

41

the table with four fingers of toast and a small serving of kippered herring. The latter was a nod to his new philosophy; he didn't actually eat it, nor much of the toast for that matter. He despised eating. It reminded him that the spirit, the breath of life that was Sir Reginald Prance, Bart., was reduced to a physical animal when all was said and done. He severed an inch from one toast finger with his knife and fork and nibbled at it reluctantly.

"Is Phoebe up yet?" Coffen asked.

"She will be down presently," Prance said. "I had a word with her. She's looking better after a good night's sleep."

"She didn't have a good night's sleep," Corinne said. "She was up in the middle of the night, hiding Simard's gun."

This alarming statement had to be explained in detail.

"Are you sure it was Simard's gun?" Prance asked.

"I've never actually seen Simard's gun, but what other gun would it be? It's in the pot of the lemon tree in the corner, if you want to have a peek before she comes down." She described it to him.

"That sounds like Simard's," he said, and leapt up to fly off to his conservatory. He was soon back. "It's Simard's gun right enough, and it's been fired recently. I could still detect a whiff of gunpowder."

"What did you do with it?" Coffen asked.

"Put it back where she hid it. The safest place for it. McAlbie won't find it there. This looks bad for poor Tante P, does it not? She has a reason, opportunity, and now weapon."

Coffen lifted his head from his plate and said, "Someone fired it. That ain't to say she did."

"Why would she hide it if she hadn't used it herself?" Luten asked.

"To protect someone else. Bertie is who I'm thinking of. We haven't heard where Bertie was at the time."

They fell silent at the sound of approaching footsteps. Within seconds, Miss Dauntry came sailing through the doorway. She may not have slept the night through, but she had recovered remarkably from the day before. She looked

42

very like her old self as she came swanning in, her full figure encased in a lutestring gown of red and white stripes that would have looked garish on a young dasher and made Phoebe look like an awning that had magically grown legs. Her Titian hair was arranged in a steeple of curls that added six inches to her height. Prance winced at the sight.

"Tante P. Surprise!" he said. "Luten has joined us."

She patted Luten on the shoulder. "You wouldn't want to let this Incomparable out of your sight for long," she said, nodding toward Corinne. "Not with two such dashing bucks as Reg and Pattle here to amuse her." She greeted the others, then went to the sideboard and loaded her plate from force of habit, but when she sat down, she only toyed with her food. "Of course, they've told you about poor Simard's death?" she said to Luten.

"We were just discussing it, Tante P," Prance said, and leveled a questioning look at her.

"Dreadful luck, the poor man, being hit by a stray shot like that. Mind you, he never kept the poachers in line as he ought. Bertie has warned him any number of times." She lifted her dark eyes and looked around the table, from one to the other. Every eye was staring at her with disbelief.

"Of course, it was an accident," she said firmly.

"Did you see anyone about outside?" Coffen asked.

She lifted her chin and said defiantly, "Yes, I saw a poacher in the bushes directly before he was shot."

"Sure it was a poacher?" Coffen said. "The reason I ask, Mary, the upstairs maid, says she saw a fellow in a blue jacket. The sort a gent wears, she said."

"Mary is mistaken. It was a snuff-colored coat of fustian."

Whatever the color, she could obviously not have determined the material from a distance.

"How do you know when he was shot?" Coffen asked.

Phoebe's pink face paled noticeably. "Why, I assume it occurred shortly after I left, as he was still chirping merry then. I saw the poacher as I was leaving. I regret now that I didn't send the fellow off with a flea in his ear. Who was to know he would accidentally shoot poor Simard?" Simard was more usually called "that wretched Simard" or worse. "Poor fellow," she added, drawing out a handkerchief and dabbing at her dry eyes.

"Sorry to distress you," Coffen said, "but there's one more little thing. Did you happen to notice how many brandy glasses were on his desk when you was there? Used ones, I mean."

"One, I believe. The tray was on top of a side table. He brought the bottle to the desk, poured himself a drink, and offered me one. I refused. Ladies don't drink brandy, and so I told him. Why do you ask, Pattle? He was not poisoned. He was shot—accidentally."

"There was two used glasses on his desk when we got there."

She frowned. "I could not swear there wasn't another glass on his desk. I wasn't looking in particular. In the heat of argument, you know—" She came to a guilty stop. "You know how old friends fall into foolish arguments."

"He's reneged on Bertie's inheritance," Prance explained to Luten.

Phoebe left off pretending. Her eyes snapped and she said in a waspish voice, "He refused to budge. You cannot think me fool enough to shoot him before I got him to reinstate Bertie in his will, if that is what all these questions are in aid of."

Prance directed a warning glance at his colleagues. "Of course not, Tante," he said soothingly. "But McAlbie will be coming to question you, and you must explain why it took you an hour to accomplish the short walk from Atwood to Granmaison."

"I told you! That hound of Simard's chased me up a tree."

Coffen shook his head. "Then you'd best tell McAlbie he kept you marooned there for the better part of an hour, Miss Dauntry."

"He did," she said. "And now if you are through with this interrogation, I shall retire to my room." She rose despite their protests and sailed to the door. Before leaving, she turned and said, "Don't forget Mr. Malton in your investigations, gentlemen. He is the only one who profits from Simard's death."

"Pity. I would not have upset dear Phoebe for worlds," Prance said.

"None of us would," Corinne said. "You should have asked her about burying the gun," she added.

"I'll have a word with her in private later."

"She's right about one thing," Coffen said. "When you get right down to the *kooey bono* of it, it's Malton who comes out on top. He's the heir. Does he need the blunt, Prance?"

"Ho! Do foxes need chickens? He needed it desperately. Pockets to let—unfurnished, in debt to his ears, according to rumor. And that is not the worst of it. Simard was letting the estate go to rack and ruin. There'd have been nothing left to inherit but the title in another few years."

"Gambling?" Luten said.

"Simard was indiscriminate in his smashing of the commandments. Every vice that has a name. Gambling, wenching, to say nothing of bad farming practices. He paid no heed to his estate and refused to hire a bailiff, though the house itself was kept up for his comfort. As he had no son of his own to inherit, he seemed determined to see that Malton got nothing. A thoroughly bad apple. There's not a soul in the parish will be wearing crape to mourn his passing. Which reminds me, I expect I ought to put a black band on my jacket and some crape on my hat," he said uncertainly.

"You just said not a soul would," Coffen reminded him.

"It is known as hyperbole, Pattle."

"Eh?"

"An exaggeration not actually intended to deceive, but to lend emphasis to an utterance."

"Ah."

"I notice Phoebe wasn't in mourning," Corinne said. "Should she not wear black, for the looks of it?"

Prance nodded. "I'll mention it to her. I doubt she'll do it, but Bertie really ought to don his crape. And I shall celebrate. I now get back the ten acres he stole from me. I don't know why Papa let him get away with it. He didn't want to become involved in a lawsuit and agreed to let Simard have the acres until his—Simard's—death, at which time they were to revert

45

to Granmaison. Most felicitously, as those acres are to be the backdrop to my *nina*. You have not seen my *nina*, Luten."

"I wouldn't be in a yank to reclaim them acres if I was you, Prance," Coffen said.

"Why not? They're mine."

"They're a dandy motive for murder. Not for the ordinary fellow, but for a luna—a Hindoo like you, they are."

"Buddhist, Pattle. And for your information, violence is against the Buddhist faith."

"Pity them *neenyas* ain't against it. Rubbishing thing, no flowers." He rose to replenish his plate.

Prance gave a scornful "Bah! One cannot expect a plebeian like Pattle to appreciate the austere beauty of a *nina*, but I am convinced your refined taste will adore it, Luten. It is nature reduced to its basic elements. The lyricism of water, the timeless beauty of rocks, the muted glory of mosses, a few gnarled branches for contrast, with a *shumisen* behind it all for a backdrop. I shall plant bamboo on those ten aces. The graceful swaying of those linear stalks will give a marvelous effect, whispering in the wind—if they can tolerate our climate."

"It sounds stunning, Prance, but shall we take a quick trip down to Atwood first, to see what is going forth?"

Prance pouted. "Just as you wish. I daresay it is too much to hope that you would put the contemplation of beauty before the seductive allure of murder."

"You've got that right anyhow," Coffen said, and snabbled down his gammon and eggs to join them.

Chapter Seven

The gray sky of yesterday had brightened to a deep azure blue. Autumn sunlight dappled the countryside to all shades of green and yellow. A light breeze moved the branches. Prance delivered a lyrical lecture on his *nina* while they all made the short trip to Atwood.

Luten listened with half an ear, and said, "Very interesting, but a garden without flowers sounds like a contradiction in terms."

Prance had heard that complaint before and had his answer ready. "*Au contraire!* In old Anglo-Saxon, a garth, which is the origin of the word *garden*, meant only an enclosed space. My *nina* is certainly that. It will be enclosed all around, with the *shumisen* in the rear."

"Ah, of course."

Prance continued with his lesson. As the group emerged from the spinney, Luten gave a mental groan to see the surrounding fields lying fallow. Wild grass grew; it might have provided cattle feed, but Simard had neither put his cattle in the field to pasture nor harvested it.

Coffen looked at the derelict field and said, "Was Simard into *neenyas* as well?"

Prance ignored him. He said to Luten, "Dreadful waste. The mind revolts to see such poor management. Similar signs of neglect are everywhere about the estate. He doesn't harvest the fruit from the orchard, but lets it rot on the ground—and shoots at anyone who goes after the windfalls. I had it from Malton that Simard doesn't even bother to breed his cattle, and you know what a pelter that puts the cows in, to say nothing of the bull. It is cruelty to dumb animals. Really, the man was asking to be killed. I told Malton he ought to have the running of Atwood looked into. There are laws about that sort of thing, when an estate is entailed."

"Why didn't he do it?"

"He was afraid of riling the old boy. Said he wouldn't put it a pace past Simard to set fire to the place if he brought the law down on his head. Simard might very well have done it."

As they neared Atwood, the stone walls rose impressively against the blue sky. Dolman had lowered the flag to half-mast to indicate the death of Simard. Someone, presumably the butler, had also had the funereal hatchment hung on the front door. Dolman answered at the first knock and bowed politely.

"Mr. McAlbie is in the study with Mr. Puitt," he said. "I shall tell him you are here."

He led them down the corridor and into the oak-paneled room. Lord Simard's body had been removed. Having memorized the general geography of the room, Luten began to assess the details. He was happy to see the broken decanter was still on the hearth, the brandy glasses on the desk. McAlbie, looking as provincial and unkempt as ever, came forward to greet the guests. With him was Phoebe's nephew, Herbert Puitt, a younger version of the same type.

Like McAlbie, he was several pounds heavier than the ideal. Unlike McAlbie, a part of the extra weight was muscle. His hair was brown, not gray, but its uneven cut suggested he used the same local barber. His jacket was poorly cut and dusty, as were his top boots. The familiar aroma of the stables was discernible at close range. Yet with all his sartorial faults, no one would ever take him for anything but a gentleman. His face was pleasant without achieving anything like handsomeness. His manner was mild and friendly, beneath the facade of grief demanded by the occasion.

"Good day, Prance, Luten," he said, making his bows around the group of newcomers. Being uncomfortable in the company of ladies, he saved Corinne for the last, and just nodded shyly at her. "A terrible thing, this death. I wager Aunt Phoebe is pretty upset. I went to call on her last night. Blakeney

48

told me she was sleeping, so I didn't disturb you when you had company, Prance."

"Blakeney didn't tell me. You should have come in," Prance said. Then he turned to McAlbie. "Are you getting any forwarder with your investigation, McAlbie?"

"The inquest will be tomorrow. I think we may count on a verdict of death by misadventure. Accidental, by person or persons unknown," he added vaguely, to cover all bases. "I sent a notice to Granmaison asking Miss Dauntry to attend, if she is up to it. If not, I daresay we can hobble along without her evidence. We have Betsy Jones, who discovered the body and heard the shot, you know. The coroner says 'twas likely a rifle shot that got him—because of the distance the shot traveled, from the cedar hedge."

"A rifle, you say!" Prance exclaimed. He felt a great wave of relief wash over him. Phoebe was in the clear. The pistol in the planter was innocent, then. He would contemplate the mystery of it later.

"Or it could have been a pistol shot at closer range, eh?" Coffen mentioned.

"Oh, aye, hard to tell from the size of the ball the coroner pulled out, but since there's no gun, it couldn't have been suicide," McAlbie pointed out. "A poacher got him, as we thought. Mary, the upstairs maid, saw someone in that little stand of cedars. She will be at the inquest as well. The only one who stood to gain anything from this death is young Malton, and his whereabouts at the time of the accident is well accounted for. I had a word with him yesterday. He was in Lewes, visiting a friend."

"And I was overseeing the planting of that east corner of your forest, Prance, in case anyone thinks I had a hand in it," Puitt added. "Looks like an accident, right enough."

Looking at Puitt's innocent, open face, Luten thought the man incapable of dissembling.

"Any word on the will?" Luten asked.

"It was read last night. Sinclair, the lawyer who is handling it, had instructions it was to be read on the day of his death. Puitt was there," he said.

49

They all looked with interest to Puitt. His sorry demeanor told them he had received no magnificent bequest. "I only got a bunch of worthless stocks for dead companies. P'raps they were worth something when he bought them. Sinclair tells me the companies are defunct. It means I don't get a sou. Malton gets the lot." He shook his head in bewilderment. "An odd will. Very odd."

"Shabby treatment," Prance said.

"I believe Puitt is referring to the burial arrangements," McAlbie explained. "Whoever would have thought old Simard would be so superstitious? He wants his burial delayed two days. During that time, his body is to be watched around the clock by two reliable persons who are to be paid for their vigil."

"There is a grisly job for someone," Coffen said.

"Did he give a reason for this bizarre request?" Prance asked.

"No, but I believe I know the reason. You are all too young to recall the few cases in the last century where a wrong diagnosis was made and a few bodies climbed out of the coffin, giving rise to a fear that others were buried alive. One of them was on his way to the burial ground. The mourners heard a wail and dropped the box. Imagine their horror when the lid opened and a live man stepped out. If, at sunset on the third day, Simard has shown no signs of life, he is to be buried."

"At night?" Coffen asked.

"That is what he wishes."

"How he enjoyed being outrageous," Prance said, smiling in admiration. "I wonder if this evening burial has anything to do with his days in the Hellfire Club. It sounds their sort of jape. The business of hired guardians during the period he is laid out is to prevent Malton from finishing the job, in case the corpse breathes?"

"That is my understanding," McAlbie agreed.

"The man was mad! You ought to challenge the will, Puitt."

"There'd be nothing in it for me but the cost of a lawyer," Puitt replied.

The major interests of murder, will, and burial attended to, McAlbie began to discuss parish business with Prance. Coffen began chatting to Bertie Puitt, and Luten wandered to the fireplace. Corinne accompanied him. He stared for a moment at the shattered decanter, then said, "Was there brandy splashed on Simard's clothing when you saw him?"

"No, he had a hole in the toe of his slipper. Other than that, he was tidy."

"How about Phoebe's gown when she returned? Was it splattered with brandy?"

"No, her skirt was dusty, and her hands were dirty. There was earth under her fingernails, as if she had been digging in the soil, but there was nothing splashed on her skirt. We would have smelled brandy. It has a strong odor."

He frowned at the shattered decanter. "She says Simard dropped it?"

"Yes."

"Then why did none of the brandy splash on him? You can see it splashed for over a yard." Dark droplets were congealing on the stone apron and the oak floor beyond. Even the chair and table by the grate bore traces of dried brandy.

"That is odd!"

"It's impossible," Luten said. "Someone else must have been here and dropped the decanter. Someone Phoebe is anxious to protect."

"Bertie! But he has an alibi."

"He has convinced McAlbie he has one. I doubt McAlbie even bothered to check it. Or Malton's alibi, come to that. He is the one who inherits the estate and title."

"Phoebe wouldn't protect Malton."

Luten stood a moment, frowning in concentration. "Would she not—if he promised to give Bertie that five thousand Simard had promised him and reneged on?"

"Oh! Of course she would. She despised Simard. They all did."

"With good reason. But that is not to say anyone had the right to kill him. If we could get a look at the clothes Puitt and Malton were wearing yesterday . . ."

"It might be possible to examine Puitt's. He works for Reggie. Reggie pays his servants."

51

"Malton's will be more difficult to get a look at."

"Well nigh impossible, I would say."

"A word with his valet, perhaps. My own valet will be arriving today with my trunk. I'll have Simon strike up an acquaintance with him, ask him what he uses to remove stains from clothing."

"If Bertie's jacket and trousers prove innocent, that is to say."

"And even if they don't. With such an unpopular gent as Simard, we may be dealing with collusion. Puitt and Malton could both stand to gain."

While Luten and Corinne were busy at the grate, they saw Coffen and Puitt stroll out of the study.

"I was just wondering, McAlbie," Luten said offhandedly, "did you actually check up on Puitt's and Malton's alibis?"

"Puitt?" McAlbie exclaimed. "There is no vice in the lad. Why, he is every other inch a gentleman. He would not kill his own papa. There is a word for that."

"Patricide," Prance said, nodding.

"Eh? I meant scoundrel. Bertie is no scoundrel. As to Malton, it is no secret he has a *chère amie* in Lewes. He is there two or three times a week. A fellow don't like to pry into that sort of thing. Where a bachelor seeks his pleasure is his own business. But in fact I happen to know he did go to Lewes yesterday afternoon. Mrs. Bucket saw him leave, heading south toward Lewes around two. We've established that Simard was shot around three. Malton would have been miles away."

Luten did not think that a man being seen heading in one direction a full hour before a murder prevented him from turning around and going the opposite way. In fact, it made a good alibi for an undemanding jury. Malton's *chère amie* would, no doubt, be happy to verify that Malton was with her—for a price.

"Who is Malton's mistress?" he asked.

"A Mrs. Warner. She owns a millinery shop in Lewes. Calls herself a milliner, but she don't make the bonnets and she don't stand behind the counter. She has girls that do the work for her while she reaps the profit. There's the way to get rich, gentlemen."

"Speaking of getting rich," Prance said, "how did Malton take the news of Simard's death?"

"He expressed shock and grief, said all that was proper, but between you and me and the bedpost, he was thrilled to death, and who can blame him? The whole parish will profit from having a responsible hand running Atwood."

"I'm surprised he is not here, taking the reins."

"He is tending to the legal business and arranging the funeral. He will come here later today. Plans to move right in and start repairing the damage of twenty years of neglect. Well, I must be off, gentlemen, Lady deCoventry." He bowed all around and left.

Prance lifted a cynical eyebrow. "*Plus ça change, plus c'est la même chose*. If Malton runs Atwood in the same manner that he has been running his life until now, there won't be much change. Except that he is not vicious and cruel. Merely a lazy spendthrift who enjoys indulging all his appetites."

"And he is a bachelor," Corinne added. "That, you must know, excuses a good many faults in a gentleman—eh, Luten?"

He turned a laughing eye on her. "Why, Countess, you make me wonder whether I ought to turn in my eligibility for the ball and chain."

"No one is rushing you," she replied, with a glinting smile.

He noticed she was not wearing her diamond engagement ring. "So I have noticed."

Chapter Eight

Coffen was trying his skills on Bertie Puitt.

"My throat is dry as a lime kiln," he said. "Would there be a drop in the house?"

"Dandy ale in the kitchen," Bertie replied, his eyes sparkling with anticipation.

"Ale, eh? I fancy something a tad stronger. Talking about dying does that to me."

"It don't bear thinking about. Hell's fire and all that. There's wine in the dining room."

"Any brandy about the house?" Coffen asked.

"In the study, but McAlbie won't like our touching it."

"I would like a gargle of brandy. You wouldn't have any at your place?"

"I never touch the stuff myself. It gives me the megrims the next morning, but I can put you on to a bottle if you like. I know the fellows who haul it from the coast, where it comes in from France. Or very likely Prance can oblige you. He keeps his bottle."

"Glad to hear it. Meanwhile, let us have some of that wine," Coffen said, and sauntered off to the dining room, satisfied that Puitt had not drunk from the other glass in Simard's office.

They stood by the window, looking out at the park beyond, chatting in a seemingly aimless way about Simard's death. Coffen raised the window and stuck his head out. The harsh barking of a dog came from the rear of the house.

"That'd be Hannibal," Bertie said. "He took a bite out of the gardener last week. He's kept chained up during the day. Simard lets him roam loose at night to attack anyone who tries to break into the house. Used to, before he was dead, that is. He's on the chain night and day now. It would be kinder to have him put down."

"Was Simard having trouble with ken smashers?" Coffen asked, wondering if it was a common criminal who had shot him.

"No, he was just naturally nasty, liked having a vicious brute like Hannibal around. Hillman—he's the head groom—is good about keeping him chained during the day, though. He's not roamed loose since he bit the gardener. The only one Hannibal will mind is Phoebe. She feeds him."

Coffen's ears perked up at this. A clue! Definitely a clue. "He might turn on her, though," he said blandly.

"Not a chance. He's too fond of her mutton. Half the reason he's so vicious is that he's starving to death. Simard kept him hungry on purpose to worsen his temper. A mean sort of thing to do to an animal. I fancy I'd bark and bite someone myself if I was starved on a regular basis."

"Enough to make a saint bite. If Hannibal ran into Phoebe when she didn't happen to have any mutton on her, though," Coffen said, trying valiantly to make Phoebe's story credible, "he might attack her, eh?"

"Nay, he'd follow her home meek as a lamb to get his teeth into a piece of meat. Well, I must be off. I have the wood choppers in Prance's forest this morning. Prance is very strict about which trees he wants down. If I ain't there to keep an eye on the lads, they'll cut an oak. He don't want any oaks down. They're not mature yet. Why don't you drop around to the gatehouse tonight and we'll have a gargle?"

"Thankee kindly, I will. Does half past nine suit you?"

"Nine would be better. I have an appointment at ten."

Sensing another possible clue, Coffen made a mental note about that appointment. "Nine it is."

"I'm off, then."

When Bertie left, Coffen poured himself another glass of wine and sat at the table to consider his gleanings. He hoped Puitt was innocent. He liked him. Easy to talk to. Friendly. His reverie was interrupted by the sound of feet in the hallway. It was

McAlbie leaving. Coffen returned to Simard's study to find the other three members of the Berkeley Brigade gathered around the grate, looking at the shattered decanter and brandy stains.

"It's impossible," Luten was saying. "Neither Simard nor Phoebe dropped that decanter or their clothing would have been splashed. Someone else was here."

"But who?" Prance asked.

"Malton, I shouldn't wonder," Coffen said.

"Or Puitt," Luten added.

"No brandy stains on Puitt's clothes. He don't drink brandy either. I asked him."

Prance adopted the supercilious expression that so infuriated Coffen and said, "It is quite possible he guessed the reason you asked and told a little untruth."

"I didn't blurt out and ask him. I was sly," he said, "let on I wanted a gargle. Puitt said he never touches the stuff. Gives him the megrims. Besides, as I said, there were no stains on his clothes."

"Some of us change our clothes when they are soiled," Prance said, with a pointed look at Coffen's far-from-immaculate toilette.

"Aye, and some of us think it's smart to wear a dressing gown in public, which it ain't. You looked a dashed quiz in that *keeryomoan* thing. Anyhow, if you think Bertie's hiding his dirty jacket in his room, I'll have a look tonight. Visiting him at nine o'clock."

"How will you arrange to see his wardrobe?"

"I'll think of something. You ain't the only one with an imagination."

"That's fine, Coffen. You do that," Luten said. "And if you find nothing interesting in his closet, then look under his bed and around the room."

"Dash it, Luten, now *you're* starting to treat me like a moonling. This ain't the first time I've gone tracking a murderer, you know. I've been learning all sorts of things."

"Such as?" Prance inquired.

"Such as your dashed Tante P was lying her head off about Hannibal. He's kept on a chain, and even if he had got off, he

56

fair dotes on Phoebe, because of her feeding him when the poor hound is starving to death. I warrant you knew it all along and never said a word to us."

A tint of rose suffused Prance's pale cheeks. "A gentleman instinctively protects a lady. Phoebe is like a mama to me. She would never murder anyone. It is merely muddying the water to concentrate on her. We now know it was a rifle, not a pistol, that killed Simard, so the pistol she buried is a red herring."

Coffen considered this with interest. "So what we've got is a gun that was shot but didn't kill Simard, a smashed bottle of brandy that didn't splash whoever broke it, and a poacher lurking in the bushes wearing a gentleman's blue jacket and a snuff-colored fustian jacket. And every soul within miles hated Simard. It'll take us two or three days to solve this one."

"What McAlbie actually said is that the shot that killed Simard *could* have been from a rifle," Luten pointed out.

"The pistol she buried had recently been fired," Corinne added.

"Perhaps it will never be solved," Prance said, "and I, for one, think it no bad thing if this particular assassin should get off scot-free."

"Someone getting away with murder is never a good thing," Coffen informed him. "That's what turning Hindoo has done to your morals."

"It is Buddhism that I am studying, not to join the faith, but merely to broaden my theological horizons. You malign the Hindu faith, ignoramus."

Coffen ignored him. "Oh, I learned another thing," he said to Luten. "Puitt has a date tonight at ten. I don't know who with, might only be a lady, but I'll follow and see if he's up to anything."

"Perhaps meeting Malton to collect his five thousand," Corinne said.

This had to be explained to Coffen a few times. When he had grasped the principle of collusion, he sighed. He liked Puitt, but there was no denying collusion was a possibility.

"Let us go back to Granmaison," he said.

Corinne was staring at the grate. She turned and said, "No!

Wait a moment. There is something wrong here. If Simard was killed by a rifle shot, then it must have been that first shot that Betsy heard outside, and mistook for Bertie shooting rabbits. But if that is true—" She stopped a moment, then continued, "But if that is the shot that killed Simard, then he was already dead when Betsy heard the second noise from inside the study and went to the study door. Betsy thought it was a shot being fired. Phoebe told her Simard had dropped the decanter. She wouldn't let Betsy in. I believe Simard was already dead at the time."

"But Phoebe didn't shoot the rifle. She was in the study. The sound came from that stand of cedars," Prance said.

"I know. I'm not saying Phoebe shot him. I'm saying she let on he was still alive when she knew perfectly well he was dead. She must have seen Bertie out there among the cedars. He is the only one she'd lie to protect."

They all considered this for a moment, mentally constructing the scene. "That must be what happened," Luten said. No one disagreed.

Coffen said, "It could still have been an accident. But if it was, then somebody else must have been in the room with Phoebe. Mean to say, she didn't drop the brandy, and it's demmed sure Simard didn't, for he was dead. It wasn't Bertie, not if he was out in the cedars, accidentally shooting Simard."

"Malton?" Corinne suggested.

Coffen added, "And the three of them colluding about it. There's a murder *à trois* for you, Prance. You like a foreign twist to things. But why did Phoebe take the gun?"

"And shoot it and bury it in the lemon tree pot," Corinne said, frowning. "And where was she for the hour it took her to get back to Atwood?"

"When we've got this many questions with no answers, it seems to me we're barking up the wrong tree," Coffen said.

"So what should we do?" Prance asked, looking to his friends for guidance.

"Keep looking for clues," Coffen said.

Corinne turned to Prance. "You should have a long talk with your aunt, Reg. She knows more than she is telling. Now that we know the pistol did not necessarily kill Simard, she may be forthcoming."

"Yes," Prance agreed. "I daresay she is really sleeping now, after her busy night, but let us return to Granmaison. You have still not seen my *nina*, Luten."

Luten smiled politely and lied, "I have been looking forward to it eagerly. Lead on."

"I've already seen the *neenya*," Coffen said. "I believe I'll have a word with Simard's head groom and just make sure Hannibal was chained yesterday afternoon. And have a word with Betsy Jones and Mary. You mind there was some talk of Mary's fellow hating Simard. I'll have a word with Tom as well."

Corinne said, "I really must attend to my toilette, as I did not bring Mrs. Ballard with me." Luten lowered his brow at his beloved, who smiled mischievously. "You go with Prance and let him show you the lovely *nina*, Luten."

Corinne was finding Prance's latest enthusiasm even more trying than the preceding one, which had been a perfectly dreadful book of poems on King Arthur. *The Round Table Rondeaux*, he had called it. He had omitted all the interesting bits from the old tale and concentrated on battles and arguments and footnotes, but at least it could be read in the comfort of one's saloon. It did not require standing about in the cold autumn breeze, seeking for praise of rocks and weeds.

She walked home, with Luten holding on to her elbow. From Luten's other side came the enthusiastic voice of Prance, saying, "The lyricism of flowing water, originating, perhaps, from the *shumisen*. Did I tell you about the *shumisen*, Luten?"

"Is that the humpbacked bridge you mentioned?"

"No, no, that is the bridge of Wu. You are, perhaps, confusing it with the *shima*, the island in the pond, beyond the bridge of Wu."

Accustomed to long, foolish harangues in the House, Luten said with perfect politeness and even some sign of interest, "Very likely. Do tell me more." When he heard a suppressed giggle from his fiancée, he gave her elbow an admonishing squeeze.

Chapter Nine

Luten's viewing of the *nina* was postponed. When they reached Granmaison, Lady Fairchild and her daughter, the Honorable Miss Coleman, were just arriving. Had Lady Fairchild not had the good fortune in her youth to catch the eye of Baron Fairchild, she would have made a likelier wife for McAlbie. Since the death of her husband a decade before, she had left Fairchild's ancestral estate in Somerset and returned to her birthplace to live on a less grand estate left to her by her papa. This estate, Meadowvale, was only three miles from Granmaison. She had never cared much for the aristocratic life, but the handle she acquired by marriage permitted her a freedom of behavior that would never have been tolerated in Miss Smiley, which had been her maiden name.

She was a deep-dyed provincial from the crown of her late husband's curled beaver, which she wore in lieu of a bonnet, to the gentleman's top boots covering her feet and lower legs. The small dame sat astride a brute of a gray gelding which none of the gentlemen would have cared to tackle. Her full skirt was hitched up in an unsightly bundle around her knees, showing the edge of unadorned muslin pantalettes above her top boots. Her face was not ugly and with even a modicum of attention could have been tolerably pretty. She had rather fine hazel eyes with long lashes. But between the wisps of grayish-red hair sticking out from under her curled beaver, the chapped condition of her skin, and the cross expression she wore, she looked a perfect quiz. Her dark green riding habit was a size too small, and her York tan gloves two sizes too large.

Beside her on a smaller, milder bay mare her daughter,

Sidonie, sat in the proper sidesaddle mode suitable for ladies. Sidonie gave some notion how the mama looked when she was younger. Her face was still round, where Lady Fairchild's had developed a pair of pouches at the corners of her chin. Sidonie's eyes were blue, as was her fancy riding habit. Her reddish-blond curls were protected by a round bonnet tied in a large pink bow beneath her pouchless chin. Despite some physical resemblance, the ladies looked completely dissimilar. Sidonie with her pink ribbon looked somehow like a birthday present, whereas her mama was more like a consolation prize.

But what Lady Fairchild lacked in elegance, she more than made up for in character. When the mother and daughter were together, it was at the mama that gentlemen looked. Prance, who cherished Originals the way a gossip cherishes scandal, was enamored of her. He rushed forward to assist her from her gelding. Scornful of the proprieties, she threw her leg over the brute's back and was on her feet before he could reach her.

"You might give Sidonie a hand down, Reg. There's a good fellow," she said in a brusque, rough voice.

Prance rushed to do her bidding. Sidonie fell like a bag of oats into his arms and smiled coyly at him. Luten and Corinne had met these local ladies before and greeted them as old friends.

"Is Phoebe at home?" Lady Fairchild asked.

"At home, but perhaps resting," Prance said. "Let us go in and see. You will want a nice cup of tea after your ride."

"A mug of brandy would go down well," the lady replied, and preceded her host into the house.

Phoebe had taken advantage of Reggie's and his guests' absence to return belowstairs and eat the breakfast denied her earlier. She had finished breakfast and sat in the saloon, staring into the blazing grate with a journal open but unread on her lap.

"Dorothy!" she exclaimed. "I am so glad to see you. You have heard the wretched news about Simard?"

"It is all anyone is speaking of in Heath," Lady Fairchild replied, striding to the most comfortable chair in the room and dropping gracelessly into it. "Nothing wretched about it in my view. I'm surprised no one has had the initiative to put a bullet in the old slice before now. Good riddance, say I."

Sidonie removed her bonnet and fussed with her curls. The intricate arrangement of twists and knots made her hair look as if someone had been tatting with it. She came simpering forward to make a curtsy to Phoebe, who nodded and then ignored her.

The company took up seats in the saloon, and Prance called for wine and brandy. Blakeney, accustomed to Lady Fairchild's habits, brought the brandy decanter and placed it on the table by her side.

"Good lad," she said with a wink, and took a gulp. "I had a chat with that fool McAlbie yesterday afternoon," she said. "Met him while I was in Heath picking up a turbot for dinner. An inordinate price they are charging for a turbot nowadays. One would think someone had to raise it and feed it, instead of pulling it out of the sea ready for the pot. But never mind that. Quite a little crowd gathered round us at the whiff of gossip. McAlbie was prattling on about your being at Atwood when Simard was killed, Phoebe. I told him it was no such a thing. I was there after you left. I know that, for Simard mentioned you had just left a few minutes before. I didn't care much for what the gossips were implying. Oh, McAlbie said the death was accidental, as it was, of course, but you know how people talk.

"I got the impression some were thinking you had a hand in it, because of his treatment of Bertie, you know. I could not have that sort of talk circulating about my bosom bow. I squelched the story, never fear. Just thought I would let you know, in case you were concerned."

Phoebe wore a curious expression while this tale was being told. Then her pinched face eased into a smile. "Very kind of you, Dorothy. Whatever possessed you to call on Simard? I didn't think you and he got on, especially since—" She stopped and glanced at Sidonie, who colored up and began twisting her fingers in her curls.

Lady Fairchild shot a warning glance at Phoebe. "I was collecting for those new benches for the church," she said. "Didn't get anything out of him, of course, the heathen. Reg, perhaps you would like to contribute? Not that we often see your handsome phiz in the family pew. You will see that he goes this Sunday, Lady deCoventry."

"Reg pays no heed to me, milady," Corinne said perfunctorily. Her mind went darting off in another direction while Prance handed some money over to Lady Fairchild. Was it possible there had been something going on between Simard and Sidonie? He was old enough to be her— She looked at Sidonie more closely. The lady was not quite as young as those shy glances and the girlish toilette suggested. Corinne had known her for seven years now, and she had not been a youngster when they first met. Say she was nineteen that first summer. She would be twenty-six now, pretty firmly attached to the shelf and no sign of a beau. Sidonie was the sort of lady who wanted very much to get married. Her talk was all of gentlemen and toilette. Ladies found Simard attractive. . . .

Lady Fairchild was not the sort of mama to tolerate any illicit romantical doings. If Simard was after Sidonie, or vice versa, Lady Fairchild would certainly take a hand in the affair to see it led to the altar. And she was fond of brandy, which could explain that second glass in his study. She glanced at Luten and noticed he wore a wary, pensive look. She wanted to ask Lady Fairchild a few questions, but knew that forthright dame would not reveal any secrets. She would try to get Sidonie alone later.

Before Corinne could think of an excuse to do it, Lady Fairchild suggested that Prance take Sidonie out to show her his Japanese garden. It would be difficult to say which of the two found this idea more delightful. Prance was always happy to show off his *nina*, and Sidonie was *aux anges* to be alone with an eligible gentleman. It did not seem a likely time for Corinne to try to pump Sidonie about Simard, so she stayed behind to see if she could learn anything from Lady Fairchild.

Nothing of the least interest transpired, however. The discussion turned on the high cost of fish and peas, and from there to conjecture as to what sort of lord of the manor Malton would make.

"He will be looking for a wife, eh?" Lady Fairchild said hopefully. "I mean to say, Mrs. Warner is well enough for a bit o' muslin, but he will want a real lady for wife. I shouldn't think he'd waste any time setting up his nursery. Simard's case will be a lesson to him. I hope he stays at Atwood and does not take into his head to scramble off to London to find himself an heiress. Sidonie has ten thousand," she added, revealing the reason for her interest in all this.

When Prance and Sidonie returned twenty minutes later, Prance looking somewhat harried and Sidonie smiling archly, they were accompanied by Coffen and the new Lord Simard, formerly Mr. Malton.

The newcomer was tall, dark, and handsome. Even, Corinne had to admit, darker and more handsome than Luten, though not quite so tall. It was his eyes that gave him the edge in looks. They were heavily fringed and the shade of black coffee, with something of the iridescence of oil on water. They ought to have been dangerous eyes. It was, she decided, his youth and the sweetness of his expression that robbed them of peril. He was young, not much older than her own four and twenty years. His lips curved in a shy smile as he bowed in her direction. His shimmering eyes did not make that hasty tour of her anatomy to which she was accustomed, but gazed deeply into hers, as if admiring her soul. She was unaware of her answering smile, which vexed Luten to no small degree.

As Malton made his bows around the group, she observed that his casual manners did not have the ease that would have made them acceptable in the best society. He would begin a speech in hardy, masculine tones that soon petered out to a hesitant, nearly inaudible murmur. It was a forced casualness, as if he was determined that the company he was in should not imagine itself better than he, but he could not sustain the charade.

She concluded it was his long wait to become Lord Simard that accounted for it. Simard had never treated him as the heir, yet he knew he would one day be master of a great estate, however dilapidated. And in the meanwhile, he had to keep up appearances on whatever small competence his own papa had left him. Prance had showed her the little farm on former visits, but Mr. Malton had never been at home. He traveled a good deal. The farm, Greenwood, consisted of five hundred acres that could not give him more than a thousand a year.

"Well, Malton, how does it feel to be Lord Simard at last?" Lady Fairchild asked, in her blunt, forthright way.

He took up a seat beside Corinne and answered, "Not so pleasant as I had expected." A frown creased his handsome brow. "It would feel better if there were no cloud hanging over the manner of Simard's passing," he explained.

"No one has pointed a finger at you, so far as I know," she assured him. "You were at Lewes with Warner, I hear. You will want to give her her congé and find yourself a proper lady now, eh?" Her hazel gaze went to the corner where Sidonie was rolling her eyes at a thoroughly disinterested Prance.

A flush of pink suffused Malton's pale cheeks as his flashing eyes turned to Corinne. Her engagement to Luten had not been announced publicly and had not reached his ears, here in the provinces. He had never seen any lady so lovely. He had a particular fondness for raven-haired ladies, especially when they came with a complexion like rose petals. The sparkling green eyes added to this made her irresistible.

"Yes, I expect I shall be going up to London come spring," he said.

"Spring?" Lady Fairchild said querulously. "Why wait so long to take a wife when there are plenty of handsome gels nearer to home? Only see what happened to Simard."

Corinne knew the exact moment he realized the match-making mama's meaning. His eyes flickered in Sidonie's direction, before returning to the mama. "I shall take care to keep clear of flying bullets," he responded lightly.

"I was just telling Phoebe I was at Atwood after she left yesterday. You would have heard the wretched stories running around Heath about her visit to Simard," she said. She repeated her tale, while Coffen sat with his ears stretched. It was his first exposure to this new clue.

"Of course, I didn't get a sou out of him for the church

benches," she said. "All I got for my trouble was a glass of brandy, but it was welcome on a chilly day."

"We must remedy that," Malton said, then his voice petered out into an uncertain whisper. "Have to look into Simard's accounts. Very happy to make a contribution."

Coffen's forehead was corrugated with thought. He said to Lady Fairchild, "You must have come in by the French door into his study."

"Yes, I did, and left the same way, which is why Dolman didn't know of my visit. I only stayed a minute, but Simard said Phoebe had left, so she is in the clear. That is the important thing, eh?"

"Did you see anyone lurking in that stand of cedars?"

"No, I didn't happen to notice."

"About that brandy," Coffen said, "where did he get it? The decanter was broken while Phoebe was there."

Lady Fairchild cast a look of loathing at him. "He got it from that cupboard beside the French door. He keeps a spare bottle there. He mentioned having dropped the decanter. He was quite angry about it." Coffen said nothing, but he remembered perfectly well the spare bottle had been in the bottom drawer of the desk. Lady Fairchild had been there before Phoebe, if she had been there at all. The second brandy glass suggested she had been there, but why was she lying about the time?

Malton listened closely, then said, "I hear Simard's pistol is missing. You didn't happen to see it about, Lady Fairchild?"

"I didn't see it, but he mentioned it. Said it was broken and he got rid of it."

"Where?" Coffen asked.

"He didn't say, but he used to take it along when he went fishing. He was after the foxes that were devastating the home garden. You'll want to take care of them, Malton. I expect that was when Simard found out the gun was broken, when he tried to take a shot at the rabbits. I imagine he simply tossed the gun into the lake. McAlbie mentioned it could have been a rifle that killed Simard, Pattle. That sound Betsy heard outside, you know. Why so curious about his missing pistol?"

"Thought it might be a clue," Coffen replied.

He decided there was no point quizzing her any further. She could lie like a rug. There was little more chance to quiz her in any case. She soon rose, gathered up Sidonie, urged Malton to call on them soon, and said she must fly. Phoebe accompanied her to the door and did not return, but went abovestairs.

Malton stayed a little longer. While Prance and Luten discussed the visit, Malton turned to Corinne.

"You will think me no better than I should be," he said, with an apologetic smile. "I am referring to Mrs. Warner. As I am a bachelor, you know . . ." She could not quite hear the mumble that followed, except for the word "lonesome."

"I am sure you will not be lonesome once you make your bows in London, Mr. Malton," she replied.

"Dare I hope I may count on you for my first friend?" he asked.

"Certainly, but do you not have any friends in London?"

"No doubt I shall find some old school friends. Socially, I am quite a deb. My finances until the present have not permitted me to enjoy the luxury of a Season. One would not want to go and hang about the fringes of Society." When he smiled and said, "You understand," in a softly intimate way, she felt it a great compliment. "Pride is a poor match for poverty. I had the disadvantage of both."

"I am not English myself, but I have always had the impression that you English consider pride quite a virtue," she replied, rather flirtatiously.

He glanced to the grate, where Luten and Prance were talking. Luten's cold gray eyes stared at him for a moment. "Only when it is accompanied by wealth and privilege, Lady deCoventry," he said.

"Then your pride will soon become virtuous, Lord Simard."

It looked strange to see a grown man blush. "That is the first time I have heard myself called by my new title. I am happy it was you who christened me."

Luten could no longer keep up his show of unconcern. He took a seat beside Corinne, and Prance sat on the nearby sofa.

"Well, my dear," Luten said to Corinne in a thin voice, "what are you two finding so interesting?"

"We were discussing Simard's going to London in the spring," she said.

"Simard?" Coffen said, frowning. "He's dead."

"Mr. Malton is now Lord Simard," she explained.

"Oh, you mean Mr. Malton."

"Yes, that was my meaning, Coffen."

Malton/Simard turned to Luten and asked, "Is it by chance that the Berkeley Brigade has gathered at Atwood, or did Prance summon you to solve our little mystery?"

"Purely fortuitous," Prance told him.

A gleam of mischief Corinne had not noticed before flashed in Malton's dark eyes. "Like Lady Fairchild's happening to call on Simard yesterday at the crucial time to prove Miss Dauntry is innocent," he said.

Prance sensed an implication that Lady Fairchild's evidence was a tissue of lies, as indeed he suspected it was. "And your happening to be with Mrs. Warner, Malton," he snapped.

"Just so. Odd that one's vices should prove helpful. In any case, it is delightful to see you again, and to have finally met Lady deCoventry, about whom I have heard so much," he said. "You must call on me at Atwood and give me some suggestions as to how I should repair the ravages Simard has wrought there, Lady deCoventry."

Luten glared at his beloved. Prance chewed back a grin.

Prance considered himself quite an expert in the matter of decor. "My dear Malton!" he said, all animosity forgotten. "We need not bother Lady deCoventry with that. I will be happy to lend you a hand. You have only to say the word."

Malton repressed a grimace. "I have heard you are busy putting in your new garden, Prance. The whole village is speaking of it. I should like to see it sometime."

Prance's voice, when he replied, had much the quality of a purr. He loved to be discussed in the village or anywhere. "My *nina*. Yes, it is a Japanese garden. You have not seen it, Malton. Do allow me to show it to you now. And by the by, we must get together with our lawyers to arrange the transfer back to Granmaison of my ten acres. You do realize those ten acres Simard stole from Papa are to return to Granmaison now?"

"Yes, certainly. We neighbors do not want to get off on the wrong foot. There will be no difficulty, I promise you."

"Good, good. Shall we go out to the *nina*?"

Malton made his adieux all around, with a special smile for Corinne, and allowed himself to be led out into the brisk October breeze to enjoy the flowerless garden.

Luten turned a questioning eye on his fiancée. "Another conquest," he said.

"And with the stiff competition of a milliner, too," she replied. "Take care, or you will dally too long in getting the ring through my nose, Luten."

"Speaking of conquests," Coffen said, "I believe Miss Coleman has an eye on our Prance."

"Better him than you," Luten replied.

"What—didn't you think she was pretty?" Coffen asked.

"Not pretty enough to be that coy, simpering and rolling her eyes."

"A good figure, though. I don't care for scrawny girls. I like them well marbled."

Luten's lips moved unsteadily. "Like a good beefsteak."

"That's it. I may give her a hurl in my rig, if she's willing." Coffen was known not to be demanding in his ladies. As long as she didn't have a tail and bark, he was game. He was getting to that age when he felt the pull of the ball and chain. "But never mind that," he said. "We've got to talk about them lies Lady Fairchild was spouting. What is she up to, eh?"

Chapter Ten

Malton did not linger long at the *nina* when he discovered the nature of a Japanese garden. He soon recalled urgent business with his lawyer and left. Prance was back in the saloon within minutes. The rogue in him was happy to see signs of pique in Luten and a smug satisfaction in his fiancée. If Malton kept up his flirting at this pace, there would soon be fireworks. Meanwhile, civility demanded that he, as host, must try to keep his guests comfortable and busy.

"Well, folks," he said, rubbing his hands together in a jovial, hostish sort of way, "a new set of clues for us to conjure with. You now all know what I have known all along. Tante P is innocent."

"What we know," Coffen informed him, "is that Lady Fairchild was lying her head off. Very likely she is in on the collision, along with Malton and Puitt."

"I trust you are referring to Luten's notion of Puitt and Malton colluding—not colliding," Prance said, with a sniff in Luten's direction. "As to that story about Simard throwing the gun away—I grant you that is fiction, but not her own visit to Simard after Phoebe left. Lady Fairchild would hardly pitch herself into the fray by pretending she had been there if she had not."

"Why did she lie about the gun, I wonder?" Corinne said.

Luten said, "She might have been trying to protect Phoebe. Does she shoot herself, Prance?"

"Nobody shoots herself," Coffen said. He could always be depended upon to misinterpret a statement.

"Does she, herself, shoot," Prance explained. "Yes, she can

shoot like a soldier—pistol or sporting weapon. She has plenty of guns—fowling pieces, hunting rifles—which does not really explain the why of her fibbing. Something else has just occurred to me. That green habit she was wearing this morning—she usually wears a blue one. Mary saw a blue jacket in the cedar hedge."

"She wears a curled beaver, too," Corinne said. "But she rides that gray gelding. Mary saw a brown horse. It is Sidonie who rides a bay and wears a blue habit."

"Hard to think of that dumpling of a gel shooting anyone," Coffen said.

"We are overlooking that Malton wears a blue jacket as well and rides a bay mare," Luten said.

Coffen said wisely, *"Kooey bono."*

Corinne nodded to acknowledge this hit. "As to the why of Lady Fairchild's pitching herself into the midst of it," she continued, "she is obviously trying to protect someone. We thought Phoebe was protecting Bertie. Perhaps Lady Fairchild was trying to protect her bosom bow Phoebe, as Luten said. She may have invented this tale of having been at Atwood after Phoebe left when she learned the gun was missing."

"That makes sense to me," Prance said. "They are close friends."

"That's going pretty far out on a limb for a friend," Coffen said. "Now, if it was Sidonie she was trying to protect—You don't suppose the daughter is the killer, hiding behind her smirks and pink ribbons? I know she don't seem the sort. More interested in landing a fellow than killing him, I'd say. And why did Lady Fairchild lie about the brandy when I asked her? Simard didn't keep his spare bottle in a cupboard. He kept it in the bottom drawer of his desk. Handier to get at."

"She lied because she didn't know the truth. She was never there," Corinne explained. "She only said she was, to ensure Phoebe is not charged. When you asked her, she had to say something."

The four exchanged a puzzled look. At length Luten said, "We discussed the possibility of Puitt and Malton being in collusion. Is it possible Lady Fairchild and Miss Dauntry are

71

cohorts? Miss Dauntry shot him, with the prearrangement that Lady Fairchild would 'prove' her innocent? Your aunt was there, Prance," he said, when Prance emitted a protesting "Bah!" "It seems she was there when Simard was killed, as no later shot was heard. Who is to say she didn't shoot him? Why else did she carry away the pistol and hide it?"

Prance colored up. "I doubt Phoebe could hit the side of a barn door. She never shoots. No, Phoebe is out of it."

"Then why did she bring the pistol home?" Coffen asked. No one had an answer. "Anyone could hit a target the size of Simard at close range. It'd be hard to miss."

Corinne said, "There is some mystery about Sidonie and Simard. I daresay he had been chasing after Sidonie. If that is the case, then both Sidonie and her mama may have a motive."

"Are we not overlooking the obvious, that Simard was carrying on with Lady Fairchild?" Prance said. "She is far the more attractive of the two ladies, and Simard, you know, was quite elderly. Frankly, I don't see Sidonie running too hard if a man was chasing her."

"No man in his right mind would try any tricks with Lady Fairchild," Coffen said. "She'd haul off and knock him down."

"Perhaps you're right," Prance said. "The lady is unflirtable."

After a moment Corinne said, "Perhaps Sidonie had been chasing Simard and compromised herself. If he refused to marry her, Lady Fairchild would certainly take steps. I mean to get Sidonie alone and quiz her. I shall call on her soon."

"Half the trouble with this case is that everyone keeps lying to us," Coffen said. "I stayed behind to have a word with the servants. Hillman did have the dog chained up yesterday right enough, so Phoebe wasn't chased by no dog. Not by Hannibal at least. Now Mary has changed her tune. She says it wasn't a blue jacket she saw in the cedars yesterday. It was a poacher. Yesterday she told me with her own tongue it was a blue jacket, like a gent wears. I believe that's what she did see. Someone has got at her."

"We know who was at Atwood," Luten said. "Puitt was there when we arrived this morning."

"Aye. I like Bertie," Coffen said, "but that don't mean he's

72

telling the truth. No one else is. Except Betsy Jones. Her story hasn't changed. Did I mention it's been embroidered a little? She says Mary was carrying on with old Simard. Round-heeled wench, it seems, falls on her back if you look at her. Carrying on with Tom as well—which gives Tom a motive."

"And half the other footmen, if Mary is that lax in her morals," Prance added.

Coffen looked doubtful. "It's Tom that has the inner track, though. He's one of those fellows the girls like."

"It would be very unusual for a servant to shoot his master," Luten said. "How many houses do we know where the master carries on with his maids, without murder resulting?"

"Dozens," Prance replied. "In some houses it is considered a compliment. The girls expect a few perquisites. Tom is the pushing sort who would encourage Mary to get what she could out of Simard. I cannot see Tom as a serious suspect. Who stands to gain is Malton—and by the by, he mentioned he was at Atwood last night. He might have got at Mary. He certainly has a way with the ladies, eh, Corinne?" he added mischievously.

"He did not strike me as the murdering sort," she objected.

"I noticed he was on his best behavior," Prance said. "What we must do is go to Lewes and find out if he was really at Mrs. Warner's yesterday."

Coffen screwed up his eyes in thought. "Mrs. Warner will say he was even if he wasn't."

"Others besides Mrs. Warner will have seen him if he was there. He drives a showy yellow curricle. You don't see many of them hereabouts."

"Or he might have ridden his mount, I suppose, if he was in a hurry," Coffen said. "That will be more difficult to trace. Shortcuts through fields and all that."

"One does not ride when he is calling on his mistress," Prance said. "It is too disheveling."

Coffen laid no claim to knowing how one carried on with women. His experience with females was pretty well limited to actresses, where any behavior short of murder was acceptable. "I didn't know that," he said, chastened. He reached back in memory to an unsuccessful romantic venture in his youth and added, "It does cause a bit of a stench, of course. I wonder if that is what put Miss Ball off me."

"I shouldn't wonder," Prance said. "Someone should drive over to Lewes this afternoon. Why don't you come with me, Pattle, and leave the lovebirds alone?"

"I'll tag along," Coffen agreed. "I'd like to get a look at Warner. Malton will be dumping her now. She'll be available. Pretty, is she?"

"A stunning redhead," Prance replied. "What will you and Corinne do, Luten?"

Corinne said, "I shall drive in to Heath and call on Sidonie en route to ask if she would like to go with me." She looked to Luten to see if he meant to accompany her.

"I'll go with you, Prance," Luten said. "I am rather curious to meet Mrs. Warner."

Prance realized at once that this was to repay Corinne for Malton and added his mite to the imbroglio. "If you are going, Luten, there is no need for me to go." Corinne would hate for Luten to visit the pretty wench alone.

Luten's thin lips parted in a mischievous smile. "I daresay I will have better luck alone."

Without looking within a right angle of his beloved, he sensed her body stiffen. He knew exactly how she would look, with her pretty little face frozen in a pose of indifference, and her eyes flashing to betray her vexation.

"She doesn't work in her millinery shop," Corinne reminded him. "How will you meet her? You can hardly call on a perfect stranger."

"She has rooms above her shop," Prance said.

"Excellent," Luten said. "I shall require some distinguished sort of bonnet that is not on the shelves. I shall ask to speak to the proprietor."

"She'll come trotting when she hears the word *Lord*," Prance said. "A very ambitious piece of mischief."

It was obvious to Corinne that this errand would make more sense if a lady went, or at least accompanied Luten. His not asking her to go with him was nothing else but an insult. He was planning to set up a flirtation with the milliner and was not even bothering to conceal it from her.

"You forget Mrs. Warner's current lover is now a lord, Prance," she said. "A bird in the hand . . ."

Prance smiled impishly. "But when the bird in hand is a sparrow, and a peacock beckons . . . *Vous comprenez?*"

"You are assuming the woman has a taste for peacocks," Corinne said through thin lips. "They are not to everyone's taste, you know. Malton is a shy, modest sort of gentleman. Charming."

"I like peacocks," said Coffen, who had not yet grasped the mood of the conversation. "You ought to have a couple in your *neena*, Prance, since you ain't having any flowers."

"I shall see what my *Sakuteiki* has to say about birds in his treatise, *Notes on How to Make a Garden*. The elegant simplicity of his title causes me to blush when I recall the striving for effect in the title of my own poem on the *dux bellorum*." He gave his audience time to praise his poem. When no praise was forthcoming, he said, "I shall spend the afternoon with *Sakuteiki*. What will you do, Coffen?"

"I'm going to see Mrs. Warner, ain't I?"

"It might be better if I go alone," Luten said.

"Why?"

Corinne explained, "Because Mrs. Warner is a woman, Coffen. Luten hopes to beguile her into saying Malton was not with her."

"I shall take her some flowers," Luten said.

Corinne simmered. "Would bonbons not be more suitable? I daresay a milliner is sick to death of looking at flowers."

"I'll take both," Luten said.

"Perhaps you'd like your diamond engagement ring to take as well?" she said, her eyes flashing dangerously. "Pity I had not brought it with me."

"I noticed you were not wearing it," Luten said, revealing no more than polite interest.

"It's such a showy thing, I cannot wear it for every day. I can't get my gloves on over it."

"I never heard a lady complain that her diamond was too big before," Coffen said.

"Ladies can always find something to complain about," Luten said airily.

"Some ladies do not have to look far," she shot back. "And who ever heard of taking a milliner flowers and bonbons when you are pretending you only want to buy a bonnet?"

Coffen scowled. "I hope you two ain't going to have another of your spats. We need all our wits for this case."

"I was only explaining to Luten why I was not wearing his engagement ring," Corinne said.

"I did not ask for an explanation! I merely mentioned you were not wearing it."

Prance smiled tolerantly. "Children, children! Coffen is right—for once. Let us not fall into arguing amongst ourselves. So, Coffen, as Luten does not want you along on his flirtation, what will you do?"

"Look for clues," he replied.

"One hardly needed to ask." He turned to Corinne. "You had best take my carriage. There is no hope of Fitz finding his way the five miles to Heath." Pattle's coachman was notorious for getting lost. He could scarcely drive around the block with any certainty of getting back the same day. Not only could he not read a map, he had a positive knack for going the wrong way.

Luten said, "I'll get Simon working on meeting Malton's valet, to see about spilt brandy. And while we are all adding our mite, it would help if you could wring the truth out of your aunt, Prance."

"She might be more approachable now that she has been proven innocent."

Coffen snorted. "If a lie is all it takes to prove the killer is innocent, we've no hope of catching anyone, for the whole parish is a parcel of liars. It's because they all wanted Simard dead. I wonder he lasted this long, when no one could stand the sight of him. One thing I want to find out is why the French doors in Simard's study were open when it was cold outside, and he had the fire raging in the grate. The two don't go together. Betsy didn't know why. She said he don't usually open it except in the summer, to let his cat in and out."

"His cat was the only creature Simard respected," Prance mentioned. "He quite doted on it. How do you expect to discover why the door was open, now that Simard is dead?"

"I'll keep my eyes open for clues," was Coffen's answer.

Before they parted on their various ways, lunch was served. Prance had brought his French chef, André, with him from London. Like Lucullus, Prance never dined simply, or alone. When he had no other company, Sir Reginald dined with Sir Reginald, who demanded the best, and did no more than nibble any of the delicacies prepared for his delectation. He had relented regarding the menus. As a host, pleasing his guests took precedence over converting them to a life of simplicity. His guests appreciated the *sauté de merlans aux fines herbes* and *les poulets à la reine, à la Chevry. Croques en bouche à la pistache* and *gateaux glacé aux abricots* had been prepared especially to satisfy Coffen's sweet tooth. Prance was not pleased when Coffen asked if there was any apple tart.

Phoebe did not join them.

"She has the megrims," Prance explained, when he returned from abovestairs to try to convince her. "Oh, she did explain why Lady Fairchild was wearing that wretched old green habit. It seems she took a tumble from her mount and ripped the hem of her blue one."

"Funny she told you that. Did you ask her?" Coffen said.

"No, she just told me. What I find stranger, though, is that Lady Fairchild told Phoebe. Dorothy is not the sort who apologizes for her toilette—or to cease wearing a habit only because the hem was torn, come to that. I've known her to come to a ball wearing her late husband's jacket in lieu of a shawl. She dresses quite independently of fashion, to put it politely."

"When did she tear the blue habit?" Coffen asked.

"Two days ago, thus making it clear that hers was not the blue jacket seen lurking in the bushes outside Atwood yesterday."

"I'm surprised she didn't go whole hog and let on Sidonie's

77

bay mare was lame as well, to convince us it couldn't have been her."

Prance gazed out the window and murmured, "I wonder if an albino peacock would not be permitted by *Sakuteiki*. It would eliminate the garish effect of blue and those staring eyes when the peacock displays his tail feathers, yet add the echo of color and motion.

"To say nothing of their dashed screeching," Coffen said.

"True," Prance said. "It must be a mute albino peacock. Now, where would one find such a treasure?"

Chapter Eleven

Luten decided the swiftest way to get to Lewes was to ride. As he hadn't brought a mount with him, he borrowed one from Prance. Sir Reggie's mounts, like his carriages, his toilette, and all his belongings, were chosen for show. Luten found Black Satin a thoroughly unreliable animal to actually ride. Before he had gone a mile, he wished he had taken his carriage. Black Satin had an unfortunate tendency to rear up on her hind legs at every passing rig, and Luten wanted to keep to the road to inquire whether Malton had been seen passing. He learned at the first inn he came to that Malton had not only passed yesterday afternoon around two, as he claimed, but had stopped for an ale. Odd he would be thirsty so soon after leaving his own home. He had been riding his bay mare, not driving his curricle as one would expect for a social call.

When Luten learned at the next inn two miles farther on that Malton had stopped again—to have the buckle on his rein repaired on that occasion—he felt certain Malton had been establishing an alibi. He had stopped at two inns to "prove" he had gone to Lewes, then cut quickly through the fields back to Atwood and shot his cousin. No further word was heard of Malton at succeeding inns.

The ride through the south downs in autumn would have been enjoyable had it not been for Black Satin's tricks. The sky was a deep cerulean blue. Golden-leafed trees stood out dramatically against the blue. There was just enough breeze to cool the brow without causing a chill. Black Satin became so intractable when he entered the ancient county-town of Lewes, with the Ouse River flowing peacefully by, that Luten dismounted and walked the troublesome mare along the High Street. From near the middle of the town the Norman Castle rose against the skyline.

He had learned from Prance that Mrs. Warner's shop was on the High Street, a block past St. Michael's Church. As he advanced, he saw the round Norman tower and knew he was close to his destination. He stopped at the George Hotel to stable his mount during the call on Mrs. Warner. He was so certain Malton hadn't been in Lewes that it hardly seemed necessary to inquire. He said offhandedly to the ostler, "You haven't seen Mr. Malton about lately?"

"Not today, sir," the man replied. "He was here yesterday."

Luten came to sharp attention. "Oh yes? In the morning or evening?"

" 'Twas yesterday afternoon, around half past two." He gave a lewd wink. "His usual visit, twice a week. Regular as clockwork. Comes at two or three and stays until after dinner."

"And the same yesterday?"

"That's right, sir. No, I tell a lie. He left earlier yesterday, just before five. You heard he's now a rich man?"

"I have heard of Lord Simard's death."

"An ill wind that blows no good. Malton will settle up his bill now, right enough." He glanced at Black Satin. "This here is Sir Reginald Prance's nag!" he said, looking suspiciously at Luten. A glance at the face and jacket of his customer assured him he was not dealing with a horse thief. "I hope you didn't buy this nervous filly, sir."

"No, just borrowed her—and I shan't do so again!"

The ostler led the mount off, laughing. "I'll give her a quart of ale before you leave. 'Tis the only way with Black Satin. Sir Reginald ought to have told you. He will have his little prank."

Luten went, cursing under his breath, to find the milliner. Not that it was really necessary now. He knew Malton had been here in Lewes at the time of Simard's death. Perhaps it was an accident after all. Interesting, though, that Malton's pockets were to let. The timing of the death was certainly convenient for him. Odd, too, that he had stopped twice en route.

Luten's mind was so deeply engaged he nearly missed seeing his destination.

Madame Chloe's was an elegant little shop squeezed in between a lawyer's office and a drapery shop. In the bay window one navy straw bonnet rested on a dummy head, surrounded by a drift of white tulle. A bloodred rose drooped over the rim of the bonnet. The name of the shop was inscribed in gilt Gothic script over the window. The sophisticated presentation seemed out of place in quaint Lewes. It would have been more at home in London. Of course, he had never had any intention of taking either flowers or bonbons. That had merely been said to annoy Corinne.

When he entered the shop, a bell attached to the door gave a tinkle, which brought a clerk rushing out to greet him. One glance at the woman told him she was not Chloe Warner. This middle-aged woman was no one's mistress, but a comfortable wife or widow. The plain gold ring on her left hand said she was not a spinster in any case.

It proved difficult to gain access to Mrs. Warner. Anything Luten asked for, the clerk—her name was Mrs. Pettigrew—could show him. Bonnets of glazed straw and leghorn bonnets, ostrich feathers and egret, grosgrain ribbons and satin, she had them all.

"Charming," he said. "Who designs them?"

"Mrs. Warner is the designer," she said, "but she doesn't work in the shop. She has ladies about town who do the work. She has her own rooms abovestairs."

"I wonder if she would design a special bonnet for—a friend," he said, to let Mrs. Warner believe he was eligible. "Tell her Lord Luten would like a word with her."

Mrs. Pettigrew's friendly smile grew wider. "I'll just nip up and ask her," she said.

Luten expected Mrs. Warner would come down at once. He was a little surprised at the length of the delay. When Mrs. Pettigrew appeared ten minutes later, she said, "Mrs. Warner will see you abovestairs, milord, if you'd just step this way."

The dark, uncarpeted staircase at the rear of the shop led him to expect a modest apartment. He was astonished to be shown into an elegant set of rooms with Persian carpets underfoot, decent paintings on the walls, and furnishings by such a recognized name as Chippendale. The greatest surprise of all was Mrs. Warner herself.

Luten had assumed Prance's description of the woman as a stunning redhead had been designed to infuriate Corinne. He had done Prance an injustice. Mrs. Warner was more than pretty—she was ravishingly gorgeous. And there was nothing common about her. "Too much woman for Malton" was his immediate assessment. The ray of sunlight from the window shone on her Titian hair, which was bound into a bundle of curls on top of her head. Her face, while not in the first flush of youth, was still lovely. A set of high cheekbones, a straight nose, and dark, flashing eyes lent her beauty, and the proud set of her head added an aristocratic touch. She wore a modest afternoon gown of deep green worsted, with a fichu of lace at the throat.

She did not rise, but smiled a welcome. "Lord Luten, welcome to Madame Chloe's. What can I do for you?" she asked in a well-modulated voice.

While he examined her, she returned the compliment, but in a subtle manner that did not reveal any romantic interest.

He bowed. "Good afternoon, ma'am. It is kind of you to see me. I have heard of your skills in designing bonnets and come to ask your help. I want a special bonnet for a friend."

She indicated a chair. He sat and found himself feeling nervous. Those penetrating eyes saw too much.

"What sort of bonnet?" she asked. "Is it for a gala occasion? A little late for Ascot. Is it to wear to court?"

"Er . . . no. It is for a special tea party being held in London."

"An afternoon bonnet, then?"

"Just so. Something showy but elegant. A trifle more fancy than one would wear out for a stroll."

"I see. What age is your friend?"

"About your own age."

"An older lady," she said, her lips tilting in a conspiratorial smile. "Lady deCoventry would not appreciate being called about my age. I wager I could give her five years." Her smile stretched to a grin as he gasped in surprised embarrassment. "Cut line, milord. You have come to have a look at Malton's lady friend. I shall tell you what you want to know. Mr. Malton was with me yesterday afternoon. He did not murder his cousin—though I, for one, would not blame him if he had. Wretched man, Simard."

"You knew him?" he exclaimed.

"Oh yes, I knew him quite well."

"Were you and he . . ." He came to an embarrassed pause.

Mrs. Warner displayed not a jot of embarrassment. "I was not his mistress. That was not the sort of relationship between us. It was business. He lent me the money to set up my shop." Her dulcet voice hardened as she added, "I repaid him—with interest."

"How did you meet him?"

"Mr. Warner, my late husband, had some business dealings with him. When Ronald died, Simard offered to help me. Ronald was a solicitor. He handled some affairs for Simard. Unfortunately, Ronald did not handle his own affairs so well as he handled others'. A case of the cobbler's wife going unshod. Any more questions—or shall we have a glass of wine and become acquainted?"

"You leave me with nothing to say but 'I apologize.' It was ridiculous of me to think I could fool you by my transparent story of wanting a bonnet. I didn't know you knew who I was."

"Malton dropped by this morning. He came to tell me of Simard's death. He mentioned Sir Reginald had company. This death will make a great deal of difference to him."

"And to you?" Luten asked. "As we are being quite frank with one another . . ."

"Will he give me my congé or marry me?" She held out her left hand, where a fair-size diamond sparkled. "We must wait for a decent interval of mourning. Malton feels my degrading past of having been in trade will be forgotten once I don my tiara. I never appeared in the shop," she added.

She lifted a small silver bell by the sofa. A maid appeared. "Wine or tea, milord?" Mrs. Warner inquired.

Luten had discovered what he had come to discover. In the

interest of saving time, he opted for wine and rather wished he had asked for tea. Mrs. Warner proved an amusing lady. After five minutes he did not hesitate to call her a lady. She was obviously well educated and well behaved. Her conversation was a little racy, but no more so than that of married ladies in London. She was Malton's mistress, but she was a widow after all, and Malton was a bachelor. Worse went on among the ton. The only wonder was that he had not married her before now. The lack of funds, of course, and her being in trade, must account for it.

They flirted discreetly, but never passed the bounds of good breeding. When he left, the only question remaining was what the beautiful dasher saw in that young cawker of a Malton. She might have had her pick of patrons. Well, what she had seen, of course, was a young heir she could lead by the nose—the future Lord Simard and herself by his side.

He turned his mind to other suspects as he rode home on a much more docile Black Satin, lulled to acquiescence by a judicious dose of ale.

Chapter Twelve

Luten found the others waiting for him when he reached Granmaison. They sat around the grate sipping tea from strange, small cups without handles. He saw at once that his fiancée was unhappy with him and decided it was foolish to waste these few days together in squabbling. He had come here to be with Corinne, and they had scarcely had a moment alone together. He would not praise Mrs. Warner. He would merely say that she had corroborated Malton's alibi. But first he would ask Corinne what she had accomplished. Whatever she had discovered, he would praise her ingenuity and cleverness. Byron had told him success in dealing with ladies was to praise the brains of the beauties and the beauty of the brainy ones. "If the lady has neither one nor t'other, you compliment her on her voice, or the way she walks, or her sense of humor, or some demmed thing she lacks."

"And if she has both?" Luten had asked.

"Then you run away from her as fast as your legs will carry you, my friend, or she'll end up your tenant for life."

Corinne had brains, beauty, and a lovely voice besides, and Luten was impatient for her life tenancy to begin.

"How did your visit to the Fairchilds go?" he asked her.

"Miss Coleman said she did not care to go shopping. I could see she was eager to, but her mama glared at her so belligerently she didn't dare to go. Lady Fairchild did not leave us alone for a minute. It is clear as a pikestaff she was afraid Sidonie would reveal some secret. I only stayed a quarter of an hour. All we talked of was her charity works. She made me feel quite a slacker in that regard, even after I had given her five guineas for the orphans."

"Lady Fairchild is the glue that holds the parish together," Prance said. "If there is a sick mama, she is there to feed the children. If the winter is cold, she is delivering blankets—and hounding one to pay for them. She is a sort of bad-tempered angel."

Luten found it uphill work praising his fiancée in the face of this story. "It was a good try," he told her with a warm smile. "Miss Coleman may be more forthcoming the next time. You have established that you want to be her friend."

Corinne realized it was an olive branch, and she seized it eagerly. Her answering smile was like a ray of sunshine. "Prance has been telling us all about *Sakuteiki*," she said, with a look that suggested her weariness with the subject, and her pleasure at his return.

"And making us drink our tea without any milk or sugar," Coffen added. "In these little jugs with no handles. My fingers are scorched."

"Do try a cup, Luten," Prance urged. "We ought really to be taking our tea in a tea garden to escape the cares of civilization. The rustic little earthenware cups are to keep us humble. Or rather to make us humble."

"It's like drinking from a stone jug," Coffen complained.

Prance poured Luten a cup of tea. Luten sat beside Corinne, looked a question at her, and drank. He was relieved to see it was only green tea, not some abomination.

"It seems the Hindoos have never heard of gingerbread," Coffen said, with a black scowl at their host.

Luten said, "Coffen, did you have any luck at Atwood?"

"I didn't go into the saloon. When I saw Malton's rig in the stable I was going to leave. Betsy Jones had spotted me coming in and came to the back door. She told me Malton was there with the solicitor going over Simard's books. She says Malton will be spending his days there, but he sleeps at Greenwood."

"Or perchance at Lewes," Prance added with a waggish look. "He does not want to scandalize the servants by telling them he is visiting Mrs. Warner. By the by, how did it go with Mrs. Warner, Luten?"

"Fine. She says Malton was with her yesterday afternoon."

"Told you she would," Coffen said. "Don't mean to say he was."

"He was there, all right. The ostler at the George told me his mount was there all afternoon. Odd, though, Malton stopped at the first two inns along the way. And he rode his mount. Speaking of mounts, Prance!" He cast a darkling brow at his friend.

"Don't tell me you had trouble with Black Satin? Why, she is docile as a lamb."

"Yes, when she's full of ale. You might have warned me."

"You would have taken a pet if I had. Felt it was a slur on your riding ability."

As this was true, Luten said no more. The ability to ride the wildest beast ever saddled was a point of honor among sportsmen.

Prance adopted an innocent expression and said, "What did you think of Mrs. Warner? A handsome creature, is she not?"

"Handsome enough."

"That hair! Her admirers call it Titian, but it is much closer to the softer, prettier tints of Giorgione. And the face, of course, is pure del Sarto. Classical lines, but with a minxlike expression never seen on a del Sarto virgin. That expression adds immeasurably to her allure."

Corinne listened to Prance and looked obliquely at Luten. She saw the signs of discomfort in the latter and wondered. Why was Luten not raving about this charmer of a woman to make her jealous? That was why he had gone. And why had he made a point of complimenting her earlier? In a split second she leapt to the conclusion he had misbehaved with the red-headed beauty.

"What age is she?" she asked with an air of indifference.

"Older than you," Luten said, to appease her. Corinne was becoming sensitive on the matter of age. Most young ladies were married long before twenty-four.

"She is twenty-nine and looks nineteen," Prance informed

her. "In the face, that is to say. The figure is more mature. Delightfully so, would you not say, Luten?"

"I didn't really notice. I didn't stay long."

"You were gone long enough," Prance said. "Come now, fess up, Luten. You are among friends. What were you two up to, eh?"

"We had a glass of wine and talked. Mrs. Warner did say one interesting thing," he said, hoping to change the subject. "It was Simard who set her up in business when her husband died." He gave the few details he had gleaned.

It was Coffen who said what the others were thinking. "Don't sound like Simard. She must have had something on him."

"There was certainly something between them at one time," Prance said. "I didn't know he had financed the millinery shop. That is unlike him. But then, Mrs. Warner is such a ravishingly lovely creature that even Simard may have made an exception. I know he was more than usually fond of her."

"You mean she was his mistress?" Corinne asked.

Prance gave a graceful shrug. "He would never tolerate a breath of scandal about her. Always insisted they were just friends. That was unlike him. He more usually boasted of his conquests. And with a ravishing beauty like Mrs. Warner!"

"Foolish of Malton to take up with her," Coffen said. "Bound to set Simard's jaw against him."

"Yes, it was unwise, but the great affair between Simard and Mrs. Warner was over when she and Malton became lovers."

Coffen scowled deeply. "You might have given us all these clues before, Prance."

"I did not see that Mrs. Warner was involved, except indirectly through Malton. What do you glean from knowing the whole story?"

"I glean she has a pretty good motive to kill Simard. A woman scorned, taking up with the heir to make him jealous. Or maybe Simard was pressing her to pay him back for the money he lent her to set up business."

"She says she had repaid him, with interest," Luten said.

Coffen gave a disparaging *tsk.* "Another liar, I shouldn't

88

wonder. It'd be in Simard's business papers, but Malton will never let us get a peek at them."

"Mrs. Warner cannot have shot Simard," Prance reminded him. "She was at Lewes with Malton yesterday afternoon."

"Just because his horse was there don't mean he was. She might have sweet-talked him into killing Simard for her. A ravishing beauty like that would have him wound round her thumb."

"Do you think she would perjure herself for him when it is a case of murder?" Corinne asked. "Especially when he will likely be rid of her, now that he's inherited the title. I mean, he can hardly marry a milliner."

Luten cleared his throat. "Actually, she says they will marry, after a decent mourning period. She was wearing an engagement ring."

Corinne managed to read a slur into this, as Luten had mentioned she was not wearing hers. Before she could retaliate, Prance spoke up. This bit of local gossip was of keen interest to him.

"You don't mean it! Set a milliner up as lady of the manor? Good God, he'll be cut dead by all the old cats. Lady Fairchild will never accept her, and she wields a large stick hereabouts."

"I am only telling you what Mrs. Warner said."

Coffen sat musing as he stared into his earthenware cup. "How did she come to tell you all this, Luten? Said you was only there a minute. Going to order a bonnet, you said."

"She knew who I was before I saw her. Malton had been to call on her earlier. She knew we are all here. That being the case, we did not have to parry and thrust. She knew why I had come, and told me at once that Malton had been with her at the crucial hours." Without realizing it, Luten slipped into praise. "She is a very straightforward lady, no coyness about her. Clever as can stare and surprisingly ladylike. She wore a very elegant gown and had her hair arranged simply but attractively. Her saloon would not be out of place on Berkeley Square. Other than her occupation, she would not disgrace her tiara. Actually she does not work in the shop, but only designs the bonnets."

Prance said slyly, "Just as well you only stayed a moment, or Corinne might become vexed with you, Luten."

Luten jerked to attention and looked at Corinne, who was staring at him with unmistakable signs of hostility.

It seemed the minute he was out of her sight, he found some fair enchantress. Her pride demanded that she ignore his philandering ways, however.

She pointedly turned away and said to Prance, "Oh, did I mention Lady Fairchild wants to have some sort of do while we are here? She says she will be in touch with Phoebe soon."

"There will be your opportunity to get Sidonie alone," he said.

"Speaking of alone," Coffen said, "does your aunt always spend her days alone in her room?"

"No, it is unusual. Something is bothering the poor old dear. I wish she would confide in me."

"It's that gun that's plaguing her. Wonder if it's still in the lemon tree, or if she's gone and got rid of it."

The group exchanged a look. It was Luten who made the first step toward the conservatory. The others were not far behind him.

"The lemon tree in the corner," Corinne told him.

They looked about to see the gardener was not present. Luten snatched a trowel from the worktable and began digging in the large earthenware pot. He dug down on all sides until he hit the root ball. Then he looked up and said, "It's not here."

"She's got rid of the evidence!" Coffen exclaimed. "Dash it, she did shoot Simard, Prance."

Chapter Thirteen

"What we ought to do," Coffen said, "is lure her out of her bedchamber and one of us slip in and search it. Stands to reason she has the gun there, where she can keep an eye on it."

They had returned to the grate to discuss the matter. Coffen refused to be fobbed off with milkless, sugarless green tea. He had poured himself a glass of wine and passed the bottle on to Luten, who was not tardy to fill his glass and one for Corinne. Prance took the bottle and poured wine into his earthenware cup while his back was to them. Tea was fine in its place, but too tame a drink for murder.

"Does it really matter what she's done with the gun?" he said, turning back. "We know it is Simard's; we know it's been fired."

"We don't know who by." Coffen scowled. "You ought to make her tell you." He heard a sound at the doorway, and looking up, saw Miss Dauntry herself entering the saloon, her red hair arranged in a tall spiral of curls, her corpulent body swathed in a crepe gown of emerald-green, with a few yards of gray tulle floating about her like steam from a kettle. "Speak of the devil," he said, in no soft voice.

"Were you speaking of me?" Phoebe asked, and laughed.

Phoebe loved company. It was hard on her to stay away when she could be hearing all sorts of delightful *on dits* about London, which she felt was her true home. Her light shone too brightly for the provinces.

"Missing you madly, my pet," Prance said, and went forward to bring her to the grate, where he settled her in his own chair. He noticed she was carrying her netting box. Phoebe did not possess any skills that involved needle, thread, or wool. This large rattan box usually resided on her toilet table. In it she kept hartshorn, headache powders, perfume, whatever gothic novel she was reading at the time, ribbons, combs, pins, and the other accoutrements necessary to her complicated toilette. She settled her tulle around her, tucked the netting box in at her ankles, and said, "Having wine? Excellent. I'll join you, folks," before Prance could pour her a cup of tea.

Prance poured the wine and handed it to her. She apologized profusely for her laxity in not entertaining the guests. "But this business of Simard has simply undone me," she said. "I have so often read horrid mysteries of lurking murderers and that sort of thing, and even thought what fun it would be if it should happen here, for there is no denying life can be dull in the country. But the reality of it! I find I am as prone to swoon as any of the unfortunate damsels in these novels from the Minerva Press. Are you folks making any discoveries?"

"Luten has been to call on Mrs. Warner," Prance replied.

Phoebe turned an alarmed face on Luten. "My dear, do you think it wise? You don't want to encourage the creature, or she will be setting herself up as a lady."

"You have not heard the cream of it," Prance said. "She says she and Malton will wed, after the mourning period."

Phoebe liked to call herself broad-minded. She had read Mary Wollstonecraft's essay on the rights of women, after which she had once made herself ridiculous by insisting on remaining at table after dinner with the gentlemen for port and cigars, until the smoke drove her gasping to the saloon. She had asked Prance to put in a word for a serving maid the Parish Council wished to ship out of the parish when she became pregnant, to save the ratepayers the cost of maintaining mother and child. Lady Fairchild, that ubiquitous benefactress, had settled the matter by taking the maid into her own home, where she gave good and faithful service for a year before running off with a stable hand and leaving the baby behind. But what Phoebe could not tolerate was to see Chloe Warner, a common milliner, lording it over her at Atwood.

"Marry her! You can't be serious!" she cried.

"Well," Prance replied, "Mrs. Warner is serious, and she, you know, is not the sort of woman who is easily thwarted."

"That is true. She's the only woman who ever gave old Simard a run for his money."

"What do you know about her, Miss Dauntry?" Coffen asked. "About where she came from, I mean, her past history. A local woman, is she?"

"Not in the least. She only appeared on the scene five years ago. Her husband was a solicitor. Simard did some business with him. When Warner died, suddenly Simard was calling on the wench three nights a week. The *on dit* is that they had a falling out. Her servants heard them screaming and shouting at each other. We thought it was the end of her, that she would go back where she came from, but she opened up that shop and has been at Lewes ever since. And now you say she has caught Malton."

"Where was the husband from?" Coffen asked.

"Up north somewhere. Birmingham, was it, Prance?"

"Manchester, I heard. He was said to have a thriving business, too. Odd he would leave at his time of life."

"Surely he must have been quite young five years ago," Corinne said.

"Oh no! He was an older gent," Phoebe said. "He robbed the cradle when he married her. It was obviously a case of cream-pot love on her part. When a pretty young wench marries an older man, you may be sure she does it to better herself. She has an eye for the lads. I heard a whisper she was carrying on with some gent in Manchester, which is why Warner decided to leave. A trollop. She cannot be anyone or Simard would have mentioned it. He always referred to her as a lady."

She lifted her netting box and began to root amid the ribbons and headache powders. "I seem to have the sniffles," she said. "I know I have a handkerchief in here somewhere."

Coffen stepped forward to offer his. As he stretched out his hand, he "accidentally" knocked the netting box onto the floor with a clatter. Pins, ribbons, book, hartshorn, and papers of powder flew onto the floor. At the bottom of the box sat

93

Simard's pistol, with an incongruous pink ribbon entangled around the ivory stock.

Phoebe emitted a strangled gasp, then looked up at Prance. Her eyes made a quick tour of the group, looking for anger or, hopefully, sympathy.

"Well, you have seen it," she said, and handed it to Prance. "I daresay there is no point in my exclaiming, 'How did that get there?'"

Coffen began picking up the debris and tossing it into the basket. "Sorry, Miss Dauntry," he said, and stuffed his handkerchief into her fingers. She took it and brushed idly at her nose.

Prance sat beside her and put his arm around her shoulder. "Share your problem with us, Auntie," he said. "We only want to help, you know. If you were—obliged to shoot Simard, your secret won't leave this room."

"I didn't kill the old buzzard!" she said angrily.

Coffen leaned forward. "Did you see who did? We know you was there at the time, Miss Dauntry. You must have seen something."

"I saw him open his eyes wide, grab at his chest, and sink onto his desk. I saw him die, I did not see who killed him."

"Was you alone with him at the time?" Coffen asked.

"Yes. I had gone to try to talk him into restoring Bertie's five thousand, as I told you. The French doors were open, although it was quite chilly. Missie, that old brindled cat of his, was missing. She had been mauled by Hannibal the day before when she got too close to him. Simard had seen her outside his window earlier on, and hoped she would come in if he left the doors open. With his gout, he did not wish to be hopping up and down to open the door if he spotted her. She comes and goes that way in the summer, you know. The shot must have come through the door. I heard the noise—it came from that stand of cedars. Someone was hiding there and shot him. I cannot believe it was an accident. A poacher or hunter would not shoot when their shot might hit a person or a house. Dorothy tells me they are careful in that respect. No, someone took aim at Simard and shot him on purpose."

"Why didn't you go for help?" Prance asked.

"My first thought was that Bertie had done it, for they had had an argument the night before. I darted to the window, and that is when I saw the man in the blue jacket. Not fustian, as I let on. He had hopped on his horse—a bay like Bertie's—and was flying away. All I really saw was a flash of blue shoulder, a curled beaver, and the rump of a bay mount. Imagination did the rest. I went to see if I could help Simard—it was too late. He was dead. I didn't know what to do. I just waited for someone—Dolman or Betsy—to come rushing to the door and discover him. Strangely, no one came. If they heard the shot, they took it for a hunter or poacher.

Coffen scowled. "You saw exactly what Mary saw. She's lying, as I suspected."

"Of course she is," Phoebe agreed. "Anyway, I began to wonder if I could somehow make it look like suicide. I got out Simard's pistol that he kept in that drawer, wondering how I could fire it off without anyone hearing, for his death would hardly be taken for suicide if the pistol had not been discharged. But then as no one seemed to have heard the shot, I did not want to draw them to the room by shooting it until Bertie had gotten well away and hopefully found himself an alibi. I paced the room for what seemed like forever, watching the clock. I decided to wait ten minutes. After seven minutes, the brandy decanter just exploded of its own accord. It was on the mantel. Simard put it there when he offered me a drink.

"It must have fallen off, eh?" Coffen said. "That is why none of it got splashed on anyone."

"I don't see how it could have happened," Phoebe said. "It was not close to the edge, but pushed safely enough in. I thought it must be Simard's ghost, come back to frighten me. I was fair trembling when Betsy came to the door and asked if something was the matter, for she heard the noise. She had ears the size of cabbages. I couldn't let her see Simard was dead until I had discharged the pistol, so I just told her Simard had dropped the brandy decanter, but there was no hurry to clean it up. Simard and I were having an important discussion and didn't want to be disturbed. She looked pretty suspicious.

"After she left, I chatted to myself a bit in case she was listening at the door, as servants will do, you know. Then when I felt pretty sure she had gone, I couldn't wait any longer. I fled outside with the pistol, out into the garden and on a hundred yards or so into that patch of wild grass and nettles and thorn bushes where I could not be seen from the house. I dug up a bit of earth with my bare hands, pushed the tip of the gun into the soil, and pulled the trigger—to kill the noise, you see. It was not all that loud. My plan was to clean the gun off, put it in Simard's hand, and let McAlbie think Simard had killed himself. Not that he would ever have done such a thing.

"But when I got back, I saw Dolman was there, just looking at Simard's body with the most shocked look on his face, poor man. So I carried the gun home. I stopped for I don't know how long, just sitting on a rock, worrying. When I got here, Lady deCoventry and Mr. Pattle had arrived. I don't know what you must have thought of me. I knew I was all a mess from the nettles. I remembered Hannibal attacking the gardener, and said he had chased me up a tree, which was a foolish mistake, but I forgot in the excitement that Simard had finally chained the brute up. Well, when everyone was asleep that night, I took the gun to the conservatory and buried it beneath the lemon tree. When Lady Fairchild landed in the next morning and said she had been at Atwood after I left, I knew no one would say I had shot him, so I unburied the gun in case my digging about had disturbed the lemon tree, and your gardener would dig it up to have a look at the roots, Prance, for he is so fussy. I did that this afternoon while you were all out."

Her audience sat spellbound throughout her recital, mentally checking her story against the facts they knew. It seemed to tally except for one thing.

Luten said, "About Lady Fairchild's visit—"

Chapter Fourteen

"I don't know what got into Dorothy to tell such a tale," Phoebe said. "She was not there at all. Certainly not after I left. Simard was dead long before that. I can only conclude she thinks me guilty and has told that plumper to save my skin, and I thank her for it. I would have done the same for her. She is my best friend in the world, even if she is always asking one for money for the poor. She knows I have little to spare and is happy with the few pennies I give her."

Her story told, she handed her glass to Prance for a refill. She drank deeply, then said, "Well, what are you going to do about it? Will you tell McAlbie?"

No one replied. After a longish silence, Prance said, "About Bertie, you thought it was he who shot Simard?"

"I did think so—a man mounted on a bay horse, making himself at home in Simard's cedar hedge. Who else would I think of? But I had a word with him this afternoon. He says he didn't do it. He was very worried that I had done it myself. Bertie is not a sly boy. You know that, Prance. He couldn't fool a child. And besides, he was in your forest with the wood choppers at the time. No, I am convinced now that he is innocent, and I regret my rash actions, but what's done is done. Really I don't see that confessing the whole to McAlbie would help him find who did shoot Simard." She looked around the group hopefully.

"All a red herring," Coffen said, "but I'm glad you told us, Miss Dauntry. It saves us checking Bertie's and Malton's trousers for splashed brandy. I expect Lady Fairchild took the cherry cordial away with her as it would point to you." Phoebe nodded. "We know now that Mary is lying about what she saw. She did see a blue jacket, as she said the first time, before she let on it was a poacher. We know why the French doors was open as well. Did the cat ever show up?"

"I haven't heard. Does it matter?"

"I like cats. Missie will need a new master. Odd about that bottle busting. Was it shot like Simard, do you figure?"

Phoebe shook her head in confusion. "I had already seen the man in the blue jacket ride away."

"Would it have been a rat, I wonder, that jiggled it loose?" was Coffen's next effort at finding an explanation. "It might have been attracted by the smell of the brandy."

"There are no rats at Atwood," she said. "A few mice in the larder, perhaps, but a little mouse could hardly jiggle a crystal decanter nearly full of brandy off a shelf."

"Dashed odd."

"It is the strangest part of the whole affair," she agreed. "I wanted to confess all my part in it sooner, but feared that one thing would make you disbelieve me. It is the God's truth. The thing just exploded with no rhyme or reason—unless it was Simard's spirit playing a last prank. I would not put it a pace past him."

They discussed the matter for some time, verifying a few details, but her story did not change. By the time the inquisition was over, they believed her.

"What should we do with it?" Phoebe said, looking at the pistol that Prance had placed on the sofa table.

"Put it back in your netting box," Prance said, handing it to her. She buried it beneath a welter of ribbons.

"Time to change for dinner," Prance said, as the French ormolu clock on the mantel emitted seven tinny chimes.

Coffen said, "You won't mind if I wear my top boots. My man forgot to pack my slippers. I would come in my stockings, but I have a hole in the toe. I have asked Raven to mend it a dozen times. He is not much good with a needle, Raven."

"Nor a clothes brush, nor a hairbrush, nor an iron," Prance said, his eyes drifting over Coffen's untidy toilette. "No doubt he has other sterling qualities."

98

"He has," Coffen said. "He can whistle through his teeth."

"How useful. Never mind. I have something you can wear," Prance said, with a mischievous smile.

Coffen looked from his own short, broad feet to the long, lean foot of Sir Reginald. "I've heard about the Chinese binding up their feet. No, thankee."

"Not my slippers, Pattle. It was to be a surprise, but with so many more exciting things going on, I have not had a chance to give you all your present. We shall do that later."

The group dispersed. Coffen, deeply worried at what Prance could be giving him, went abovestairs with Prance and Phoebe. Luten took Corinne's arm as they went to the staircase.

"We are a step forward now with the case, eh?" she said. "A few mysteries have been cleared up."

"Yes. Phoebe's story is too bizarre to be anything but true. About Mrs. Warner, my dear—"

Luten's hope was to conciliate his fiancée by speaking freely and openly about the woman. He had fallen into difficulty in the past by trying to conceal from Corinne his innocent doings with ladies. But by mentioning Mrs. Warner the minute they were alone, he only annoyed his beloved.

"Are you returning to continue your acquaintance tonight?" she asked with forced lightness.

"Of course not! I have no interest in the woman outside of this case. I was going to suggest you and I spend tonight together."

She tilted a sly, questioning smile at him. "Unless your invitation involves a minister and a ring, I am afraid I must decline."

"What a lurid imagination you have. I am flattered at your high opinion of me."

"So you don't want to spend the night with me."

He took a deep breath. "We could use your skills at verbal manipulation in Parliament. If that is an invitation—or even a challenge—I accept. My room or yours?"

"What did you really mean?"

Luten lifted an arched eyebrow, murmured, "Coward," in an insinuating voice, and watched in admiration as a flush colored her ivory cheeks. "I should have said 'spend the evening' with me. It was that thoughtless 'night' that misled you. What I was thinking, before you distracted me with your mischievous suggestion, was that we might investigate Atwood tonight, after Malton leaves."

"What sort of investigating do you have in mind?"

"Discovering why that brandy decanter exploded."

"You don't believe in ghosts?"

"I am not Irish," he said with a charming smile that robbed the gibe of offense.

"I have often noticed the lack of a silver tongue."

"I leave Irish blarney, along with cabbage and a belief in leprechauns and fairies, to you Celts."

"We are notably gullible, of course, but not so gullible as to believe you learned all those details about Mrs. Warner in two minutes," she replied lightly. "She must be vastly pretty."

"Prance is pretty. Mrs. Warner is handsome, and you, my darling shrew, are beautiful when you're jealous."

"How would you know, Luten? You have never seen me when I am jealous. I am only annoyed when my fiancé does not tell me the truth. It suggests that he is hiding things from me. Strangely, he only becomes evasive about his doings when they involve women."

They reached her door and stopped. Luten leaned against the doorjamb, crossed his arms, and said, "And here I flattered myself you cared enough to be jealous. No doubt it is your green eyes that led me astray."

"No doubt, but they are equally green when I am pleased with someone. And if you ever do anything to please me, you will see the phenomenon for yourself."

He detached himself from the doorjamb and inclined his head over hers. "What can I do to please you? I had hoped my rushing here, *ventre à terre* through the night, abandoning my duties at Whitehall, would please you."

It had pleased her very much. She said, "I am naturally thrilled to be accused of making you neglect your duty. So gentlemanly of you to place the blame in my dish."

"I blame it on your insidious charm." He lifted his hand and grazed her cheek with warm fingers. When he spoke, his voice was rough with emotion. "I never get enough of hearing you denigrate me. Without my daily dose of insults, I found I could not concentrate on the probability of Napoleon retreating from Moscow. It was Corinne's retreat from London that disturbed me." His fingers fanned out, cupping her chin and tilting her face up to his.

She saw the love and tenderness glowing in his eyes, and felt a rush of warmth swell her lungs. This was the Luten she loved to distraction and only saw in rare moments when his guard was down. "You should have told me that before I left, Luten," she said softly.

"Would you have stayed?"

She reached up and placed a quick kiss on his cheek. "Of course not. But I would have been happy to write every day with a fresh list of insults."

"Wretch!" His arms went around her, crushing her against him for a long, deep kiss. When he lifted his head, he said, "Or we could forget about the case tonight and just—"

"Oh, but I really don't want to get married at night in a *nina*, Luten. And naturally you are not suggesting we spend the night together before we are married."

He took a deep breath. "Naturally. Be sure you wear your most unbecoming outfit tonight for our investigating, in case it gets soiled. That gown you're wearing now will do fine."

She looked down at her afternoon gown of mauve serge, which everyone always praised, then up at Luten, with a look of hurt and shock on her face. "Idiot," he said, and went, laughing, to his room.

Corinne stood at her door a moment, looking after him with a rueful smile on her face.

Chapter Fifteen

Prance was late joining the group who met in the saloon before dinner. It was utterly unlike him to keep his guests waiting.

"I wonder if he's taken ill," Corinne said.

"Got his death of pneumonia from drinking tea in that chilly gazebo in his dressing gown," Coffen suggested.

"Don't worry, he's not ill," Phoebe said, chewing back a smile. Having made her toilette before her first foray to the saloon, she had not changed, but only replaced her gray tulle with pink. "The gray was my nod to mourning, but why should I mourn a man I despised?" was her explanation.

Although none of the guests wore any mourning symbols, they had changed into evening outfits. Prance did not permit the small size of a party to excuse any deficiency in toilette. Luten was a pattern card of restrained elegance in a close-fitting burgundy jacket that displayed to advantage his broad shoulders and board-flat abdomen. His immaculate white cravat stood out in dramatic contrast against the jacket. Pattle was his usual rumpled self in a mud-brown jacket that he found the optimum color for concealing spots. Unfortunately Raven had not brought sufficient cravats, and had been reduced to the trick of sprinkling talcum powder over a few gravy stains, with the result of turning them from brown to pink. Corinne was resplendent in a gown of bronze taffeta that enhanced her impertinent shoulders and rustled enticingly when she walked.

The assembled guests were looking to the doorway, wondering what was keeping their host (for they were hungry), when he appeared—or someone who vaguely resembled him appeared. Prance had rigged himself out as a full-fledged Oriental. Having no actual acquaintance with any Asians, he relied on old woodcuts for inspiration. His hair was oiled and slicked back on his head. His eyebrows had been shaped with a kohl pencil to give them an upward tilt. He had not colored his face, but his natural swarthiness lent a suggestion of ocher. These cosmetic changes, while bizarre, were but the icing on the cake. The major treat was his *kirimon* with flowing sleeves, a wide black band around the waist, and felt slippers. The *kirimon* was not the traditional blue and white seen previously, but a flaming red affair. He made an excuse to turn around to let them see the back, which was decorated with a painted dragon. Its hideous head covered his shoulders, its body twined sinuously down his back. He joined his hands as though in prayer, touched them to his chin, and bowed nearly to the floor.

Luten and Corinne exchanged a speechless glance.

Coffen blinked and said, "If it's a masquerade party, you ought to have warned us, Prance."

Prance shimmied forward without either toe or heel leaving the floor. Blakeney came behind him at a stately pace, bearing gifts.

"You would not believe how comfortable this is," Prance said. "I have had a *kirimon* made up for each of you—my gift. And the slippers. Coffen is wearing his."

"Dashed comfortable," Coffen said, lifting a felt-clad slipper and smiling at it.

"But—but where do we wear these?" Corinne asked, as Blakeney handed her the ensemble. Her *kirimon* was a brilliant yellow silk. Japanese ladies peeped at her from behind raised fans.

Coffen's was blue. He shook it out and was satisfied with the reproduction of the bridge of Wu, with a fellow dangling a fishing rod into the water.

"That is very kind of you, Prance," said Luten, ever the gentleman. He accepted his gift and examined the elaborate red silk affair, with an intertwining pattern of white lotus blossoms and what looked like ferns. "It's a lovely—er, dressing gown," he said.

103

"No, no! It is your wedding outfit, Luten! The ordinary *kirimon* would be much simpler. This is my own design for special occasions. Think of it as the Eastern equivalent of a grand toilette. I thought with you being so dark and with Corinne's raven hair dressed high on her head with combs wedged in like a geisha, the Far East would make a fascinating theme for your wedding in the *nina*."

A profound silence fell on the room. Luten received an imploring look from his fiancée. Prance, in an excess of enthusiasm, had gone to great trouble and expense to please them. He was one of their closest friends. How could they say what they both thought: that he was as mad as old King George?

"This will take some thinking about," Luten said in a nearly normal voice. He cast a commanding eye at Corinne. "Lovely as these are—really you have done a marvelous job, Prance. Quite delightful. The problem is, Corinne was saying just this afternoon that her mama was looking forward to holding the wedding at Ardmore Hall. I daresay she has gone to inordinate trouble to arrange it."

"Oh, indeed!" Corinne exclaimed. "And she wants me to wear her wedding gown—white lace, with pearls embroidered down the front. Much as I would adore to wear this beautiful gown—"

"You never told me this!" Prance pouted. "Not a word, all the time you were here."

"I—I thought perhaps Luten would want to go ahead and be married in your *nina*, Reg, for it is such a—an original idea, but after we discussed it, we agreed we cannot offend Mama."

"Thing to do," Coffen said, running his fingers over his *kirimon*, "wear these for an engagement party before we go to Ireland for the wedding."

Luten heard that "we" with deep foreboding. Yet even a wedding, and no doubt a honeymoon, with Coffen and Prance in tow would be preferable to being married in a cold, flowerless garden in a dressing gown.

Prance considered it. "Followed by a traditional wedding in Ireland," he said pensively. "The contrast of the two ruling principles, yin and yang, coming together in a cosmic whole."

Coffen said what he always said when he lost track of the conversation. "Eh?"

"Yin and yang, Pattle," Prance said, in a faraway voice. "Actually a Chinese notion, from the followers of Tsou Yen, but then, Japan is weak in the area of philosophy. Its strength is assimilating and tailoring others' ideas to suit its needs. Their culture is heavily influenced by China, so it is not entirely irrelevant."

"What's it got to do with getting married?" he asked suspiciously, suspecting a Hindoo trick.

"Literally yin means the dark side, yang the sunny, but yin can also represent the feminine principle, yang the masculine, as in a wedding. My thinking was that the engagement party is the yang—bright and sunny—while the wedding in Ireland, with its dark past, is the yin. Corinne is right to insist on returning to the land of her birth to begin her new life, for it is she who must complete the cycle—marriage, birth, death. One does feel the pull of tradition at such times. Late autumn is hardly the ideal season for it, but then, Ireland has benign weather, and if it is cloudy, it will be appropriate for the yin."

Prance struck his oratorical pose, alerting his audience to the danger of a long screed on matters Oriental.

Corinne was struck with inspiration. There was little dearer to Prance's heart than dressing up in outlandish outfits and playacting.

"Could we wear these lovely *kirimons* now, Prance, to get accustomed to the feel of them?" she said. "I can see these flowing sleeves will take some getting used to."

It worked like a charm. "Let me arrange the stomacher for you," he said, and rushed to assist her.

Their well-simulated enthusiasm went a long way toward satisfying him. He really did not want to wait until the wedding to be wearing his own *kirimon* and seeing his friends in theirs. Truth to tell, now that the cold weather was setting in, he was finding the *nina* an inconvenience. In his mind's eye, a trace of Capability Brown and Repton was creeping into *Sakuteiki*. His luxury-loving eye missed the flowers.

The three donned their *kirimons*. Phoebe watched in amusement, thankful that Prance had taken her at her word when she had declined his offer of one.

"Tomorrow I shall dress your hair *à la Japonais*, Corrie," he said.

She cast a wicked grin at Luten. "And Luten's, too. However do you get yours to sit so tightly to your head, Reg?"

"A special unguent of my own decoction, based on Macassar oil. My servants are in the boughs. It comes off on the pillowcases. I find putting a tea towel over the case helps, though of course, it destroys the tea towel."

"I must say, I do like these felt slippers," Coffen said, as he struggled into his *kirimon*. "You're on to something here, Prance. I hope this notion catches on. I'd never know my bunion is there."

"Marvelously comfortable, are they not? I could attach a suede sole, to permit them to be worn outside."

"Or one could carry them, and put them on once she was inside," Corinne suggested.

"Oh no! One removes them when he enters a house," Prance said.

"I see," she said, bewildered, wondering why they were now putting them on.

"In autumn one needs something more than a stocking in England. We must make allowances for climate."

Coffen wiggled his toes and smiled beatifically. "You can take yours off if you want. Mine ain't leaving my feet—ever. Hoby never shod me so comfortably. Where can I order a few more pairs?"

Prance was close to purring in delight. "The local seamstress, Mrs. Leach, made them up for me from my own pattern. And at a very good price, too. I wanted to make them of shagreen, but it was not available locally. We don't challenge our craftsmen in England. They are capable of a good deal more than we ask for."

When they were all arrayed in *kirimons* and felt slippers, they were allowed to shuffle into the dining room. Corinne was relieved to see they were to be allowed to sit on chairs. Other than chrysanthemum petals sprinkled on the soup and Prance eating his turbot with wooden sticks, the dinner was not painfully Oriental. His usually elaborate centerpiece had dwindled to one perfect orchid, cleverly taped to a gnarled branch, but no one minded that. Prance pretended not to notice when Coffen poured milk and sugar on the rice he served with the mutton.

Corinne, observing it, gave Luten's toe a gentle tap under the table and made a choking sound into her serviette.

"This is lovely, Reg," she said, when she had recovered her sobriety. "I would never have thought of serving rice instead of potatoes with mutton."

"Folks say travel is broadening," Reg said, smiling benignly, "but I find reading is equally so. One need not endure the hurly-burly of carriages and the commotion of ships to learn from another culture. We have only seen the tip of the Orient's influence on English culture. Every saloon has its japanned table, and of course, Prinney has raised China to preeminence with his pavilion at Brighton. There is a great allure in the inscrutable East. I wish I had more books on the subject. We know so little of it. *Sakuteiki* says—"

They feared they were about to hear a great deal more about *Sakuteiki*, but Prance got sidetracked to the wedding in Ireland, and so far forgot himself as to use his knife and fork to eat a few bites of raised pigeon pie.

At the dinner's end, Phoebe and Corinne left the gentlemen to their port, served in proper footed glasses, and retired to the saloon.

"That was very clever, Lady deCoventry, deciding to be married in Ireland," Phoebe said. "Poor Prance. He hasn't enough to do, that is his trouble. Bertie handles everything about the estate for him, and he does not involve himself in politics to the extent Luten does."

"He is one of life's butterflies, Mrs. Dauntry, who enhances the world by just flitting about, being beautiful."

"Yes, it is you others who will solve this mystery at Atwood. Who do you think murdered Simard?"

"You know more about the situation here than I. Who do you think did it?"

She shook her head. "I wish I knew. The whole parish despised the man. Yet if Malton is to land Mrs. Warner in on us, I don't know that I would not be glad to see Simard back. Sidonie would have made a better countess."

"Was she seeing Simard?" Corinne asked.

"Oh no!" Phoebe said at once, too quickly. "It is just that there are not many eligible young ladies about, you know. No one else, really. As Simard was such a scoundrel, Lady Fairchild and I hoped that he would remain single, that Sidonie would marry Malton and eventually become Lady Simard."

"Would she have accepted an offer from Malton?"

"Ho, would a dog snatch at a bone? Sidonie would marry the rat catcher. If Malton marries Mrs. Warner, I begin to wonder whether Bertie may not have a chance with Sidonie. I doubt Lady Fairchild would permit it. She is proud of the title. To see her daughter marry an illegitimate man—well, it would go against the pluck. It would be better than Sidonie sinking into a spinster, though. I know the troubles of that state."

Corinne nodded her sympathy and said, "She is hardly an ape leader, but she is getting on."

"Indeed she is, and so eager to marry that—" She came to an abrupt halt. "Not that she has ever compromised herself, exactly, but she runs after the men too hard. She was here the very day Reggie arrived. Tossed herself off her mount and claimed she had twisted her spine, to get an excuse to stay here. Reggie was busy in his garden. He never went next or nigh her. When she discovered he meant to pay her no heed, she recovered the next day and rode home. Very odd, is it not? She is not at all bad-looking, and has ten thousand pounds besides, yet she cannot get a soul to look twice at her. It is the eagerness that does her in. It blends poorly with that varnish of shyness she applies. Let a gentleman stand up with her once and she starts sending him notes and scolding him for not calling. No one wants what is shoved at him."

"Could you not drop her a hint?"

"I have, but she pays no heed. She is more likely to listen to you. You managed the magic trick of landing yourself two very eligible gents. I would not dally in getting Luten to the altar if I were you, milady. There are plenty of other ladies who would not hesitate to snap him up from under your nose. You see how long Mrs. Warner kept him entertained at Lewes this afternoon," she said with a sage look. "They were doing more than talking if she had anything to say about it. Mark my words. She would drop Malton in a flash if she thought she had a chance with an out-and-outer like Luten. She really is an extremely pretty wench, if you like that bold sort. Men seem to, in any case. Any woman who could bring Simard round her thumb . . ."

Corinne remembered Luten's prevarication about the woman. "Handsome," he had called her, but Prance praised her more highly. And Luten had been there longer than he admitted. Long enough to discover all her past history. Perhaps long enough to fall under her spell. She shook herself back to attention.

"So you have no idea who might have killed Simard?" she said.

"I have plenty of ideas, but I was wrong about Bertie, and might be wrong again, so I'll keep them to myself. But when you come down to it, Malton is the one who comes out on top."

"Are Malton and Bertie good friends?"

"Everyone likes Bertie," she said with satisfaction.

Corinne wondered if they were close enough to have struck a bargain about the killing of Simard. She hoped the matter was soon resolved, before Luten found another excuse to call on Mrs. Warner.

Chapter Sixteen

Sir Reginald was still in the dining room with the gentlemen when the door knocker sounded. With a mind to his master's *kirimon*, Blakeney showed Mr. McAlbie into the saloon. Their caller had abandoned his ill-fitting blue jacket for an evening suit of equally poor tailoring. He smiled and bowed to the ladies.

"I thought Sir Reginald and Lord Luten might like to hear how the case is going," he said. With a shy leer at Corinne, he added, "No hurry."

"Fetch them, Blakeney," Phoebe said at once.

Blakeney disappeared. Corinne waited with some interest to see the effect on Mr. McAlbie of three Englishmen wearing Oriental garb. He had not appeared to find anything strange in her own *kirimon*. Nor did he turn a hair when the gentlemen arrived. Perhaps it was their nonchalant bearing that accounted for it. One would think they habitually dined in dressing gowns of such lavish splendor.

"I hope I am not keeping you from your beds," was the only indication McAlbie was aware of their dishabille.

"A bit early to hit the tick yet," Coffen replied.

Luten said, "Has there been some new development in the case?" and they all found seats.

"Nothing significant. I have been looking into Puitt's doings." Phoebe sat bolt upright, with the aggressive air of a mother bear about to defend her cub. "He was in your woods, as he said, Sir Reginald, but it seems he was overseeing the cutting at two ends half a mile apart. As he had his mount, he might have made a quick dart to Atwood and never been missed. He was not carrying any firearm, but that is not to say he hadn't a rifle or fowling piece hidden in the bushes, which would make it a premeditated killing. Betsy Jones says she overheard Simard and Puitt arguing the night before about money. Simard was very angry."

"Puitt would hardly kill his own father," Prance said.

"Oh, as to that, his lordship hardly behaved like a father. They do say folks are most often killed by their own kin. A sad thing, but there you are. Cain and Abel—it goes back that far. I have looked into Malton's doings as well. He was certainly at Lewes. He was seen heading in that direction at two o'clock. I checked at an inn along the way. Luckily for him, a buckle on his rein had come loose and he stopped to have it fixed, so Malton is out of it. About your own visit, Miss Dauntry. You mentioned seeing a poacher in the cedars."

"That's right," she said.

He peered at her sharply. "What color was his jacket?"

A sort of snuff color," she answered promptly.

"Now, that is odd. Mary swears up and down and all around the fellow was wearing a catskin weskit with a black shirt beneath it." His gimlet eyes bored into her. "Was your poacher wearing a hat at all?"

"I—I'm not sure. Yes, I think he was wearing a sort of slouched hat of some sort. Grayish." She looked to hear what Mary claimed to have seen.

"Mary's was bareheaded. Long brown hair worn in a tail," he said triumphantly, and stared at her with something close to accusation.

"She was mistaken. Or he had taken off his hat when Mary saw him—or there were two poachers." Prance scowled her to silence. Such a plethora of choices sounded unconvincing.

"Or no poacher at all," McAlbie retorted. "Come now, Miss Dauntry. The truth. You do your nevvie no good with these prevarications. Who did you see?" She sat mute, glaring. "Mary's first story was that she saw a gent in a blue jacket, curled beaver, and mounted on a brown nag. Most gentlemen wear a blue coat and curled beaver. More than half of them ride

111

bays. It might have been anyone, but until we find out and capture the scoundrel, we have a murderer running loose in the parish. It will be on your head if he kills again."

Her fat face turned an alarming shade of pink that just matched the tulle in which she was swathed. "I saw a poacher," she said.

McAlbie drew a long sigh. "I wish it were so." He looked around and said, "Have any of you anything to add?"

"Kooey bono," Coffen said. "Bertie Puitt don't gain anything from Simard's killing."

"Except satisfaction," McAlbie declared, his tone becoming belligerent. "Men have killed for revenge before."

"That is true," Prance murmured. Then he lifted a mischievous eye to McAlbie and said, "Did you ever manage to unload that lame colt Simard sold you? I cannot recall ever seeing you so angry. There were threats, *n'est-ce pas?*"

"Aye, in jest. You were none too happy when Simard diddled your papa out of those ten acres and chopped down the oaks."

"Touché," Prance said.

"If none of you have anything sensible to say, I shall leave." He rose stiffly, bowed, said, "Good evening, ladies, gentlemen," and walked away. At the door he turned and added, "The inquest will take place tomorrow afternoon at four in the assembly room of the inn in Heath. You are welcome to attend."

"Thank you, McAlbie. Blakeney will see you out," Prance said, as unfailingly polite as if McAlbie were the premier duke of the realm.

They were silent until they heard the front door close, then Prance turned to his aunt. "Well, Tante P, much as it galls to admit it, the man is right. Puitt did have opportunity. What have you to say?"

"Bertie wouldn't hurt a fly, and well you know it. Why should I tell him what I saw, when he has already decided Bertie is guilty? McAlbie couldn't find an elephant in a clothespress. We cannot count on him to find the murderer. You must get busy, Reg, if you don't want to see your cousin hang."

On this speech she rose and billowed from the saloon in a cloud of pink tulle and indignation.

Coffen rifled beneath his *kirimon*, eventually drew out his turnip watch, and glanced at it. "I'm off to see Puitt," he said, and left, presumably to change into trousers before making his visit.

Luten turned to Prance. "Corinne and I are going down to Atwood to have a look around. Will you be coming with us?"

"I shall try my luck with Phoebe again. McAlbie's lecture shook her up. I believe she has told us the truth, but perhaps I shall glean some new sliver of information."

Luten rose and helped Corinne from the sofa. "It will be good to get out of this *kirimon*," he said, when they were beyond earshot. "I was afraid to reach for my wineglass at dinner in case I knocked it over. These sleeves are like skirts."

"I noticed Coffen's sleeves are already soaked in gravy. But the slippers are comfortable."

"I wonder where Prance plans to hold this Oriental engagement party. Here at Granmaison, I hope, where no one from London will hear of it."

"If in London, we shall let it be known it is a masquerade party, with an Oriental theme."

"And that puts us in jeopardy of Prinney inviting himself. He loves to dress up and takes an interest in the East."

They parted at the top of the stairs and met again in the saloon. Luten had changed into his day clothes; Corinne wore her plainest gown with a hooded cape for warmth, and walking shoes. They walked hand in hand through the darkness of night, with the scents of autumn filling the air. A big white moon turned the countryside into a gothic scene of menacing trees that whispered as they passed. Behind them, the poignard turrets and swelling bartizans of Granmaison rose in fantastic splendor against the pewter sky. One half expected to see the wan face of an imprisoned princess in the tower.

"What do you hope to discover at Atwood?" she asked, as they entered the spinney. She drew closer to Luten in the darkness as the rustle of night creatures echoed ominously in the surrounding darkness.

"I want to rifle the desk, for one thing, as well as discover what caused the brandy decanter to explode."

"How do we get in?"

"I took a look at that French door when we were there. I figure I can pry it open—and utterly confuse McAlbie tomorrow when he discovers someone has broken in."

"The servants won't be in bed yet."

"They won't be on the qui vive either, with Simard dead and Malton in Lewes with Mrs. Warner. I wager they'll be in the kitchen, gossiping and drinking ale, or Simard's wine."

The darkness of the house, when it came into view, suggested that Luten was right. No lights shone on the main floor. Above, only one light burned, reminding them that Simard was laid out, with hired observers watching to see if he moved, if he drew breath. Odd to think of that worldly old lecher harboring such childish dreads.

A dull yellow glow from the half windows of the kitchen below suggested the servants were there. They went around the side of the house to the French door. It was locked, but the lock was centuries old. Luten pried it open with his clasp knife. He entered the study, looked all around, then drew Corinne in after him.

The scent of brandy still hung in the air. In the moonlit interior she could distinguish the large bulk of desk and cupboards and fireplace.

"Dare we light a candle?" she whispered.

He felt around the desk for a tinderbox, struck a flint, and lit a lamp. He lifted the light and said, "Now, where would he keep letters and account books going back a few years? I am curious to see just how much Simard gave Mrs. Warner. She says he set her up in business."

"The lawyer may have taken them."

"As Malton spends his days here, I fancy Sinclair comes to him." He saw a pile of leather-bound books on the edge of the desk and drew them forward. He went back to one marked 1807, when Warner had first removed to Lewes. The ledger showed a quarterly payment of five hundred pounds to Mr. Warner "for services rendered."

114

"No one pays his solicitor two thousand pounds a year!" he exclaimed. "Warner was said to perform some small duties for Simard. This smells fishy."

He leafed through the pages to determine the payments were made on a regular basis over three years. At the time of Warner's death two years before, the payments stopped. There was a lump payment of five thousand pounds to Mrs. Warner.

"They were holding the old boy to ransom," Luten said grimly. "Now, what could Warner have had on him?"

"Simard was no saint," she said. "It could have been anything. Probably something involving Simard's lechery."

"He made no secret of that. It seemed he gloried in it."

"I wonder if he was carrying on with Mrs. Warner all that time. But then why the five thousand payment at the end of the affair? That was at the time Simard and Mrs. Warner had their falling out. Very likely she was hounding him to marry her, once she became a widow, and he paid her off."

"Or perhaps she was enceinte—a payment to take care of the child. Yet there was no hint of it. The gossips would certainly have known if that were the case."

He turned to the more recent books and saw that Simard could well have afforded to give Bertie his five thousand. His rack-rent way of running Atwood had devastated the estate, but it had filled his own pocket. It was an old trick for the incumbent lord to siphon cash from an entailed estate when he did not like his heir. But whom did Simard intend to leave the money to?

"Interesting," he murmured. "Now for the other item of business."

He took up the lamp and went to the grate. The broken decanter had been removed. Some effort had been made to clean up the spilt brandy, but traces remained on the stone apron. Luten set the lamp on the mantel over the fireplace and began to examine the shelf and the oak wall above it. He gave a little "Aha!" of triumph, drew out his clasp knife, and pried something out of the oak paneling, where it had lodged between the crossed swords.

"What is it?" Corinne asked.

He held out his hand. A little black metal ball rested on his palm. "A lead ball. Someone fired a shot. It broke the decanter and knocked it off the mantel." He felt along the back of the mantel with his fingers. "Yes, there are traces of brandy and shards of glass here, at the back of the shelf."

"He must have missed Simard on his first shot."

"According to Phoebe, the first shot killed Simard. The decanter broke a few minutes later—after she saw the man in the cedar hedge riding away. Someone else was out there as well."

He went to the French doors and began gauging the angles of fire. The stand of cedars was in a direct line to Simard's desk, where he had been shot. A good marksman could have hit his target with one bullet. But the grate was on the side wall. A shot from the cedars could not have hit it.

"He had to be standing roughly—there," he said, pointing to the left of the open doorway, where a growth of roses climbing up a trellis wall offered concealment. There was an archway in the wall, leading to the park beyond. He took up the lamp and said, "Let us have a look out there."

"For clues," Corinne said, and snickered nervously.

If any clues were there, they were not visible by moonlight. They returned and closed the French doors.

"I have just had a horrid thought, Luten," Corinne said in a frightened voice. "Was it Phoebe that second shot was fired at? Where was she at the time? Where in the room, I mean?"

"Pacing to and fro, she said. She wasn't close enough to the grate to be splashed by the brandy."

"But if she was between the grate and the French door and he missed her, the ball would have landed there, where you found it."

Luten gazed from rose trellis to grate. "You're right."

"He must have thought she saw him when he shot Simard." Then she looked puzzled. "No, it can't be that. The man who shot Simard had already left. It doesn't make sense. It must have been an accident."

"There were two people here besides Phoebe," Luten

116

repeated. "What we have to deal with is a successful murderer and an unsuccessful one, both on the loose. Or perhaps a pair, working together."

"You mean Bertie and Malton?"

"It cannot be Phoebe and Lady Fairchild, or Phoebe would not have been an intended victim. Nor would Bertie shoot her, I think."

"That means Bertie shot Simard—and Malton took a shot at Phoebe and missed."

Luten looked doubtful. "Why would Malton shoot Phoebe? If she had not seen him shoot Simard, he had nothing to fear from her. Of course, he might have lost his head."

As they stood discussing the matter, they heard a quiet sound at the French door. Glancing to discover its cause, they saw a pale face staring in at them. Corinne emitted a light shriek. Luten blew out the lamp and drew her behind him.

"Has someone just returned to the scene of the crime?" he asked in a low voice that sounded as if he were smiling.

"I hope you brought a pistol!" she whispered.

"Er, no. I didn't think it necessary, but I have my clasp knife."

She felt about in the darkness and handed him the poker from the grate. "He's trying to break in," she whispered, as the sounds grew louder. "Stand by the side of the door and hit him as he enters."

"It's probably Dolman. He's heard us and is checking up."

"Don't hit him hard enough to kill him. Just stun him and let us get away unseen."

The lock gave a click and the door began to open.

Chapter Seventeen

"Psst! Don't shoot. It's me," a familiar voice hissed into the shadowy silence.

Corinne cried, "Coffen!" at the same instant as Luten said, "Pattle, what the deuce are you doing here?"

Coffen came tiptoeing into the darkened study. "I saw the light moving about. Thought maybe it was the murderer come back, but when I got up to the window, I recognized you two. Did you find anything?"

"Let us go back to Granmaison and discuss it at leisure," Corinne suggested.

"We'll not be disturbed here," Coffen said. "I took a look in at the kitchen window. The servants are celebrating there, making inroads into Malton's cellar, to judge by the number of bottles on the table. A regular Irish wake. Tom and Mary was dancing a jig."

He sat down in Simard's desk chair as he spoke, then rose again when he saw the bloodied blotter on the desk. "P'raps we ought to toddle along home," he decided.

They left by the French door, closing it carefully behind them, though the damaged lock would no doubt be discovered in the morning. As they walked back to Granmaison through the dark spinney, Luten outlined what he had discovered at Atwood. Coffen listened and agreed that there must have been a second person at the scene of the crime.

Prance was waiting for them in his saloon with, unfortunately, the handleless earthenware cups and a pot of tea. He had had the wine removed from the room to encourage his guests' acceptance of *chanoyu*.

"This is better than wine, after being out in the cold," Corinne said. She liked her tea—if only he would let them have milk for it!

"So soothing for the nerves," he said. "I am quite distraught. I have been hammering at poor Tante P until I feel like Torquemada convincing an innocent he has sinned." When Coffen's forehead corrugated in question, he added, "The inquisitor general in charge of torturing heretics during the Spanish Inquisition, Pattle, to save your inquiring. Nothing to do with Hindoos."

"Phoebe ain't popish."

"No indeed, nor is she at all forthcoming. I learned nothing. I am slowly coming to the conclusion she has revealed all she has to reveal. In short, the lady is innocent, and I am a brute." He sensed his audience's impatience and said, "Your eager faces tell me you folks have enjoyed some luck. No, that belittles your work. Not luck but effort and intelligence are your tools. Tell me all. I am famished for some good news."

Luten showed him the bullet pried out of the wall above the mantel, and again the matter of who had shot it, and why, was discussed.

"It was obviously intended to kill Auntie!" Prance cried. "I must warn her at once—except that she has dosed herself with laudanum, a sure sign she is worried, poor dear. She normally sleeps the sleep of the just—accompanied by such a cacophony of snores that— But there is no need to go into that. If it bothers you, Corinne, say but the word and I shall move you to another chamber."

"I'm a sound sleeper. It doesn't bother me."

"What an untroublesome guest you are—and with a murderer on the loose, too. I shall let one or two hounds out of the greenyard to roam free and warn us if the murderer returns to get Phoebe." He rose and did this at once.

"If anything should happen to Phoebe," he said when he returned, "I should hold myself accountable. She is my nearest and dearest relative, and next to Puitt, I believe I am hers. Speaking of Puitt . . ." He turned a questioning look on Coffen.

119

"He's acting queerly, but there might be an innocent explanation for it, Prance. You tell me."

"First you must tell me the nature of his behavior."

"He was normal enough when I got there. Showed me into the parlor, handed me an ale, all right and tight. Talked of a boxing match he'd been to and a cock he's having trained up to fight. After we'd done the pretty, I told him of McAlbie's visit, that McAlbie said he had time to ride to Atwood and shoot Simard. He admitted he had time, but insisted he hadn't done it. I believed him. But then after I left, I loitered about outside to follow him and see who he was meeting. Thought it might be a lady. No such a thing. He was wearing awful clothes. An old jacket I wouldn't be caught dead in."

"That bad!" Prance murmured, with a disbelieving look at Coffen's rumpled jacket. "One can only wonder where he got it."

"From the rag and bone man, p'raps," said Coffen, undismayed. "Not from a cat anyhow. Not a catskin weskit, is what I'm getting at. He wore a misshapen hat pulled low over his eyes as if he was hiding his face. Only there was no one to see him but sheep and me, and he didn't know I was there.

"I followed him a mile to a little ramshackle farmhouse. A fellow came out to talk to him—a tall drink of water. Puitt handed the fellow something—I believe 'twas money. The fellow lifted the door of his dark lantern and seemed to be counting it. Then they parted. Puitt headed for home and I went along to Atwood and met Luten and Corinne. My thinking is that he could have hired the fellow to shoot Simard and was paying him off."

"Was it a little clapboard cottage with a thatched roof, a mile or so west of here?" Prance inquired.

"That's it. You know the lad?" Coffen asked eagerly.

"That's Chris Hawken. He works with the Gentlemen. Puitt buys brandy from him to distribute to the local gentry."

Coffen frowned. "Dash it, a red herring. Still, a smuggler wouldn't balk at murder, eh? Bloodthirsty lads, the Gentlemen."

"Not hereabouts. Hawken is a good fellow. He is the sole support of his mama. You'll find him in church every Sunday."

As they were talking, the door knocker sounded. Blakeney came to the door and announced, "Mr. Puitt."

"Show him in," Prance said. Four eager faces turned to the doorway.

Bertie had stopped at home to repair his toilette before calling on Sir Reginald. "Evening, Pattle, folks," he said, making a jerky bow all around before joining them at the grate. "I left your—er, merchandise—with Blakeney," he said to Reg.

"These are my friends, Puitt. No need to mince words." He turned to the others. "Puitt has brought me my quarterly supply of brandy. Blakeney paid you, Puitt?"

"He did. I wanted a word with Auntie, but Blakeney tells me she has retired."

"Yes, with a sleeping draft, so I fear you cannot see her tonight. I'll tell her you came. Drop by tomorrow morning, if it's urgent. Or you can tell me." He poured Bertie a cup of tea. Bertie accepted it and seemed to appreciate it.

"It's nothing important," he said. "Just a visit. I knew she would be worried about—what McAlbie thinks. He has been quizzing me, but I had nothing to do with Simard's death. They can't prove I had when I hadn't, eh?" He looked to Coffen. "Did you tell them about Mary and Tom?"

"Not yet," Coffen said. "We got chatting of other things."

"What about Tom and Mary?" Corinne asked.

"I was telling Pattle earlier, I overheard them arguing this afternoon," Puitt said. "I saw them strolling in Simard's orchard as I was coming home from the woods, around suppertime. I was going to have a go at Mary, for I know she's lying about what she saw in the hedge. Not that it would help me. I wear a blue jacket, not a catskin weskit. Anyhow, I know she's lying. She said she was making up Simard's bedchamber at the time, and you can only see the far edge of the cedar hedge from there, and you can't see anyone leaving unless he goes round to the front of the house. The master bedroom looks out on the front park. I figure where she was if she actually saw anything was the Rose Suite, which overlooks the cedars. But it's a guest suite, so she had no reason to be working there. Simard seldom

121

has guests. An unsociable fellow. I wager she was waiting for Tom to join her and cut up some larks."

"Are you saying that the man left by the front road?" Luten asked.

"Not really," Puitt said. "What I'm saying is she lied. She would have made up the master bedroom in the morning. She was in the Rose Suite. She'd get a dandy view of the cedar hedge from there. And she has eyes like a hawk. I'm sure she knows exactly who was there. That's what I'm saying."

"Did you quiz her about it?" Prance asked.

"I didn't, Prance. The two of them were arguing, so I just slipped behind a tree and listened. Not the thing, of course, but when my reputation's at stake, I did it anyhow. Tom told her she shouldn't ought to do it, it was too dangerous to be going out alone at night. She told him she'd do more than whatever it is she's doing for a hundred quid. Tom was pretty pleased with that, but then after a while he said she ought to hold out for a thousand. That's when my eyes opened up wide, I can tell you. A thousand pounds! It's more than she'd earn honestly in a lifetime. She said she'd try to raise the ante, but it might be best to wait awhile, until things settled down and the blunt was more readily available. I don't think Tom was with her when she spotted the murderer or he'd be running the show."

"Who was going to pay her such a sum?" Prance asked.

"She never said. They got to snuggling and talking about what they'd do with the blunt, so I slipped away."

"What was they going to do with it?" Coffen asked.

"Mary wanted to waste it on silk gowns and bonnets. Tom said they'd open up a public house somewhere near London."

"Where they could use one is on the way to Brighton," Coffen said.

"Is that so? Someone should tell Tom."

Luten stirred restively. "Did you hear anything else relevant to Simard's murder?" he asked. "That mention of when 'the blunt was more readily available' suggests Malton."

"That's what I thought," Bertie said, "but they didn't name names, worse luck. I think we ought to keep an eye on her, see who she meets. I meant to do it myself tonight, but I had invited Pattle to call, and I had to meet Hawken as well, to pay him for the last load of brandy. The Gentlemen get rusty if you're late in paying."

Corinne said, "It sounds as if Mary saw who was in the cedars and is planning to make him pay her for holding her tongue. That is why she suddenly changed her story about seeing a blue jacket. She knows who the man is."

"Extortion is a dangerous game," Luten said. "She didn't say when she was to collect the money, Puitt?"

"She didn't. They were already into their talk when I got close enough to listen. I took a run past Atwood before I came here. Just peeked in at the kitchen window. The servants are there, drinking up Simard's cellar. I didn't see Mary or Tom."

"They were there a while ago," Coffen said.

"They might have slipped up to the Rose Suite or Mary's room," Puitt said. "With the servants all three sheets to the wind and no master in the house, they won't be too careful."

Corinne felt a tremble of apprehension quiver up her spine. "Or she could be out collecting her hundred pounds," she said.

"Your second sight sending a message, is it?" Coffen asked. "Now, don't squint at me, Corinne. I ain't making fun of you. I mind it worked before, the night Lady Chamaude was killed." Prance uttered a shuddering sigh at the memory.

"As long as Tom's with her, I wager she's safe," Puitt said. "There was no talk of him being in on the extortion. I fancy he'd keep clear of it, but be dodging behind her and get the money out of Mary. He's a slippery sort of fellow. Knows how to look out for himself."

"But does he know how to look out for Mary?" Corinne asked.

"Dangerous for her to be out alone at night," Luten said. "If she's lying to help a murderer, they'll meet tonight. She's not with the other servants. I wager she's out now, this very minute." He was already rising from the chair as he spoke. His nervousness communicated itself to the others.

"We should spread out, go in different directions," Corinne said. "What are the likeliest meeting spots, Puitt?"

123

"It would be somewhere close to Atwood. Mary would have to walk. And of course, they'd want someplace they couldn't be seen, so they won't meet in an open field. There's the spinney between Granmaison and Atwood."

"And the orchard where Mary met Tom," Prance added. "Or perhaps at the end of Simard's road, where it meets the road to Heath. I'll change and join you." He ran from the room, already struggling with the stomacher that held his *kirimon* in place.

"No one should go alone," Corinne said.

"I'll go to the orchard," Coffen said. "You come with me, Puitt. Show me where Mary was with Tom. If she got to choose the spot, that might be it."

"Luten, let's you and I go to the spinney," Corinne said.

"You stay here, love. I'll go to the spinney. Tell Prance to saddle up a mount and go to the main road. Tell him to take one of the grooms with him."

"I'll tell Blakeney," she countered. "I'm going with you."

"Stay!" he said in a sharp voice, as if he were commanding one of his hounds. Then he strode out of the house, troublesomely aware of her mutinous glare following him.

Corinne told Blakeney to have two mounts saddled up at once. When Prance returned, she said she was to accompany him to the main road. He was so keen on the hunt that he didn't realize her stunt. When they went out, one of his hounds came barking up to him, yelping loudly. Another could be heard barking at the rear of the house.

"They'll give the show away. I'll ask the groom to put them back in the greenyard," he said, and rode around to the stable to do it.

They rode halfway to Atwood, tethered their mounts to a tree, and walked the last part of the way on foot, clinging to the shadowed edge of the road. They continued, looking all about in the darkness, to where Simard's private road met the main highway. Tall trees grew along the road's shoulder. The metaled road stretched into the distance like a white ribbon in the moonlight. Not a soul was on it. A fox barked in the distance. A bird, a nighthawk it looked like, swooped through the sky.

"I doubt Mary would agree to go any farther than this," Prance said. "Does your second sight tell you anything?"

"No. I am worried for her, but I don't feel anything here. Let us return. The others may have seen something. Did you notice, Reg, Coffen said Mary and Tom were in the kitchen, but Bertie said they were not? Do you think Bertie might have invented this story about Mary extorting money?"

"He is too honest and too simple to do anything of the sort. Puitt was there after Pattle. Tom and Mary left during the interval. *C'est tout.*"

"I expect you're right. In any case, Mary's changing her story actually helped Bertie as well as the murderer."

"True, Puitt is no Brummell, but I am happy to say he does not own a catskin weskit."

When they reached Granmaison, Prance let one of the hounds loose. It darted off toward the *nina*. They followed the animal. It stood with its nose at the gazebo door, howling like a banshee.

"Hush, Nellie," Prance said. The howling eased to a high-pitched whining in the throat. "A badger or stoat has gotten into my teahouse again," Prance said, collaring the hound and drawing it by main force back to the greenyard. "I shall have a proper door put on it. The hounds are obviously no protection for Auntie. I tremble to think that second shot was meant for her. Perhaps Malton will lend me Hannibal for a few days. I see Malton is keeping the brute chained at night, or he would have savaged us."

When they returned to the saloon, they discovered none of the searchers had been shot or attacked, nor had anyone discovered anything of the least interest. It was not until the next morning that the second murder was discovered, and by then, of course, it was too late to save Mary's life, or to learn her secret.

Chapter Eighteen

"All a hum. We upset ourselves for nothing," Coffen said, when they all sat around the revived fire. He and Puitt had got back first. As well as refurbishing the fire, they had run a wine decanter to earth in the dining room and were making free with it, while sparks snapped and flames leapt in the grate.

"No reason to think whoever Mary was meeting was going to harm her," Bertie replied. "Mean to say, if she's lying for someone, he'd be eager to keep her alive, wouldn't he?"

"She's already given McAlbie her evidence," Corinne said. "The safest thing would be to silence her before she changes her mind. I am assuming it is the murderer she's shielding."

"What we need is a bite to eat to stir up our brains," Coffen suggested, with a hopeful glance at his host. "We can't think on an empty stomach." Coffen's horror of an empty stomach was well known to them all.

"I have already spoken to Blakeney," Prance said. "Sandwiches will be here shortly, glutton."

"You're a fine host, Prance. Demmed fine." Coffen topped off his glass. In this mood, he was willing to forget insults, *chanoyu*, *ninas*, and other heathen matters.

Rather than enlivening their minds, the sandwiches and tray of sweets and wine put them all in a restful mood. They went upstairs, assuring themselves and each other that they would watch Mary like a hawk tomorrow night. Coffen volunteered to be at the back door of Atwood at twilight and follow her to see who she met.

Luten accompanied Corinne to her room. "I believe we ought to run through the marriage ceremony to refresh our memories," he said, with a playful squeeze of her fingers. "I told you not to go out. I seem to recall there is something in there about love, honor, and obey. The key word, my pet, being *obey*."

"I would have said *love* is the more important word."

"That's why I asked you to stay here, so you would be safe—because I am so fond of you."

She raised her eyebrows and gave a disparaging smile. Try as she might, she could never get him to say in so many words that he loved her. "If we ever actually get around to getting married, then we shall discuss it again. In the meanwhile, I would be more likely to oblige you if you did not bark commands at me, but made a civil request, like a gentleman."

"I was worried for your safety! And in a hurry."

"Does that excuse poor manners?"

He tilted his head and scowled. "Apparently not. Do my poor manners preclude a kiss good night?" As he spoke, he reached out and drew her into his arms. Just as he lowered his head to kiss her, a stertorous snore came from Phoebe's room. It was not a light sound, but a deep, rumbling thunder that made one wait for the accompanying lightning. The embrace died aborning. Luten drew a deep, disgruntled sigh and said, "How romantic! Nothing like musical accompaniment for a courting. Why don't you ask Prance to give you another room? The one beside mine is unoccupied," he added, with a suspiciously innocent face.

"I'll be fine," she said, and turned to open her door.

"You don't get away that easily, miss!" He swung her back into his arms for a satisfying kiss. If Phoebe's snores rent the air, Corinne didn't hear them. She heard only the insistent siren call of temptation as the kiss deepened to a rising passion. She was a widow, after all, not an inexperienced maiden, and she and Luten were engaged. She wanted to be with him that night, safe in his arms, to fill the aching need inside her. Her strict Irish upbringing told her it would be sinfully wrong, but her body and heart felt it was right.

"Come to my room," he breathed into her ear, while his hands performed a warm, caressing massage on her shoulders

127

and the crook of her neck. It was a nearly irresistible temptation. Something inside her was melting to a golden glow of anticipation.

For ten seconds she trembled on the edge of going. Then she remembered her mama's warnings against the wicked melords she would meet in England who would seduce a lady, then throw in her face that she was no better than she should be. She gazed for a moment into his eyes, trying to read his mind. She saw only hope and love. At least it looked like love.

"Good night, Luten," she said, and slipped away, into her room, smiling softly.

She loved Luten madly. She also trusted him. He was not the sort who would seduce a lady and abandon her, but he just might think less of her if she gave herself to him before the wedding. He had more than once scoffed at the low morals of high society. This was the first time he had suggested that he wanted to make love before their marriage. The admission had cost him something. He was not the sort to show his weakness, even to the woman he loved. It was an odd sort of pride in him that he pretended he didn't need anyone.

She wondered what accounted for it. She knew his parents' marriage had been a loveless one, arranged by his mama's parents. Luten was an only child. An older sister had died in childbirth. He spoke of his school days with affection, yet Eton was not a gentle place for a young boy. If he had preferred it to his home, what hell must his home life have been? He never spoke of it, not even to her. The little she knew, she had gained from Prance.

Phoebe was snoring in the next room, but the sound was muffled and didn't bother her so much as the baying hounds. They seemed upset that night. She drifted off to sleep, thinking of Luten. She awoke from a bad dream several hours later. In her dream, she and Luten were back in London, discovering the body of a seamstress, crumpled in a heap behind a curtain in a cramped room in a cheap rooming house, strangled to death.

It was worrying about Mary, of course, that had drawn this sad memory to the surface of her mind. There was no reason to think Mary was dead. The baying hounds, though, had a mournful sound. She had never heard them so noisy before. Then she noticed something else. Phoebe was not snoring. Vague worries began to coalesce into an overpowering fear. Someone had murdered Phoebe! Prance had locked up the hounds, which were perfectly useless in any case. Was that why the dogs were baying, because Phoebe lay on the ground, dead? Sleep was impossible after that mental image. It would be better to take a look in Phoebe's room and see if she was all right than to lie awake for hours, imagining and worrying.

Corinne rose, lit her bedside lamp, and tiptoed from her chamber. As it was the middle of the night and no one would see her, she didn't bother with her dressing gown or slippers. Prance had had a fire laid in the occupied bedrooms. The embers still warmed it, but once she went into the hall, a draft of cold air set her shivering. She listened a moment to the reverberating silence, then tapped once lightly on Phoebe's door, in case she was awake. When there was no answer, she opened the door and peeped in. The flickering light from her lamp and the embers in Phoebe's grate showed her a tousled bed and an empty room. Phoebe was gone.

A tremble shook her from head to foot. For a long moment she just stood at the doorway staring, unable to believe her eyes. There was no sign of violence. The furniture had not been disarranged. She went into the room and looked on the far side of the bed, in the unlikely event that Phoebe had fallen out of bed. Of course, she wasn't there. What should she do? Call for help. Luten, Prance, Coffen—her surrogate family. On an impulse she went toward the window, thinking she might see someone carrying Phoebe off. As she approached it, she noticed the moving shadow, throwing a gigantic form on the golden drapery of the window where there had been no shadow before.

Her own candle, held in front of her, cast no shadow forward. Then who? For an instant that seemed an hour, she stood stock-still with her heart pounding in her throat, waiting for a sound, a movement, that would presage an attack. The shadow flickered, but there was no sound. When the shadow moved and grew larger, showing that someone was advancing silently toward her, she summoned up her courage and turned around, to see Phoebe staring at her in confusion.

"Lady deCoventry, what are you doing here?" Phoebe was carrying a large tray that held a lamp, a steaming cocoa pot, and a cup.

Corinne felt weak with relief. "Oh, Miss Dauntry! I was so frightened! I came to see if you were all right. Reggie was worried about you, and when I couldn't hear you snoring—"

"Oh my dear! I have kept you awake with my wretched snoring." She set the tray down on the bedside table and sat on the edge of the bed. "As if the barking of those dogs isn't enough to wake the dead! It was their howling that awakened me, and kept me from getting back to sleep. After an hour staring at the window, I decided some warm milk would help, so I went below and heated some up. I like a little cocoa and sugar in mine. Come and share it with me. I've made a whole pot. Here, I'll use my posset cup and you can have the clean cup. You do look shaken up. It is this murder that has us all on edge."

She poured two cups of cocoa. Corinne drew the desk chair up beside Phoebe and they had their cocoa and tried to calm each other. Phoebe was nervous, too. Her hand trembled on the cocoa cup. Corinne told her of Bertie's visit, and their looking about the estate for Mary.

"Of course, it was a blue jacket she saw, the same as I did myself," Phoebe said. "If she is trying to get money from a murderer, she is a fool. She'll end up a corpse. If she knows who it was, she ought to tell McAlbie. I shall make Bertie tell him tomorrow what he overheard in the orchard. I wonder he hadn't the sense to do it."

"Who do you think she saw?"

"Who else could it be but Malton? There is no other gentleman involved, and he rides a bay mare. There isn't a doubt in my mind. He is the one who ends up with the lot— estate, title, whatever money is left. I doubt there is much."

Corinne opened her mouth to correct her error, then shut it again. Perhaps Luten wanted to keep that quiet until they were sure Phoebe was innocent. It was not until she was preparing to leave that Corinne noticed the traces of earth on the carpet, just at the doorway. They were quite noticeable on the cream-colored carpet. They had not come from her own bare feet. As they were sitting knee to knee, it was difficult to see Phoebe's feet. But she had to know.

She lifted her spoon as if to stir her cocoa and let it fall from her fingers. When she reached down to pick it up, she noticed Phoebe was not wearing slippers, but laced-up walking shoes, neatly tied. A lady did not go to that much bother only to nip down to the kitchen, not when there was a pair of blue slippers right beside her bed. Her legs were crossed. The sole of one shoe was in plain sight. There was some fresh earth, just where the heel met the sole. Phoebe had been outdoors. She had also been to the kitchen to make the cocoa, but she had been out-doors first. What had she been doing?

Afraid that her knowledge would show in her face, Corinne drank up her cocoa quickly and left. Back in her own room, she quietly wedged the back of a chair under the doorknob, the way she and her sister Kate used to do when they were reading the servants' magazines that their mama disapproved of. She climbed into bed, extinguished her lamp, and drew the cover-ings up to her chin, but it was hard to sleep, with so much to think of. Pictures and bits of information chased each other around in her mind. She noticed then that the hounds had stopped barking. She couldn't say when it had happened. She had not heard them for a few minutes now. The silence seemed suddenly ominous.

Was it Phoebe whom Mary had met, to get the hundred pounds? Did Phoebe have a hundred pounds? She had a small competence, and Prance paid her something. Was it Phoebe whom Mary had seen from the upper window? Had Phoebe shot Simard, then gone into the study to make sure he was dead? But Phoebe didn't shoot. She hated guns. She had been swift to point her finger at Malton, who had an alibi. Was she protecting Bertie? Eventually Corinne slept.

Sunrise came late in October. It was seven o'clock before the sky began to lighten. Things seemed better in daylight. There

131

was probably some innocent explanation for Phoebe's being outdoors alone in the middle of the night, but even in daylight, Corinne couldn't think what would draw an elderly lady out alone at night, when there was a murderer on the loose. A murderer who might already have tried to kill her once.

At seven-thirty she rang for hot water and began her toilette. Prance's servants had pressed her dark green merino gown with the lace fichu at the neck. Luten liked her in that outfit. As it was early, she took the time to arrange her hair carefully, swept back from her pale face to fall in a basket of curls behind. Purple smudges beneath her eyes after her disturbed night reminded her of her age. Twenty-four, fast approaching the quarter century. Perhaps a special license and a hasty wedding were the way to go. It seemed the only way she and Luten were ever going to find time to get married. Murder always seemed to intervene.

At eight o'clock she went down to the morning parlor to find Coffen and Luten there before her. She took advantage of Prance's absence to tell them of her night's doings.

"Phoebe might have gone down to silence the dogs," Coffen suggested. "I was tempted to do it myself. What a racket. I wonder if someone forgot to feed them. Poor blighters."

"You can't be sure the earth on her carpet was fresh," Luten said. "It hasn't been raining lately."

"The servants would have swept it up if it had been there when they lit her fire this evening," she pointed out. "You know Prance's servants. They scarcely wait for you to put a glass down before they snatch it away. Everything is kept spick-and-span here."

"They empty the wastebasket in your room twice a day," Coffen said. "I accidentally dropped a packet of lemon drops in mine. Meant to fish it out later. The dashed thing was gone. I agree with Corinne. If there was dirt on that carpet, it was fresh dirt."

"It might have been on her shoes when she put them on," was Luten's next idea.

"I know what you're feeling, Luten," Corinne said. "I like

Phoebe, too. In fact, I don't believe she killed Simard, but she obviously knows more than she is telling."

"Protecting Bertie, I shouldn't wonder," Coffen said. "No reason to think he killed Mary just because he didn't see her like I did. Dancing in the kitchen, I mean."

"There is no reason to think Mary is dead," Luten insisted.

It was at that moment that Prance came flying into the morning parlor. He had abandoned his Oriental toilette, or perhaps had not yet taken time to grease his hair and paint his eyebrows. He was wearing a normal jacket and trousers in any case. His skin was bone-white and his usual cynical expression was gone, leaving his face strangely vulnerable.

"What's the matter?" Coffen demanded.

"It's Mary!" he exclaimed. "She's dead. Murdered."

Chapter Nineteen

"Where? When?" Coffen barked.

"Just now, in the gazebo." In his shock, Prance reverted to the original name of his new teahouse.

"Just murdered now, you mean?"

"No—I don't know. I just discovered the body now. I went out to silence the hounds. I could see something was upsetting them. I thought perhaps a fox—" he said disjointedly. "I let Nellie out of the pen—you know, Corinne, the one who was barking at the teahouse last night. She headed straight for it again and nagged at me until I went in—and saw the body."

"Are you sure she's dead?" Corinne asked.

"Positive."

"Is she still there?" Coffen asked.

"I would assume so. She was in no condition to walk."

"Then let us go," he said, and flung his napkin on top of his gammon and eggs, a certain sign of his alarm, for in the usual way, nothing came between Coffen and his breakfast.

Corinne and Luten rose abruptly, too. Luten cast one chiding look at his fiancée but didn't bother telling her to "stay."

"You know perfectly well you won't sleep for a week," he scolded as they hastened down to the kitchen and out the back door, the closest route to the gazebo. She knew only too well the nightmares that would ensue, but she wanted just one quick peek at Mary. She hardly knew why, except that death was one of life's major occurrences, like birth or marriage. It was not something to be ignored. One went to see it, perhaps to make its acquaintance in hopes of becoming inured to it, except that one never did become inured.

It struck Prance, as they stumbled over the uneven stones to the gazebo, that his Japanese enthusiasm had been ill advised. He had had a perfectly good set of cobblestones pried up and hauled away, to be replaced by these rude rocks. His ill-advised haste was even more obvious when they all had to hunker down to get through the lowered doorway of the gazebo. As to ever enjoying *chanoyu* there again! Serenity had fled his sanctuary forever.

He led the way in. Mary's rigid body was on the floor, with her head and shoulders on the low table, facedown. Her brown curls were uncovered. The wind moved them playfully, giving a ghoulish illusion of life in death.

"How did she die?" Corinne asked in a hollow voice.

"I don't know."

"Shot, like Simard?" Coffen suggested.

"I hadn't the nerve to examine her," Prance said, and went forward tentatively to take a closer look.

He touched her stiff shoulder but could not bring himself to raise her head. When Coffen moved closer to do so, Corinne reached instinctively for Luten's hand. His fingers tightened on hers, but he was looking at Mary as Coffen lifted her head. She saw the pain in his eyes and felt a warm rush of love. It always surprised her that this lofty lord held such deep and true feelings for life's unfortunates.

"Strangled," Coffen said.

Corinne just took one glance. She remembered too well the agonized face of a victim of strangulation, with the bluish cast to the skin. Mary looked like that.

"She's still rigor mortified," Coffen added. "It takes six or so hours to set in and a whole day to work off. A day and night, I mean, so she's been dead for at least six hours. That'd make it two o'clock this morning. Maybe earlier, of course."

"Earlier," Corinne said. "That's why the hound was barking here last night, Reg."

"I daresay you're right—and we never even thought of looking. I hadn't thought Mary would be murdered on *my* property. Why did she come here, I wonder?" After a frowning

135

pause he said, "It's not what you're thinking! This has nothing to do with my aunt."

"No, 'twas later that she was out prowling," Coffen said.

Prance bristled up like an outraged rooster. "What do you mean, 'out prowling'?"

Corinne gave him an abbreviated version of her night's doings.

"I shall speak to Blakeney," he said stiffly. "The upstairs maid is becoming derelict in her duties recently. I noticed dust on my toilet table this very morning. She forgot to sweep up the dirt from Auntie's shoes yesterday, and Auntie forgot to put her shoes out for cleaning."

"Phoebe wasn't out of the house yesterday," Pattle reminded him.

"The day before then, when she went to visit Simard. She was in that patch of nettle bushes. That is obviously when she got her shoes soiled."

"But why did she put on shoes and lace 'em up if she was just going to the kitchen to make cocoa?"

"Because the floors are cold. It is exactly what I would have done myself." When he met three disbelieving pairs of eyes, he said, "I'll talk to her. I daresay we must call McAlbie."

"I'll stay here with Mary," Coffen volunteered. "Best not to leave a corpse alone."

It flashed into Corinne's mind that Simard's corpse was being watched at Atwood, lest it show signs of life. Two murders. Folks said such tragedies came in threes. She assumed Coffen was staying behind to look for clues, not watch the corpse for signs of life. The others returned to the house, and Prance sent a footman off to Heath for McAlbie. This done, he rushed upstairs to confer with his aunt.

"This is going to be a busy day," Luten said to Corinne. They had returned to the morning parlor—not to finish their breakfast, neither of them could eat—but to have a warming cup of coffee. "McAlbie will be asking questions this morning, and this afternoon is the inquest for Simard's death. This looks bad for Phoebe, does it not?"

"I think Mary was killed some hours before Phoebe went

136

outside. Remember we heard her snoring when we went up to bed? She could hardly murder someone, then fall peacefully to sleep."

"Rigor mortis might have set in more quickly than six hours. It depends on the temperature, for one thing. It would have been cold out in the gazebo."

"Could a lady strangle someone, then calmly come home and make a pot of cocoa? She didn't seem very upset last night, just a little nervous. I don't think she killed Mary."

"Then why bother telling McAlbie she was out?"

"I don't believe I will. It will only confuse matters."

"Excellent rationalizing." He stirred restively.

"Go on back," she said. "I know you want to help Coffen search for clues."

"How did you know?" he asked, already rising.

"You forget I'm Irish. I can read minds, as well as the future."

"But are not always so obliging in fulfilling wishes," he said with a teasing grin. Then he lifted her hand and kissed her fingers, while gazing into her eyes.

She knew he was referring to last night. That, too, was unlike Luten. His little failures were not usually mentioned, once they were past. She felt it showed some new closeness, that he could reveal his feelings to her. She didn't answer, but he seemed satisfied with her smile. He left at once.

As he hastened to the gazebo, he glanced up at the darkening sky, where scudding clouds promised rain. A cold wind had blown in from the coast. It stirred the branches of tall oaks and elms, sending a shower of sere leaves to the ground. That cold wind was enough to hasten rigor mortis.

"Any clues, Pattle?" he asked, when he entered the gazebo.

Pattle was prowling the circumference of the small building and peering out the unglazed windows for signs of any unusual disturbance.

"Her hands are scratched up quite a bit. Her hair ribbon had been torn off. It was tangled up in her skirt. Trying to fight off her attacker, poor girl. Nothing seems to have been left behind, unless she's sitting on it. I didn't like to move her. It didn't seem right to jostle a corpse about." He and Luten exchanged a questioning look. "Of course, with two of us, we could move her gentlelike."

"I'll take her head and shoulders, you take her feet. We'll roll her over gently. Ready?"

They acted with all due respect for the dead. On the table beneath Mary's body, Coffen found his clue. A small brass button with a navy blue thread still attached to it. He picked it up and handed it to Luten. "This ain't from Mary's gown. It has white bone buttons."

"It didn't come off Phoebe's nightgown," Luten said.

"No, it's from a gent's jacket, looks like. A bit smaller than you usually see. Smaller than they wear in London."

"Puitt?"

Coffen shook his head. "Smaller than his, too. There was no button off his jacket last night, was there?"

"Not when he was here, but that was before the murder. In any case, the size is wrong. We'll put it back and let McAlbie find out who it belongs to."

They put the button back on the table and placed Mary as they had found her. Luten returned to the house to tell Prance and Corinne what he had found. Prance had returned to the morning parlor.

"That lets Phoebe out!" Corinne said at once. "Prance has just been telling me where she went last night."

Prance was happy to exonerate his aunt. "The dogs' barking was keeping her awake. She was afraid it would disturb my guests—you folks. She thought exactly what occurred to me, in fact, only I hadn't the common decency to do anything about it. She thought the servants had forgotten to feed them, so she went to the larder to see if the pan of kitchen scraps André sets aside for them was full. It wasn't, so she knew they had been fed, but there were some rather tasty bones. Actually André had been keeping them to make soup, but she decided sleep was more important, so she took the bones out to the greenyard and tossed them in. She really did! I checked, and the bones were there, licked clean and well gnawed. It did not stop the barking entirely. Nellie remembered the scent of that corpse, and her nervousness communicated itself to the others. But in any case, that is why Auntie was out last night."

"It's odd she didn't mention it when I was talking to her," Corinne said.

"Why—she said she did mention it to you, Corrie."

"She mentioned the dogs' barking had kept her awake. Perhaps she said she had been out. I was so frightened when I saw her missing, you know, that I daresay I didn't catch every word, but I did notice a little later that the barking had stopped. In any case, Reg, that brass button Coffen found points to a gentleman, so you can tell Phoebe to rest easy."

"A plain brass button about an inch in diameter," Luten said. "Can you think of anyone who wears buttons like that?"

"No, it sounds as if it might have come from a youngster's jacket."

"Or a footman's?" Corinne asked.

"They more usually have a crest. I don't recognize what you've described."

They were still at the table when McAlbie arrived. Prance offered to take him to the gazebo. Within minutes of their departure, Coffen came darting into the morning parlor.

"Glad I caught you before you left. I'll go with you."

"Where?" Corinne asked in confusion.

"To Atwood, of course. We want to find out what they have to say about Mary. We'll want a word with Tom for starters. He certainly knows who she was meeting last night."

Luten and Corinne exchanged a stricken look and immediately leapt up.

"Why didn't we think of that!" she cried.

Coffen preened a little. "Too busy gazing into each other's eyes. Lovebirds and murder don't mix, except in them *crimes passionels*. Come along, we'll want to be back before McAlbie leaves."

He snatched a piece of cold toast from his plate and led one delinquent lovebird off to Atwood. Corinne decided to remain behind. Mary had been murdered at the gazebo. There might be clues to be discovered at Granmaison.

Chapter Twenty

The usually dour Dolman welcomed Luten and Coffen to Atwood like long-lost friends. "So glad you have come, your lordship, Mr. Pattle! I didn't know whether we ought to bother Mr.—that is, Lord Simard, with it. At this time, you must know, he is so busy, and the inquest this very afternoon. We are all at sixes and sevens here."

"What seems to be the trouble, Dolman?" Luten inquired.

"Forgive me. My wits are gone begging. You would not have heard of it at Granmaison. Tom and Mary have taken off without a word to a soul, leaving us shorthanded, and with the guests coming here after the inquest for tea. To say nothing of the funeral this evening. The tea will be the new lordship's first social occasion, and though it will be small and informal—he plans to issue only a verbal invitation at the inquest—we had hoped to make it perfect for him. I have Betsy searching the house this minute to see if Tom took anything belonging to Lord Simard with him. I am happy to say the silver is intact. I keep it under lock and key. The late Lord Simard's valet assures me his lordship's jewelry is in the safe. Vincent, having been with his late lordship for several decades, was given the combination."

Luten listened, intrigued. "Mary and Tom are both gone?"

"A runaway match, it looks like, though why they would choose to give up such excellent positions—" He stopped. Something in the callers' faces told him they had news of their own to impart.

"I am afraid I have some shocking news for you, Dolman. Mary was found at Granmaision this morning, murdered."

140

Dolman's hand flew to his mouth. "Good God! The poor girl. Murdered—at Granmaison? How?"

"Strangled."

"And Tom?"

"No sign of Tom. We came here in hope of speaking to him, to see what he could tell us."

"You don't suppose—" Dolman pursed his lips together in silent thought.

"You figure Tom killed her?" Coffen asked.

"I have no reason to believe so," Dolman admitted, almost reluctantly. "They were both chirping merry last night. In fact, we had a little celebration belowstairs in honor of their coming marriage."

"At what time would that be?" Coffen asked.

"I'm afraid it went on for several hours, sir. With no master in the house, you know. His lordship returned to Greenwood immediately after dinner."

"Any idea what time Mary and Tom left?"

"I locked up the wine cellar at eleven-thirty and retired, leaving the housekeeper in charge. They were still there at that time, dancing a jig. Betsy, of course, does not take drink. She informed me this morning that Tom and Mary left shortly after me. She feared they had gone—er, abovestairs together," he said, blushing for their sins.

Coffen nodded at Luten, as if to say Puitt had been telling the truth. Tom and Mary had left the kitchen by the time he was there.

"There is one other thing," Dolman continued. "I noticed this morning when I was making my rounds that the study had been broken into. Nothing is missing, but the desk had been rifled. Tom would not have had to break the lock to get out, if that is the way he and Mary left. It looks bad for Tom, does it not? I mean, who else—"

Luten said not a word about the broken lock. "I shall ask McAlbie to come down," he said. "He is at Granmaison now. He'll want to hear what you have to say, Dolman. I'm sorry for your trouble. You should notify Mr. Malton at once."

"Oh, I will. I will, now I know it is more than a pair of runaway servants. Dear me, and his tea party this afternoon and the funeral this evening— So kind of you. Thank you, your lordship."

Luten and Coffen left at once.

"It looks like a falling out between the young couple," Luten said as they strode from the house. "You noticed Dolman considers Tom the prime mover. 'To see if Tom took anything belonging to Lord Simard.' It seems Tom has no sterling reputation."

"I noticed that. Wait a minute, Luten. I want to speak to John Groom."

He darted off toward the stable. Luten strolled around to the study door to see how much damage he had caused. He figured a clever footman could fix the lock up without replacing it. As he peered into the study, he saw the desk was in some disarray, but concluded Dolman had been searching for missing money or papers and, in his haste, left the mess behind.

He met Coffen on his way back from the stable and they walked hastily back to Granmaison. "What was that visit all about?" he asked.

"One of the nags was taken out of the stable last night, late. No one saw it go, but it was put back with the saddle on."

"Then it doesn't seem Tom stole a mount to put more miles between him and the law after he killed Mary."

"I didn't think he'd be such a fool. Horse stealing would land him in jail pretty fast, but that's not what I had in mind. Before I left the gazebo, I took a look around for clues. I noticed freshish horse droppings a quarter of a mile from the building. I figure whoever killed poor Mary rode to Granmaison. Tom wouldn't risk borrowing a nag for such a short trip. It lets Phoebe out as well."

"Hmmm, it sounds more like Malton or Puitt."

"Puitt has his own nag."

"Yes, but it could be a clever means of diverting suspicion to Malton. I wonder if Malton spent the night at Lewes."

"He told Dolman Greenwood. McAlbie can find that out easy enough," Coffen said. "What I'm wondering is why Tom sheered off. I wager he knows that whoever murdered Mary knows that Mary told him what she knows, if you see what I mean." Luten nodded. "He's run to ground like a frightened fox, poor soul. If he's wise, he's hied it off to London. That's the place to lose yourself."

"If he were wise, he would have told McAlbie what he knows and had the murderer locked up."

"Aye, and Tom is said to be a sharp lad. Looks to me like he either plans to continue with Mary's plan and weasel money out of the murderer, or he knows he hasn't a chance against him and has run in fear for his life. Running in fear don't look like Puitt is the culprit either, does it? I mean to say, who'd be afraid of Bertie Puitt or hope to get money from him, for that matter? Not Tom— What is his last name?"

"Gifford, Griffard—something of the sort. No, it doesn't sound like Puitt. It sounds remarkably like Mr. Malton. A footman would know he had little chance of being believed against his master, a peer of the realm. That speaks badly for our justice system," Luten said grimly.

"They have the right idea in America. All people are created equal. Of course, even there I daresay some of them are more equal than others."

Luten smiled derisively. "That's the way of the world."

"You ought to take it up in Parliament."

"Strangely, the most privileged group in the country do not consider it a problem. They're still angry with King John for signing the Magna Carta."

"You mean King George."

"No, I mean King John. He preceded George by a few centuries."

"Ah—history! I've heard of the Magna Carta. A good thing, was it?"

"An excellent document, for its time, but in need of updating."

McAlbie's investigation had moved to Prance's saloon by the time Luten and Coffen returned. Corinne was with them. She had spent a fruitless hour quizzing the servants without discovering a single item of interest. None of them had seen or heard anything suspicious the night before. McAlbie jumped up from his chair when they informed him of Tom's having run off.

"There is our culprit!" he exclaimed gleefully. "Flight is always a sign of guilt. It was her lover, Tom, that Mary was protecting. It was his red livery she saw in the cedars, not a catskin weskit or a blue jacket. She has been taunting him with her knowledge and he murdered her. Foolish chit, if she had come to me— But that is the way with girls." He shook his head and left.

"What a letdown," Prance said. "I was hoping for some more interesting murderer than an upstart footman."

"You've got your wish," Coffen said. "It wasn't Tom. You tell him, Luten. I'd best go after McAlbie and let him know about the horse droppings and the horse that was taken out of the stable at Atwood."

Prance blinked in confusion. Then he lifted the tails of his jacket and perched daintily on the arm of a stuffed chair. "Horse droppings?" he sneered. "That sounds an unusually vulgar sort of clue, even for you, Pattle. The case almost ceases to intrigue me. We have descended from the aristocratic to the servant class to the barnyard in one fell swoop."

"Aye, and you've sunk from a sensible man to an idiot in one swell foop if you think the horse rode itself." On this leveler, Coffen hurried off to catch up with McAlbie.

Prance patted his fingers against his cheek. "A hit. A palpable hit, however badly expressed," he admitted.

Luten explained what he had learned at Atwood. "Tom is in danger. It is vital that we find him before the murderer does," he concluded. "Have you any notion where he would go? Does he have family nearby, or even far away?"

Prance shook his head. "He has no family. Tom comes from the orphanage at Reigate. He may have friends hereabouts. The orphans are usually placed locally, but as to who they would be, I haven't a notion."

"How about Mary?" Corinne asked. "Would her folks know anything?"

"She's a local girl. Her papa is a blacksmith in Heath.

McAlbie will notify the family, if Dolman has not already done so. Not that they'll care. Her family disowned her a few years ago, when she began carrying on with the lads. I daresay it was her reputation that recommended her to Simard. He always had a nose for a wayward chit."

Luten sat, frowning as he listened. He suddenly rose. "I'm going to make some inquiries about Tom, see if anyone in Heath or Lewes has seen him since last night. I'll check the coach stops. If he's wise, he'll have hopped a coach to London. I may go directly to the inquest without returning here first. Dolman tells me Malton plans to invite a few folks to Atwood after for tea. That should be interesting. Do you two plan to attend the inquest?" He directed the question to Corinne.

"I would like to attend Malton's party," she said uncertainly.

After some consideration, Prance said, "I am still sufficiently intrigued to attend the inquest. It is not the sort of place I would like Auntie to go. Why don't you and she go down to Atwood after the inquest is over, Corrie? I'll send my rig up to Granmaison for you."

"All right."

Intercepting a look from Luten, she rose to accompany him to the door. "You think Malton did it?" she asked.

"You are unhappy that suspicion centers on the favored lad, but I fear it is so. Whether Malton or someone else, I feel Tom is in danger. If anyone knows who did this, it is Tom."

"Unless he killed Mary himself," she countered. "He is the logical suspect. He had a motive to kill Simard as well, if he was carrying on with Mary. In fact, doesn't the horse that was taken from Simard's stable rather point to him?"

"Why would he risk discovery by borrowing a nag to ride the short distance to Granmaison? If it were gone, I would suspect Tom, but why would he take it and bring it back if he wanted to run away?"

"He might have taken it in a panic and realized the nag would be recognized."

"He loved Mary enough to kill Simard one day and two days later he kills her?"

"Jealousy can make someone in love do strange and horrid

145

things. Or they may have argued over the money, the hundred pounds."

"And all the hundred pounds to come. No reason to think it would stop at one bleeding. They had both been drinking as well. But whether Tom is the villain or Malton's next victim, he must be found."

She noticed that casual "Malton's next victim" and realized that in Luten's view, Malton was the culprit. Was it jealousy that rushed him to this conclusion?

At the door he stopped and seized her fingers in a crippling grip. "It is a terrible thing to have happened to two young people who were in love, engaged. It makes one realize the uncertainty of life."

She knew he was thinking of their own engagement. "Yes."

He placed a light kiss on her cheek and left.

Chapter Twenty-one

Luten rode north first, as London seemed a likelier destination than the coast for a runaway footman. With the leaden sky promising rain at any moment, he took his closed carriage. Timmy Wayne, one of Prance's grooms who was on friendly terms with Tom, offered to take the southern jaunt. Prance volunteered the use of a whiskey with an oilskin roof over the seat that he used for jauntering about the estate. It was arranged that if Timmy discovered anything, he would immediately drive north and tell Luten.

No one had seen Tom passing on the road north to Lewes, but that was not surprising as it was assumed he had left in the middle of the night. He had not stopped for refreshment or to hire a nag at any of the inns. Luten stopped the few carriages he met, thinking he might hear of a horse being stolen during the night. This was considered a serious offense; it would be known if a horse thief were on the loose. No horses were missing. His hope rested on the coaching house at Lewes, but again he was disappointed. Tom had not bought a ticket for London or anywhere else. Unless Timmy Wayne had learned something, it was beginning to seem that Tom had disappeared into a hole in the ground.

Luten continued his quest for a few miles north of Lewes, but as the hour for the inquest drew near, he decided to head back toward Heath. He met Coffen's rig as it wheeled out of Granmaison. Coffen also saw Luten's rig and yanked on the drawstring. He hopped out and joined Luten, just as the first heavy drops of rain began to fall. His groom, happy to be spared the trip, took Coffen's carriage back to the stable.

"Corinne told me you was out looking for Tom Gifford," Coffen said, shaking the rain from his hat. "Thought I'd give you a hand. I had a word with Timmy, the lad you sent to Heath. Timmy called on Len Halliday—that's Tom's friend from the orphanage. He's kitchen help for the Forresters, at Heath. Len hadn't heard from Tom. Len said that if Tom was in any trouble, he'd have gone to him, his old chum from St. Giles, so it looks like Tom is either dead or has made it safe to London. It'll be like looking for a noodle in a haystack to find him."

"Needle," Luten corrected automatically.

"Aye, he's sharp as a needle, is Tom, according to Timmy. Tom had a little business going on the side. Took bets from the servants on boxing matches and horse races and cockfights and such things. Timmy said he had a bit of money put aside, so I daresay it's London he's headed for."

"I hope his sharpness doesn't get him killed. If he tries to screw more money out of whomever Mary was holding to ransom, I wouldn't give much odds on his life."

"Timmy don't think Tom killed Mary. Crazy for her. Jealous, too, but not a violent sort of lad, despite the size of his shoulders. More likely to pout than punch, according to Timmy."

"I didn't really think Tom was our culprit. An estate and title seem a likelier motive for murder to me."

"Ah, speaking of Atwood, Dolman had something to say about that broken lock. I went back there, took a peek into the study. It ain't the way we left it last night, Luten. Someone else besides us was there, rooting around. It might have been Tom, seeing if he could pick up some cash for his dart to London. That seems the likeliest explanation, eh? I mean to say, he knew the servants had been drinking and weren't likely to hear him, though it seems Betsy Jones did hear something."

Luten cocked a curious eyebrow. Coffen continued.

"Says she heard someone scuffling about in the study around three o'clock this morning when she came downstairs to look for Mary. She didn't like to say so, but I figure she checked Mary's room to see if Tom was with her first. Mary had her own little room under the eaves. They wouldn't be in

Tom's, for he shared with a couple of other footmen. We'll want to have a word with them later. When Betsy saw Mary was gone, she went looking around the house trying to catch the couple in fragrant delect—you know what I mean. Doing the featherbed jig. It's the closest a girl like Betsy would ever come to enjoying that sort of thing."

"Did she look in the study?"

"She did, but she figured they heard her coming. Someone darted out the door as she came in. In the dark, she couldn't see who it was, but she's pretty sure one of them was wearing a skirt. What made her think it might not be Tom and Mary was the broken lock, since they wouldn't have to break it to get in from the hall or to get out. Of course, you and me and the bed-post know who broke it, but I didn't say so. 'Twas her told Dolman about the lock being broken this morning. Kind of odd, though. I'd have thought Mary met whoever she met a lot earlier than three o'clock. More like midnight, which would mean Tom had shabbed off by one or two. Why make the meeting at such an inconvenient hour? You couldn't stay awake that long. You'd have to go to bed and get up in the middle of the night. If all you was after was privacy and the dark, why wait so long?"

"Why indeed?" One could always depend on Pattle for common sense. "But if it wasn't Tom in the study, who was it?"

"That's what I've been trying to figure out. The skirt don't sound like Tom, unless he disguised himself as a girl to escape to London, which he might of done since he was a sharp lad."

Luten winced. He hadn't asked for a strange girl at the coaching house.

"Prance won't like it," Coffen continued, "but it was about three o'clock that Phoebe was missing from her bed. I know she did feed the dogs some bones to shut them up, but that ain't to say she didn't slip down to Atwood as well."

"You're not suggesting she killed Mary?"

"Not really, though she could have, and gone chasing Tom down to Atwood after if he saw her. Phoebe's a big, strong lady and Mary's small. The thing is, Tom wouldn't be afraid of Phoebe, would he? Do you think maybe Tom don't know who killed Mary? He might have arranged with Mary to meet her after she got her hundred pounds, and when she didn't come, he went to the gazebo and saw her dead? Feared he'd be blamed and lit out in a panic?"

"Why would he fear he'd be blamed?" Luten asked. "He loved her. He'd just got engaged to her. And another thing— why was the meeting arranged at the gazebo?"

" 'Twould be convenient for Phoebe, but then, it points straight at her. If she was planning to strangle Mary, she'd have done it at Atwood or thereabouts, away from where she lives. The same for Puitt. He'd not murder someone on his auntie's doorstep. And there's the little brass button. It don't point to any of our suspects. It's a dashed brass herring. Er, red farthing— you know what I mean."

"My money is on Malton. Was he at Atwood today?"

"He came just as I was leaving. I loitered around to learn where he was last night. He says he was at his own little place outside Heath. McAlbie hadn't the wits to ask if anyone could vouch for it, but I expect the servants can. Still, what was to stop him from slipping out in the middle of the night after they were asleep? Them horse droppings tell me it was someone from far enough away that he had to ride to get there. And if he rode his own nag, that don't jibe with the horse taken out of Simard's stable and put back with the saddle still on."

"Tom might have taken the nag for a quick getaway and abandoned it after a few miles. The horse would find its own way back. Mary's murder and Simard's are part and parcel of the same thing. Mary was meeting the murderer. I shall have another word with Mrs. Warner. Let her know the penalty for being an accessory to murder."

"Malton's mount was stabled in Lewes all that afternoon Simard was killed, though."

"There are other mounts in Lewes. He might have borrowed or hired one. We can check the stables for starters. Does Mrs. Warner have a mount herself, I wonder, and where does she stable it?"

"There's an idea."

As they entered Heath, the rain turned violent. It clattered like a drumroll on the carriage roof, and made vision through the windows impossible. At the quaint half-timbered inn where the inquest was to be held, a servant rushed out to meet them with an umbrella large enough for a family. They darted inside and were directed to the assembly room. Prance was there, waiting for them. He wore a black band on his arm in honor of the occasion.

"I was hoping you'd beat the rain. Did you find Tom?" he asked eagerly.

Coffen shook his head, and Luten said, "No, he's vanished."

The bentwood chairs that were placed around the wall for the elderly folks when an assembly was in progress had been arranged in rows in the center of the room. Lady Fairchild and Sidonie were there, along with a clutch of local gossips. Lady Fairchild had got wind of Malton's tea party and had donned a proper bonnet and pelisse. Both were a decade old, but they were obviously of good quality, and designed for a lady. The officials sat at a large table at the far end of the room. The rain pelting against the windows added to the dismal atmosphere. The room was so dark it was necessary to light the chandeliers, as well as a brace of lamps at the official table.

Nothing new or of particular interest was learned. The magistrate brought in a verdict of death by misadventure at the hand of person or persons unknown. The representatives of the Berkeley Brigade hardly listened. Like the rest of the people present, they were more interested to see Mrs. Warner sitting with Malton, both of them heavily swathed in mourning crape. It was the first time she had appeared in public with him.

As the crowd burst into chatter upon hearing the verdict, Prance said, "Do you think Malton means to have his mistress at this tea party?"

"He can't very well send her home," Luten replied.

"It must mean the wedding is imminent!" Prance exclaimed. He was delighted. The rogue in him anticipated a great clamor of indignation. Neighbor set against neighbor as camps pro and con were formed. "What else can account for her mourning duds? The local ladies will have something to say about this!

151

We shan't hear it, though. They won't attend the tea party if she is to pour."

"You couldn't keep them away with a brigade of dragoons," Coffen said, and he was right.

Lady Fairchild stood like a stone statue when Malton went forward to proffer the verbal invitation, but her proud head nodded before he left. He went through the throng with Mrs. Warner a few paces behind him like a monarch's consort as he spoke to the gentry, every one of whom agreed to attend, including Prance and his guests.

"I do hope Phoebe bestirs herself to attend," Prance said. "I would give my favorite diamond cravat pin to see her face when she spots la Warner."

Luten was less eager to see Corinne's face when she met the handsome dame, who he sensed was casting her wicked eyes in his direction, though her black veil made it hard to be certain.

The crowd waited at the inn doorway. Malton and Mrs. Warner were the first to leave. Once they were gone, the remaining crowd felt free to voice their ire. Such phrases as "encroaching creature!" "a common milliner!" and "surely he doesn't plan to marry her!" echoed on every side.

Under the protection of the inn's large umbrella, individuals and couples made a dart to their various carriages as each one was driven up to the door.

Prance, Coffen, and Luten went to Atwood together in Luten's carriage, while Prance's rig was sent off posthaste to Granmaison for Corinne and Phoebe, withholding the wonderful news that Mrs. Warner would be at the party to surprise them.

"What a performance this will be. I feel as if I am on my way to an opening night," Prance said, grinning from ear to ear.

"It ain't night," Coffen pointed out. "It's a matinee performance is what it is."

"Or better, a dress rehearsal, to see how the new leading lady performs in her starring role. Do you know, I think she is not so poorly cast as everyone assumes. She looked quite noble, *n'est-ce pas*?"

Coffen said, "What I would like to know is what she has over Malton to make him do her bidding. He'd not want to turn the whole parish against him before he ever takes over his duties. He ought to have made himself liked first, then he could do as he wished. This way is only asking for trouble."

"It is called love, Pattle," Prance said. "Another word for madness."

"Another word for slyness. I'm beginning to think you're right, Luten. Malton used her nag to bounce back to Atwood and shoot Simard. She's got him dancing to her tune. Does she ride, Prance?"

"Oh yes. Now you mention it, I seem to recall Lady Fairchild, no mean rider herself, saying something about Warner being a tolerable rider."

"Does she own her own mount?" Coffen asked.

"I got that impression."

"Where does she stable it?"

"I am not in the milliner's confidence in such intimate matters, but I have no doubt that you, in your inimitable way, will find out before the afternoon is through, without raising a single iota of suspicion. One never suspects a simple-seeming man of subtlety."

Coffen accepted the compliment with good grace. "There's times it pays to let folks think you're dumb. I fancy this is one of them."

Chapter Twenty-two

The rain had stopped by the time Corinne and Phoebe arrived at Atwood, but the sky had not lightened to blue. The rain-drenched flag atop the roof drooped at half-mast, too wet to flap in the breeze. Many guests from the inquest had already gathered. As the ladies entered the saloon, Corinne was assailed by the funereal atmosphere. At first she attributed the gloom to the fact that Simard lay in state abovestairs with his hired guardians. Or it might have been the small number of guests, who seemed lost in the enormous room, or perhaps it was the quantity of crape in evidence. The conversation was only a dull hum.

As she gazed about the saloon, she realized it did nothing to lighten the atmosphere. While the appointments were splendid, an air of decay hung over the whole. The gold velvet window hangings had deteriorated to bronze from age and sunlight and dust. The gilt of picture frames and furniture—and there was a deal of gilt—had dimmed from lack of attention. Such a room could look either regal or tawdry. The saloon teetered on the verge of the descent. Obviously Simard seldom used this chamber.

The only bright spots amid the crape-laden guests were the footmen, wearing Simard's brilliant scarlet livery. They also wore black armbands and the proper dour faces as they moved through the small throng, passing sherry. Luten spotted Corinne and went forward to greet her.

"Not much of a crowd," she said. "Is it only a sherry party? I thought it was to be a proper tea."

"As it is a tea party and funeral feast combined, I believe Dolman has further treats in store."

Corinne looked around, nodding at Lady Fairchild and Sidonie, until she espied Malton and Mrs. Warner.

"Who is the lovely lady with Malton?" she asked, in all innocence. "Some relative of Simard's, I expect? She has a look of him around the eyes." A closer study showed her the eyes were really not that similar. "Perhaps it's her regal bearing."

Luten felt a warmth rise up his neck. "That's Mrs. Warner," he said, trying for an air of nonchalance.

Corinne's jaw dropped. "The milliner! It can't be! She looks— You don't mean Malton invited his mistress here!"

"So it seems. After all, he does plan to marry her. Not what you expected from the favored lad, eh?"

"I don't know why you call him that!"

"You are always quick to leap to his defense. What have you to say now?" he asked, chewing back a grin.

"I think he must be mad!"

"Certainly rash. It is causing a good deal of comment, though folks have not actually refused to speak to her."

"Oh dear! What should I say when he introduces her?"

"It is nothing to do with us. I would smile and say 'How do you do?' I noticed Lady Fairchild spoke a few chilly words to her, so the milliner has not been sent to Jericho."

"She is very pretty," Corinne said. But as she stared across the room, she knew it was the wrong word. Mrs. Warner was not precisely beautiful, but she was striking and had that much-prized attribute, countenance. It was hard to credit a milliner would have such self-assurance. Mrs. Warner smiled at the vicar with something very like condescension, as though she were already Lady Simard, mistress of Atwood.

Malton, on the other hand, looked tense. Not proud or embarrassed, but wary. Unhappy. Corinne felt in her bones he did not want the woman there. Yet she could hardly be there without his approval.

Coffen beckoned to Luten, who excused himself and left. Mrs. Warner caught Corinne's eye and came striding forward.

155

She extended her hand and took Corinne's in a firm grip, catching her in midcurtsy.

"We have not met, Lady deCoventry, but Lady Fairchild pointed you out to me," Mrs. Warner said in a firm voice. "I am Mrs. Warner. I'm so happy you could come. A sad occasion. We shall all miss the late Lord Simard. He was a great friend of my husband, you must know."

"How do you do," Corinne said politely. Yet she was not fooled that Mrs. Warner was here as the wife of Simard's solicitor and great friend. She was here as Malton's lady.

"You have heard of the other death here at Atwood?" Mrs. Warner said, assuming a sad face. "Only a servant, but a shocking thing. And coming on top of Simard's death."

"Yes, it is too bad," Corinne said.

"And it actually happened at Granmaison, it seems. You must be wishing you had never left London, milady."

"I cannot feel I am in any danger."

"You have plenty of protection at Sir Reginald's house," the lady said with a teasing look. "All those handsome gentlemen!"

The conversation was in some danger of flagging when Luten espied the two ladies together and hastened forward. It did not occur to Corinne to introduce them, as she knew they had met.

"You must be Lord Luten, whom I have heard so much about," Mrs. Warner said, with a mischievous smile at him.

"What a short memory you have, Mrs. Warner," Corinne said stiffly. Why should she be trying to conceal that meeting, unless there had been something improper in it? "You met Luten only two days ago, at your shop in Lewes."

"Say a *convenient* memory." Then she laughed. "Our secret is out, milord. But it was not in my shop, Lady deCoventry. I do not work in the shop. Luten came to my flat. So much cozier." Her bold eyes met Luten's and held them.

"I see you have met my fiancée," Luten said, damping down the urge to strangle the woman. Why had she adopted this flirtatious manner? It almost seemed she was trying to annoy Corinne—and him.

"Fiancée? You did not tell me that, sly rogue! Nor do I see a ring on Lady deCoventry's finger," she added playfully. "Remiss of you, Luten."

"It is I who am remiss," Corinne said coolly. "Luten has given me an engagement ring. The diamond in it is inconveniently large for every day."

"An original complaint!"

"We cannot all be boring, and say the expected thing, Mrs. Warner."

"I am sure no one ever accused you of being boring, Lady deCoventry," she replied, with another of those laughing looks at Luten, as if he made that very complaint every day. "And now you must excuse me. Our guests are all eager to put me under the microscope. Poor me!"

She dropped a careless curtsy and wafted away.

"Bitch!" Prance said admiringly. He had been hovering nearby and overheard the conversation. "Did you catch what she said—'our guests'? She certainly plans to run Atwood— but she was not wearing an engagement ring. Perhaps, like you, Corrie, she finds it too large. I shall have a chat with her and quiz her about it."

He sauntered off with an anticipatory gleam in his eye.

Corinne directed a cold gaze at her fiancé. "I wonder why she felt it necessary to pretend she didn't know you, Luten?"

"I believe Prance's description explains the matter."

"I notice you didn't tell her you were engaged to me either, when you visited her in her flat."

"Mrs. Warner is hardly a bosom bow of mine! I met her exactly once."

"You always were a fast worker," she snapped, and strode angrily away to flirt with Malton, whom everyone forgot to call Lord Simard.

He saw her from across the room and went forward to meet her. As he drew closer, she was struck by how tired he looked, almost haggard. He was too young for time to have left permanent wrinkles, but purple smudges under his eyes suggested a lack of sleep.

"My condolences on this sad occasion," she said, and offered him her hand.

He clung to it a moment. "You are very kind. Thank you for coming. I can't imagine what folks must think."

"This second murder is distressing for you, but you cannot have known Mary well. You must try to keep things in perspective."

She was aware of two things: First, that Malton had not been referring to the second murder. His eyebrows rose slightly in confusion as she spoke. Then she noticed he was staring at Mrs. Warner. It was her presence that he had been regretting.

"Yes, of course." He brushed his hand over his forehead, as if to wipe away his worries, and essayed a wan smile that made him look about twelve years old.

Her heart went out to him. Malton needed a confidante, someone older to confide in. "Or perhaps you were referring to something else?" she asked leadingly.

"I knew you would understand," he said. He seized her fingers and squeezed them tightly. Again his eyes moved across the room to stare at Mrs. Warner with something like loathing. It struck her, looking at his pale, worried face, that Mrs. Warner was worlds too old and experienced for him. This was the face of a troubled youngster, not a murderer, no matter what Luten said.

"Is there anything I can do to help, Malton? That is—I should be calling you Simard."

"No, you call me Malton. Others will call me Simard. That name has too many unhappy associations. I had not realized being a lord involved so many duties. Sinclair has been pestering me to death. The butler and housekeeper the same, and as soon as this do is over, a bunch of politicians will be landing in for the funeral. Tory politicans," he added, "urging me to join their cause. All in vain, of course. My mind is made up. Ah, there is Lord Denfield, a friend of Simard's from the old Hellfire days come to pay his respects. I shan't introduce you to him. Please excuse me. I hope we can talk again soon."

He went off to speak to a dissipated-looking old gentleman.

Chapter Twenty-three

Corinne joined Phoebe and Lady Fairchild and Sidonie, who were having a good gossip about Mrs. Warner. Mary's murder and Tom's disappearance were hardly mentioned at the party. They were eclipsed by gossip of Mrs. Warner and Malton.

"I had a good mind to stay away," Lady Fairchild was saying, "but then, you know, if he is to marry her, there would be no hope of getting any help from Atwood for the local charities if I snubbed the lady of the manor. She is certainly up to all the rigs. She spoke most leadingly of having a public day here to raise money for the orphans. Now, why would she do that if she has not already got one foot in the door?"

"She's sharp as a needle," Phoebe opined. "I overheard her complimenting the vicar's wife on her needlework, saying Malton has told her so much about it, and she would love to see it. Angling for an invitation to the vicarage, you see. She has gone to the trouble of learning all about us and is trying to turn us up sweet."

"You're not to ride out with her if she asks you, Sidonie," Lady Fairchild decreed. "Not yet, until we hear of the engagement," she added, to hedge her bets.

"Is she a good rider?" Corinne asked.

"An excellent horsewoman," Lady Fairchild admitted grudgingly. "I would like to know who bought that showy bay gelding she rides. It would not surprise me if it were Simard. She got it just after her husband's death. Prior to that, she used to hire a nag from the local stable. She has a hunter as well now, and hunts with the pack from Lewes, as I do myself from

159

time to time. Of course, that is hardly a select pack. The local solicitor and half a dozen merchants belong to it."

Corinne began some conversation with Sidonie. When the informal tea was served, the young ladies walked together toward the refreshment parlor, where the tea was to be served. Malton explained that they were dispensing with precedence. A dozen small tables had been set up, to allow folks to sit where they liked, after the fashion of the larger card parties. Sidonie kept looking at Malton and Mrs. Warner in a sad way, as she waited at the door for her turn to enter.

"To think, she will soon have a second husband, and I have not had one," Sidonie said. Then she recalled that her listener was in the same enviable position and added archly, "What is the secret, Lady deCoventry?"

"I fancy playing hard to get has something to do with it. It never pays to let a gentleman know you have designs on him," she replied, hoping to nudge Sidonie into a more successful flirting style.

"Yes, I expect I trotted after him too hard," she said. Tears started in her eyes. She tried to blink them away, but she was not the sort of lady who could control her emotions.

"I didn't realize you and Malton were—"

"Malton? Oh no, I do not mean him." A trickle began to run down her cheek.

Corinne sensed that her moment to learn Sidonie's secrets had come. "Let us leave a moment," she said, and led Sidonie back to the saloon, which was now vacant.

They sat on the sofa. Corinne took her hand and said, "Who was the gentleman . . . ?"

Sidonie's head hung in shame. "It was Simard," she said. "Oh, I know he was a good deal older than I, but I loved him."

To herself Corinne exclaimed, "I knew it!" To Sidonie she said, "My husband was three times my age, and I loved him, too. He was sweet and generous."

"Well, Simard was not exactly like that," Sidonie said, frowning in memory. "He was quite inconsiderate really. He would never call on me or answer my notes. The first time I met him was in his grotto. Mama always told me to stay away from it. It was used for bad purposes some years ago, I believe. Simard had one of those Hellfire Clubs, you know, where they—had women, I believe. Anyway, I wanted to see it. It was not very interesting. Just a cave at the back of his property, surrounded by trees, with a sort of altar thing at the back. There was a statue of Venus and a bunch of cherubs at one end. Vandals had knocked the heads and arms off most of the statues. Or perhaps the woman was not Venus, for she still had one arm.

"He came upon me there and began to tell me about how he and his friends didn't really harm women, they loved them, and appreciated that their bodies were temples of love. Is that not a beautiful thought? He stroked my hand and said I was more beautiful than Venus. He made me feel all soft and warm inside. Desirable. He said if I wanted to come again, he would tell me more stories about his club. So I went, and the second time, he kissed me. And the third time—no, it was the time after that—he . . . took liberties."

Corinne felt a rising anger grow within her at Simard's stunt. How easy it had been for a hardened rake to manipulate a gullible young virgin into seduction. "What sort of liberties?" she asked.

"The sort a man should not take, except with his wife," she said primly.

"What did you do?"

"I—I let him," she said, in a small, fearful voice. "Once he started kissing me and telling me how beautiful I was, I couldn't seem to stop myself, Lady deCoventry. Oh, may I call you Corinne, as we are being so . . . Mama refuses to discuss it. She says I am a wicked, wicked girl, and she does not want to hear any sordid details. She said I should never tell a single soul. She would not even let me tell the vicar, so I just keep it all locked up inside. I think about it all the time, trying to understand how I could have been so wicked. I felt I had to talk it over with some lady of the world, and you seemed sympathetic."

"It helps to talk about it. How long ago was this?"

"Last summer."

Corinne did a quick bit of arithmetic. The question was hard to ask, but she felt it important to know. Because if Sidonie was carrying Simard's child and he refused to marry her, she had just discovered a strong motive for murder. "Are you enceinte?" she asked gently.

Sidonie breathed a great sigh. "No. I thought I was and told Mama, for when I told Simard I was and he would have to marry me, he laughed. I remember he was in the garden, looking at some yellow roses that had black mold. He didn't answer my note or go to the grotto as I asked, so I had to come to Atwood. He just laughed and said prettier and more clever ladies than I had tried to bam him into marriage." An image of Mrs. Warner flashed into Corinne's head. Sidonie's tears were coming in buckets now. "He said a man didn't buy a hen when he could get eggs free, whatever that means!"

"It means Simard was no gentleman. What did your mama say? What did she do?"

"She went to Simard and demanded that he marry me. But he told her I had chased after him and thrown myself on him, and even I was enough temptation to make him lose control. Even I, as if I were an antidote! He hinted that he was not the only man who had had me, and he had grooms and footmen who would say so! It was untrue, of course. He said there was not a judge in the county who would hold him responsible. Oh, I was so ashamed, milady. Mama said it was the same old story—she meant like Phoebe's sister, Cybill, and she would do the same thing Cybill's mama did. Have Phoebe take me to Ireland and pretend I got married there and my husband died. In that way we could keep the baby, you see, and we both wanted to keep it, for I can never get married now, and I would like to have a baby, even Simard's.

"Phoebe said I should hold out and make him marry me, and if the baby was a boy, I would end up at Atwood after Simard died. But then I would have had to live with him in the meanwhile. We didn't know at the time how soon he would be dead. Phoebe said it didn't pay to rush things, for while Cybill was in Ireland, Lady Simard died, you know, and Simard could have been made to marry Cybill after all. Only he didn't, of course. His wife's family was very rich, and he feared they would get back Lady Simard's dowry somehow if he married again so soon and for such a reason. And in a way Phoebe was right, for as it turned out, I was not enceinte after all."

"When did you find out you were not?"

"At the end of September."

Before Simard's murder, then—but there might well have been enough anger to want revenge.

"And now no gentleman will ever marry me," Sidonie said, brushing away her tears. "Sometimes I wish I were dead, milady. I really do."

Corinne squeezed her fingers. Her own eyes were moist with pity. "You must not despise yourself, Sidonie. Ladies past counting have done the same as you. You were more foolish than wicked, and more naive than foolish. It is over. Now you must forgive yourself—and of course, not do it again," she added. "We have an old saying in Ireland. 'It's many a twist life does.' "

Sidonie peered at her in confusion. "What does that mean?"

"It means we never know when things are going to change in ways we could never imagine. You were not enceinte at least. That must be a great relief to you. You will find some gentleman who can love you despite your past mistake."

"I still have my dowry of ten thousand," she said. "And no one knows about my disgrace, now that Simard is dead. At least he didn't tell anyone. There is a rather handsome new doctor in Heath," she said, brightening.

"There is also Mr. Puitt, closer to home," Corinne said leadingly.

"Bertie? Oh, Mama would never let me marry him." She stopped as she remembered her disgrace. "Do you think he likes me?" she asked.

"I noticed him gazing at you this very day," she lied. "Shall we dry your tears and go to the tea room now?"

Sidonie bit her lip. "Mama says it would be better to die a spinster than to lower myself. That was when I stood up with Mr. Allyson, who runs the drapery shop in Heath."

"It is not your mama who will have to live alone for all her life," Corinne said. "I daresay she will feel quite differently when you present her with her first grandchild."

Sidonie smiled at the thought. "Bertie could handle the estate for us. He would seem higher if he were not Reggie's bailiff. He looks quite like a gentleman, don't you think?"

"He behaves a good deal more like one than Lord Simard ever did."

"Would I have to tell him about—you know?"

"That would be only fair. Bertie is not the sort who would cut up stiff."

"And after all, he is only Simard's by-blow, so he would be doing pretty well to get me, even if I am damaged goods. That is what Mama calls me," she said, with a rueful smile.

"So am I, come to that, but I don't think of myself in that way."

"But you were married. It is not the same."

"There is scarcely an undamaged piece of male merchandise on the Marriage Mart."

"Yes, but I'm a lady," she said. No more needed to be added. It was only ladies whose reputations were so easily destroyed.

The talk had done her some good. She drew a hand mirror out of her reticule and examined herself before being led off to the refreshment parlor.

Chapter Twenty-four

Bertie Puitt was astonished to find himself the object of Sidonie's enterprising shyness when she joined him at the table. He had always considered her miles above him. They sat with Luten, Corinne, Coffen, Prance, and the Misses Havergal, two elderly aunts of the late Lady Simard. Simard had kept up a rallying sort of romance/friendship with the pair over the years. Their fortune was said to be exceedingly large. Being spinsters, they had no children to leave their money to. They showed their disdain of Mrs. Warner by refusing to speak to anyone but each other and criticizing the luncheon, which did not prevent them from snabbling down their share of victuals.

"And having the funeral so late!" Miss Havergal declared in a voice that could be heard in the next room. "It ought to have been yesterday, or today at the latest—in daylight. It is macabre, being buried in the dark. What can Malton be thinking of? I daresay it is the custom among milliners."

Her sister, Miss Amelia, replied, "No mention of having the guests back here after the funeral, you noticed. We are being fobbed off with this tea party before the funeral. Malton ought to know better if she does not."

Their conversation did not encourage anyone to linger at the table. As soon as politely possible, the party from Granmaison rose and took leave of their host.

"Don't be a stranger. Do come again," Mrs. Warner said, aiming her words at Luten, but tossing a crumb of a smile to the others as well. Over her shoulder, Malton cast a wan gaze at Corinne, whose heart went out to him.

They left in Luten's carriage, leaving Prance's behind to

deliver Phoebe home. She remained a little longer to gossip with Lady Fairchild.

"Did you speak to the fellows who share a room with Tom?" Luten asked Coffen.

"I did. Tom wasn't in his room when they went up to bed last night. Hadn't been there at all. His bed was still made up this morning. They were pretty well foxed, admitted he might have come in later, but they don't think so. It seems he didn't take anything with him, anyhow. Not even his money. He kept it locked in a strongbox under his bed. He was wearing his livery last night. His other clothes are still there. I can't see him lighting out in scarlet livery if he hoped to hide himself, unless the murderer was hard on his heels."

"It looks bad for Tom," Luten said, frowning.

"You think he's been killed?" Corinne asked.

"I don't know how else to account for his disappearance. He would have made a better plan if he'd meant to kill Mary and run away."

"Tom's not that foolish," Prance said. "Where we shall find him, if we ever do find him, is dead in a ditch or buried in a shallow grave. McAlbie ought to get a pack of hounds out looking for him."

"I had another chat with Betsy about the woman she saw in the study last night," Coffen said, aiming his words at Prance. "About three A.M. in the morning."

"And not three A.M. at night?" Prance asked facetiously.

"No, 'twas in the morning. It only seemed like night because of the darkness."

"That, of course, makes it perfectly clear."

"Was her shawl a light one or dark?" Corinne asked.

Prance took exception at once. "I know what you are implying! It was not Tante Phoebe. She was feeding the hounds."

No one argued, but the look they exchanged spoke volumes.

"Betsy couldn't tell," Coffen said. "It was too dark."

To introduce another suspect, Corinne told them what she had learned from Sidonie. There was no need to tell them the tale was not to go beyond their own circle. They would have

166

been offended had she done so. A gentleman did not carry tales that reflected badly on a lady's honor.

"It could have been Lady Fairchild that Betsy saw leaving the study last night," Prance said at once. "Or Sidonie."

"Why would either of them go searching Simard's study now that he's dead?" Luten asked. "He would hardly have written down anything to do with Sidonie."

"Why would Phoebe have gone?" was Prance's reply to that.

"Whoever was there, it must have something to do with Tom," Coffen said. "He saw whoever killed Mary. Darted back to Atwood for safety. The murderer followed him and killed him—or tried to. It could be that Betsy's nosiness saved his life. The murderer might have got in by the study door, planning to slip up to his room and slice his throat. If she didn't know about the other two lads in his room," he added, as that thought occurred to him.

That heedless "she" infuriated Prance. "I can assure you Phoebe had no idea of the sleeping arrangements of Simard's servants," he replied.

"No more she would. My money is still on Malton."

"Malton doesn't wear a skirt," Corinne pointed out.

"He could have. What's to stop him?" Coffen said.

"Didn't you say whoever was in the study was looking through Simard's papers for something?" she asked.

"His papers were mussed up. Old papers from his cabinet, nothing to do with bills or investments. More like old family documents. That don't indicate Malton. They're his now. He don't have to sneak in after dark and rifle his own papers."

"Mary's murder might not have anything to do with the study being searched," Corinne suggested. "Sidonie wrote to Simard. I believe she wrote a note about her condition, asking him to meet her. She and her mama would certainly want to recover that."

"That makes sense to me!" Prance said at once. "You have got it, Corrie. How clever of you."

Coffen sat deep in thought. After a moment he said, "Or it might have been Mrs. Warner." Three pairs of questioning eyes turned to him. "Love letters. She might have written some as

167

well as Sidonie, since it seems she was carrying on with Simard earlier. She wouldn't want Malton to come across them if they was too hot."

"There is another possibility!" Prance chirped.

Now that Phoebe had been exonerated, so far as Prance was concerned at least, he went on to other items of interest. "I keep wondering why Malton was in such a rush to introduce Mrs. Warner," he said. "She might not know how outré that was, but surely he does. You mentioned he might have borrowed her mount, Luten, and come rushing back to Atwood to shoot Simard. If that is the case, she has him in her power. She could end up strangled next."

"I don't know that this is such a bad time to foist her on the neighbors," Coffen said. "They've got so much else to talk about just now. The murders are a distraction. I think folks'll take to her, in time. She seems pretty ladylike, for a seamstress, I mean."

"Milliner," Prance corrected. "There might be something in what you say. 'If it were done when 'tis done, then 'twere well,' to quote the Bard."

Coffen's brow scrunched into a washboard. "You mean he was wise to do it now and get it over with?"

"Precisely."

"How did the Bard know anything about it?"

"You do know who the Bard is, Coffen?"

"Of course I do. I ain't an ignoramus. It means poet. Poet means Byron. And I agree with him. I was just saying so. As to Warner's being in trade, if she owned a brewery, everyone would think Malton had done well for himself. I don't see that bonnets are any worse than beer. It's all trade."

"It is a question of degree," Prance explained. "Bonnets do not make enough money to gentrify the manufacturer."

"They would if she made enough of them."

"But she doesn't. She has only the one small shop."

Luten turned to Coffen. "Did you discover if Mrs. Warner rides?" he asked.

"I hadn't time. Couldn't one of you have done it?"

168

"She rides," Corinne said, and told what she had learned from Lady Fairchild. "Why is that considered important?"

"Horse droppings," Coffen replied. "Close to the gazebo this morning. Fresh ones."

"But why on earth would Mrs. Warner kill Mary?"

Prance replied, "If Malton borrowed her mount to fly back to Atwood and kill Simard, leaving his own in the stable, while she provides him with an alibi, then she has good reason to abet him, even to the extent of killing Mary, I suppose, if Mary was a threat to his inheritance. Her elevation in society depends totally on Malton, whom we might as well get used to calling Simard."

While Corinne listened, she kept thinking of Malton's haggard face, and the wary way he looked at Mrs. Warner. Almost as if he were afraid of her. Surely he had not murdered Simard? She remembered her conversation with Sidonie, too. During a pause she said, "I keep wondering why Simard didn't marry Sidonie, when he believed she was carrying his child. Lords usually want a son and heir. She is wellborn, she's pretty, and he was old enough that he couldn't be choosy."

After a frowning pause, Luten said, "An interesting point!"

"He was a mean old fellow," Prance said. "He would do it for spite."

"P'raps he wasn't sure he was the papa," Coffen suggested.

"Of course he was sure," Corinne said angrily. "Sidonie is hardly a light-skirt. And she has a dowry of ten thousand besides."

"Ah, now, that could very well be the sticking point!" Prance exclaimed. "Simard had a fiendish appetite for gold, *vide* his courting of the Havergal gargoyles. He probably did plan to marry Sidonie, but he wanted to screw Lady Fairchild up to augmenting the dowry first. She has a sizable fortune that will be Sidonie's when she dies. He wanted to get his hands on it before then, in case Dorothy lands herself another husband. She is still attractive, in her own outlandish way."

"That might be it," Corinne said. "And then before the matter was settled, Sidonie discovered her pregnancy was a false alarm."

169

"Either way, both Lady Fairchild and her daughter had good reason to kill Simard," Prance declared. "The mama might have feared Simard would get after Sidonie again. She is such a widgeon, I wouldn't put it a pace past her to go trotting back to the grotto. Malton also had an excellent reason, of course. If he knew about Sidonie's condition, he would be in a great hurry to finish the old boy off, would he not? Before he married Sidonie, I mean, and produced a son?" He looked around the group. "Have I just been terribly clever?" No one supported this notion.

"Malton wouldn't know about Sidonie's condition," Corinne objected. She was still reluctant to blame Malton.

"Au contraire!" Prance said. "Simard would certainly have told him, to put the fear of the Lord into him. He enjoyed that sort of thing."

"That would explain the hasty and reckless manner of Simard's death," Luten added, with a glinting look at Corinne. He noticed her defense of Malton and resented it. "Malton could have come up with a better plan, given time, one that left no possibility of being discovered."

"Like what?" Coffen asked.

"A shooting accident while Simard was away from the house. Poison in that spare brandy bottle he kept in his drawer. It could never be traced back to Malton."

"But in that way, he might have killed some innocent person besides," Corinne pointed out. "Malton would not do that. Simard did occasionally offer a guest a drink."

Luten's eyebrows arched in annoyance, then drew together in interest. "So he did. I wonder . . ."

Coffen turned and stared at him. "What?"

"I was thinking of that brandy decanter that was shot. McAlbie didn't test the contents. I wonder if it was poisoned."

"That'd be killing one bird with two stones," Coffen objected. "Poison and shooting."

"It would also mean that no one was shooting at Phoebe. In fact, as Simard was already dead and Phoebe was there alone, it might have been done in an effort to prevent her from

170

drinking it. In her state of shock, she might very well have taken some brandy."

They discussed this until they reached Granmaison. Prance's bright and cozy saloon was welcome after the chilly, faded elegance of Atwood.

"Are we having some of that *chanoyu* tea, Prance?" Coffen asked.

"If you wish, Pattle. Truth to tell, the murder in my teahouse has given me a distaste for things Oriental. Why was it chosen for the meeting with Mary, I wonder? Of course, it is 'a fine and private place.' And for all I know, some ones have been there embracing. A love tryst, is what I mean."

"I'd as lief twist in a ditch," Coffen said, reaching for the wine bottle. He was soon ensconced by the grate.

"But a ditch does not have a roof—and the privacy of hedges," Prance pointed out. "I am thinking, of course, of Malton as the man in question." Corinne gave a *tsk* of disagreement. "When I showed him my teahouse the other day when he was here, he made some leering mention of its being a cozy love nest."

"Aye, it keeps coming back to him," Coffen said. "What we must do is get busy and prove it, before he strikes again. Mrs. Warner seems a likely target."

"But how do we do it?" Luten said. He sat on the sofa beside Corinne with his chin resting on his knuckles.

The others waited to hear his plan. But when he spoke, he said only, "We really must discover what the intruder was looking for in Simard's study last night. That, I think, is crucial."

"And so is that brass button," Coffen added.

The others ignored Coffen and looked at Luten in disappointment. Before more was said, Phoebe came bustling in, her eyes open as wide as barn doors.

"It is just as I feared!" she cried. "They've found Tom."

"Alive?" Luten asked, jumping up from the sofa.

"No, dead in a ditch, with a pile of straw and branches tipped over his body. It was the vicar who found him. Actually the vicar's dog."

"Where?" Prance demanded.

"Halfway to Heath, just there where the road bends, by McCormick's place. You know, Prance."

"Thank God it was not on my property!"

Coffen drew a deep sigh. "Well, you got your wish, Prance. You said he'd be found dead in a ditch."

"I did not wish for it! I merely prophesied the possibility. Oh dear, I hope your second sight is not contagious, Corinne. I am all over weak and trembling at the horrid prospect."

"Do they have any idea when it happened?" Luten asked.

"He was stiff as a board, if that is any clue," she said.

"Rigor mortified," Coffen said. "He'd been there since last night, I wager. Halfway to Heath, that is pretty close to Malton's place. I'm surprised Malton didn't take him in some other direction, or at least hide the body better. He's getting reckless. Thinks he can get away with murder, now that he's Lord Simard."

Phoebe's black eyes snapped. "We shall see about that!"

Luten's head turned slowly. He studied her a moment, noticing the gleam of triumph in her dark eyes. Why should Tom's death put her in this mood of restrained joy? Just who, exactly, was getting away with murder?

"I wonder if I might have a word with you, Miss Dauntry. Alone."

Chapter Twenty-five

A fresh murder was enough to get Coffen out of his comfortable chair by the fireside. Prance accompanied him to the ditch where Tom had been found. As Luten was with Miss Dauntry, Corinne elected to remain behind and see what he planned to do. When he joined her a quarter of an hour later, he wore a musing frown.

When he saw her by the fireside, his frown changed to surprise, then slowly to a smile. A tender smile that softened the severe geometry of his lean face and warmed his cool gray eyes. He was fully aware of her annoyance regarding Mrs. Warner and had expected her to be gone. "Ah good, you didn't go haring off with Prance and Pattle."

"No, but I may go haring off with Luten, if he plans to join them."

"I don't, actually. There is something else I must do."

A gleam of interest showed in her green eyes. "Oh, and what is that?"

"I am going to Lewes."

"I'll go with you." Luten opened his mouth and closed it again. "You don't want me to go," she said, not a question but a statement.

He reached down and gave her fingers a squeeze. "It might be best if you stay here, love."

"No need to ask whom you will be calling on, then," she snapped, and withdrew her fingers. She picked up a magazine and opened it.

"Not Mrs. Warner," he said.

She studied him a moment, wondering if it was true. She

knew it was foolish to be jealous. If Luten was visiting Mrs. Warner, it would have to do with the case. She knew it was herself he loved, and wished she could be satisfied with that. It was just that every time he went anywhere without her, he ended up with some attractive lady. She could never get used to the way the English ladies flirted with all the gentlemen who were already engaged or even married. It was not like that in her circle in Ireland. And of course, it didn't help that she felt Luten was miles too good for her and that eventually he would discover it.

"Who else do you know in Lewes?" she asked.

"I don't know anyone, but I have a few names, and a few places of business I plan to visit. It would be tedious for you, my dear. I'll make better time alone. I plan to ride, so I shall be back for dinner."

"As you wish, Luten," she said, and returned to the perusal of her magazine.

Luten mistrusted her meek reply, but he was eager enough to be on his way that he convinced himself she could get into no trouble with Prance and Pattle at the scene of the latest crime to keep an eye on her. Of course, that was where she planned to go, as soon as he was out of the house. Very likely Malton would be there.

"What will you do?" he asked.

"I daresay I can entertain myself for a few hours."

"Don't enjoy yourself too much," he said. On an impulse, he reached down and dropped a kiss on her cheek before leaving. She did not look up, or acknowledge it in any way, but she felt a small glow of pleasure.

The backhouse boy came darting to the stable to order Pattle's team put to while Luten was there, choosing a mount. He decided against Black Satin and rode a less restive nag. A rueful smile tugged at his lips as he rode off. He must be mad, shackling himself to a headstrong Irish hoyden. But he could not even imagine a future without her to drive him insane. If she ever stopped being jealous of him, he would be furious. Was it just his vanity that enjoyed her jealousy, or was it more than that? Until he met her, no lady he loved or admired had cared enough for him to be jealous. Certainly his mama had not cared a groat, except for his physical survival to protect the title and estate.

A small crowd of gawkers gathered by the ditch alerted Prance's coachman to the spot where Tom Gifford had been killed. Half a dozen boys stood together talking and gesturing under the sullen autumn sky with the faded trees drooping sadly. A brisk breeze moved the branches. A few dead leaves twisted to the ground. Mr. McCormick, who lived in the big white frame house nearby, had come down with a few of his servants. Two or three rigs had stopped to allow the occupants to see murder firsthand.

McAlbie's men were just carrying Tom's body to a waiting wagon as Corinne arrived. The body was covered with a gray blanket. As they placed him on the flatbed, one arm jiggled loose and fell into view. Simard's handsome scarlet livery was stained with mud and rotting vegetation. The hand was well shaped and well groomed, as became a noble's footman. Corinne had hardly known Tom Gifford, except by sight, and she had not liked him much. He was one of those cocky, strutting lads, sure of himself, resentful of authority. But he didn't deserve to die in a ditch before his life had really begun. Someone said he was nineteen years old. A mere boy.

Coffen came over to join her.

"How was he killed?" she asked.

"Shot in the back. Old Ned Harper even heard the shot, or a shot at least, around one-thirty this morning. He's McCormick's groom, lives in that little cottage behind the big house. He heard a horse as well, and a boy shout. Thought it was a couple of bucks coming home late, drunk and carousing. They get a bit of that hereabouts. He didn't get out of bed to investigate. It don't really help us much, except it sets the time."

"It corroborates what you already discovered, about the horse droppings at the gazebo. It looks as if it's the same person, I mean. Or another person riding a horse, at least," she finished, knowing this was of little help.

"Aye, Tom must have gone to watch out for Mary. Malton spotted him and followed him."

175

Prance came walking over to join them. "I'm surprised Malton would be so rash as to shoot Tom on a public road like this," he said.

" 'Twas one-thirty in the morning. Not much chance of getting caught," Coffen pointed out.

"Yes, but he could have just halted him, say, 'Stop or I'll fire' or some such thing. Tom would stop. There'd be no escaping for Tom when he was on foot and Malton mounted."

"There's a ditch, though. P'raps Malton's mount couldn't take it," Coffen suggested.

"Rubbish. I would not be frightened of that ditch," Prance said, glancing at it. It was both shallow and narrow, with a few inches of sluggish water after the recent rain. "Malton is a bruising rider, better than I."

As they spoke, Corinne found herself beginning to accept that Malton must be the murderer. Why else was he under Mrs. Warner's thumb? "He had to kill him sooner or later," she said. "It would be awkward to lead him off somewhere more private. Tom was a strong lad. He might have overpowered Malton and escaped."

"When Malton had a gun?" Prance asked. "Only a woman would think of that."

"It's as I said," Coffen decided. "Thinks he can get away with murder, but he'll not. We'll catch him." He turned to Corinne. "Where's Luten? I thought he'd be here."

"He went to Lewes."

"What for?"

"Some mysterious errand. He didn't say what."

"No need to wear that Friday face. He ain't chasing after Warner."

They were interrupted by the arrival of Malton. He came mounted on a blood mare that could obviously leap the ditch where they had found Tom, or one three times its width. He wore a worried frown. Watching him, Corinne wondered if it was fear of being caught that caused it. How could anyone carry such a burden of guilt? How could he meet his friends and acquaintances? Murder should leave some indelible mark on a man. Yet she knew from past experience that murderers

176

looked like anyone else. They murdered and smiled and joked, they ate their dinner, went to the theater, flirted with ladies, and murdered again.

"I came as soon as I could," he said, dismounting. "What a terrible thing! Three murders in as many days. I am half afraid to move into Atwood. Who will be next, I wonder?"

After a curt "Good day" from the gentlemen and a nod from Corinne, Malton was greeted with a speaking silence.

A frown creased his handsome brow. "Don't squint at me like that!" he said. "I didn't do it."

"My dear Simard. No one said you did," Prance replied, but he said it with a sort of half smile that belied the words.

"They may not have said it, but I know what people are thinking, and will soon be saying. Who but myself had a reason to kill Simard? I was nowhere near Atwood when it happened. I was in Lewes and can prove it."

"Mrs. Warner has already done that for you, *n'est-ce pas?*" Prance said.

Malton's lips tightened. His nostrils flared, but he managed to hold his temper in check. "How was Tom killed? I heard he was shot."

"Yes, in the back," Prance informed him. "A cowardly thing to do. We are obviously not looking for a gentleman."

Malton glared, but he did not respond verbally to Prance's taunt. "I'd best speak to McAlbie," he said. He cast one long, hurt look at Corinne, then he turned on his heel to stride away. His back was stiff with anger.

"I was hoping to goad him into some indiscretion," Prance said. "He has himself under remarkable control."

"Either that or he's innocent," Corinne said.

Prance gave her a jeering look. "Too handsome to be a murderer, you mean?"

Coffen gave a *tsk* of disgust. "Handsome is as handsome does."

When Malton tied his mount to a tree, Coffen went forward and examined the horse's shoes. It was a big horse, with hooves and horseshoes to match. He then examined the roadway near where Tom had been shot, but it was so marked

by other horses and carriages and pedestrians that he could discover no identifiable prints. There would be no convenient
button beneath Tom's body. His murderer had not gotten close
enough for Tom to grab a button. Odd about that little brass
button. Betsy Jones hadn't recognized it either, when he
described it to her. There were none like it at Atwood, she had
said. But then, Malton was not living at Atwood yet. He
had spent the night at Greenwood.

As the wagon holding Tom Gifford's mortal remains rolled
away, Malton remounted and rode off, alone and looking
strangely pathetic. Corinne felt a wince of pity for him. The
title and estate he had waited for so long were finally his, but
they could not be bringing the pleasure he had anticipated. No
one had spoken to him except McAlbie and Prance's party. In
both cases, his reception had been extremely chilly. And to add
to his uncertain position, he was being forced to foist his
milliner-mistress on society.

Coffen strolled up to McAlbie. "Someone ought to find
out if one of Malton's nags was out of the stable last night,"
he said.

"I've made inquiries. The groom tells me no one was next or
nigh the place. Malton's nag never left his stall. Of course, the
groom would have been asleep—or is being paid for his
silence. Assuming, of course, that Malton is our lad. Come
to that, he might have used that nag from Simard's stable that
was found with its saddle on this morning. That was Simard's
hacker he was riding just now."

"The one that was out last night?"

"I'm not sure. I'll find out, discreetly. I would not want to set
his jaw against me if he is to get away with it. Lord Simard
wields a pretty big stick hereabouts. He has the mortgage on
half the county."

When Coffen and the others returned to Granmaison,
Coffen went out to the gazebo to examine the hoof marks there
by the tree where he had noticed the droppings. The horseshoes
were a little larger than most, like those on the nag Malton had
been riding that day. Coffen went haring off to Atwood to tell

McAlbie. Horses were like boots. A gentleman found one that suited him, and tended to ride it regularly.

Phoebe was in her room, where she spent most of her time.

"Your aunt seems unsociable this visit, Reg," Corinne mentioned.

"Something is bothering her. It has to do with these murders, of course. She knows something she is not telling me. Perhaps Luten got it out of her before he left. He can be strangely persuasive—but I don't have to tell you that, do I, my pet?"

"He can be uncommonly infuriating," she replied.

Prance drew a deep sigh. "I miss my *chanoyu*, and my Zen, but somehow I cannot bring myself to continue. I require a new outlet for my psychic energies. I have never really looked into Celtic lore in any detailed manner. I ought to do it, now that you and Luten plan to be married in Ireland. Yes, that might rouse me from this lethargy. Come with me to the library, love."

She accompanied him to the library to await Luten's return.

Chapter Twenty-six

Corinne was sitting alone by the grate when Luten returned a few hours later. She had dressed early for dinner, in hopes of a few minutes alone with him while the others were above-stairs. She had taken special pains with her toilette, dressing her hair as he liked, and wearing her bronze taffeta gown. His beaming smile as he looked across the saloon made her heart leap. She went to meet him, expecting he would draw her into his arms, but he just dropped a careless kiss on her cheek and took her hand.

"You look marvelous, as usual," he said.

"What took you so long?"

"I had a few places to go."

He led her to the grate just as Prance and Coffen came downstairs. He had to hear all the details of Tom's death at once. This tale was just completed when Blakeney came to announce dinner.

"Don't bother changing. Come as you are," Prance said, which was a great concession for him. "André will be in the boughs if I let his ragout go dry. Pattle will be wearing his Japanese bootees, so there is no hope of anything but an informal dinner."

"Just the rig," Coffen said, smiling at his comfortable toes, freed from the restraint of leather.

Phoebe recovered from whatever ailed her to join them just as they were going into the dining room. The table, as usual, was lovely. Relieved from the austerity of a single flower for adornment, Prance had placed an enormous cornucopia of autumn's harvest on the board. The cornucopia was of silver ribbons woven to imitate a straw basket. Apples, pears, lemons, oranges, well-scrubbed carrots, parsnips, and leeks tumbled from the silver holder. A collar of vegetable greens edged the container.

"A foolish conceit," he said, looking around for praise. "One would not hazard it in London, but here in the country I like to be surrounded by these rustic reminders of the season. Flowers in spring and summer, nature's edible bounty in autumn, soon to be replaced by holly, fir boughs, and mistletoe as winter rushes at us. The silversmith in Lewes created the cornucopia to my design."

His guests praised his ingenuity. When he had milked the last compliment from them, he said, "Speaking of Lewes, Luten, do you have anything interesting to report? It had best be good or you have put our Corinne's pretty little nose out of joint for nothing."

Luten looked an apology at Corinne, who was glaring at Prance for implying she had missed Luten.

"I visited Mr. Hutchings, Malton's man of business," Luten said. "I believe he mistook me for some aide to the attorney general when I mentioned that Whitehall was taking an interest in the case. Working under that misapprehension, he was quite forthcoming. Malton did not spend the entire afternoon with Mrs. Warner the day Simard was murdered."

"How would Hutchings know that?" Coffen asked.

"It happened Malton was with Hutchings. He could not be certain of the time, but it was early in the afternoon. It is quite possible Malton darted from Lewes to Atwood and shot Simard. The important point is, he was lying—and Mrs. Warner abetted him. She said they were together all afternoon."

"Now we know why he is in such a fever to push her into society!" Prance exclaimed. "She is putting pressure on him."

Coffen considered it while masticating his ragout. "Interestin', Luten, but it don't prove Malton ever left Lewes that afternoon."

"I'm not finished," Luten said. His mischievous smile alerted them to greater revelations. "I called on Lady Fairchild and learned where Mrs. Warner stables her mounts—she has two of them, a hunter and a hacker. I paid the stable a visit this afternoon. She sent word to have her hacker sent to her back door the morning of Simard's murder. Said she wanted to go riding. She did not return it until that evening, so it was there, right at her back door. I went to have a look at the yard. It has a high fence, which would hide from any passerby whether the nag was there or not. There is virtually no traffic in that alleyway, so there was not much risk of Malton being seen leaving. He might have nipped from Hutchings's office—it's only two blocks from her millinery shop—hopped on the mount, ridden to Atwood, and been back within the hour, to be seen by the clerk in the shop as he left. With Mrs. Warner ready to swear he was with her the whole time, he thought his alibi was secure."

"Mrs. Warner would have a lady's saddle," Corinne said. "Did she ask for a man's saddle?"

"No, but she might very well have one at her house. If they worked this out together in advance, providing a man's saddle would be no problem. Her husband probably had one, or Malton could have taken one to Lewes in advance someday when he was driving his carriage. Her hacker could easily take a man's weight." He made a dramatic pause, then announced, "She rides a sturdy bay."

"It was a bay that I saw at Atwood that day!" Phoebe exclaimed. "A man on a bay horse. It was certainly Malton!"

"There is more," Luten said, his eyes dancing. "The reason Malton was visiting his man of business was to raise funds. He had the creditors nipping at his heels. Greenwood mortgaged to the hilt, not a sou in the bank. He was on the verge of losing Greenwood. He was in desperate need of funds."

Coffen brought a slice of mutton to his mouth and lowered it again. "Odd he'd be trying to borrow money the very day he meant to kill Simard. Why draw attention to the fact he was at debt's door?"

"Perhaps it was the visit to Hutchings that pushed him over the edge. He tried his hand at post-obits, but Hutchings refused. It was always possible Simard would marry and have a son before he died. The Sidonie affair leaps to mind. Or Malton might have visited Hutchings to establish an alibi," Luten suggested.

"He already had Warner for his alibi."

"Well, if that alibi failed, he had Hutchings to fall back on. It might be the cleverest move he made. It does seem unlikely he'd try to borrow if he knew he was to inherit a fortune."

"Ergo he did not know," Prance said, nodding.

Coffen had to hear this explained two or three times before he grasped the subtlety of it. "So he made himself look guilty so no one would suspect him," was his final summation.

"That is not exactly the point," Luten said. "By unnecessarily drawing attention to his lack of funds, he gives an aura of innocence, of not knowing he was about to inherit Simard's estate."

Coffen pondered a moment, then said, "That's what I just said."

"Let us quit while we're ahead," Prance suggested. "That still leaves a few loose ends, though, Luten. That female, or person in a skirt in any case, whom Betsy saw last night in Simard's study."

Luten cast a commanding eye on Phoebe. "I believe your aunt has something to say about that."

Phoebe took a sip of wine to give her courage. "That was me," she said, trying for an air of bravado. "I slipped out of bed after dark and went down to Atwood. Bertie went with me. We arranged it earlier. Bertie watched at the window to warn me if anyone came. No one did, until Betsy came landing in on us, not leaving time for us to tidy up after us."

"What was you looking for, Miss Dauntry?" Coffen asked.

"A marriage certificate," she said, and stared around to see the effect of this stunning statement.

Prance, watching her, knew she was in her element once she got going. Tante P, he had always felt, was an actress manquée.

"Whose?" Coffen asked. "Do you think Simard was married? To someone else besides his wife, I mean."

"Someone besides his first wife, yes. I always harbored the hope that he had married Cybill. He could have done, you know, by proxy, for his first wife died three months before Bertie was born. He did write and tell her of his wife's death, and mentioned something about joining her in Ireland. He never did it, of course. The Havergals kept in close touch with him. He could not like to lose their support by marrying so soon after his first wife's death. Cybill kept hoping until the end. She did receive many letters from him. She never showed them to me, and in fact she must have burned them, for I could not find them after her death. He was not such a hard man in those days. I think if he had been able to marry Cybill, he would have turned out quite differently.

"But once she was dead, he took no interest in Bertie. Perhaps he blamed the boy for Cybill's death. And of course, he would have lost the Havergals' sympathy if he ever claimed Bertie for his legal son. He has been buttering up the wealthy Havergal spinsters forever. In any case, that is why I wanted to search the study before Malton got into those old papers. If he came across the marriage license, he would have destroyed it. I did not find anything, however. Well, I found the letters Cybill wrote to him, actually. I have been perusing them today. It is sorry reading, I can tell you. She loved him so, and kept telling him not to worry, and that she still loved him. She told him of our plan to pretend she was married, said she would bring Bertie home with her, and after a year or so, she and Simard could get married. There was no proxy marriage. I am convinced of that now."

She looked at Corinne. "I am sorry I fooled you last night, milady. I saw the light in my room as I came back, and knew someone had seen my empty bed. So I got the bones from the larder and fed the dogs, to give myself an excuse for being out. They were making a dreadful racket. Then I made the cocoa to warm me up. It was chilly outside. Oh, and by the by, Bertie knows nothing of my real reason for going. I only told him I wanted to look for his mama's letters and destroy them. I did not want to get up his hopes, in case it came to naught, as it did."

They discussed the matter until the next course arrived, at which time Coffen said, "Did you hear or see anything on your way to or from Atwood? Anything that might point to whoever killed Mary?"

"No, only the dogs barking. I believe she was already dead. He—we are assuming Malton is our man—would not have stayed at the gazebo if the hounds had been baying like that. He would have taken Mary somewhere else to do the deed."

Luten looked around the table with a triumphant expression.

"I believe that answers all our questions. It satisfies me that the man Mary and Miss Dauntry saw in the cedar hedge was Malton. We know how he got from Lewes to Atwood. We know who the mysterious lady was in the study last night."

After considering the facts, Corinne said, "We don't know who took a shot at Phoebe and broke the brandy decanter." She wondered what charm Luten had used to get all Miss Dauntry's secrets from her, when she had not told Prance, her own nephew.

Luten's smile stretched to a grin. "Miss Dauntry has something to say about that as well."

"That was Dorothy—Lady Fairchild," Miss Dauntry said. "As to why she did such an extraordinary thing, it is as follows. You will not credit it, but that fiend of a Simard had the impertinence to send Sidonie flowers after he learned she was not enceinte. Dorothy realized at once that he intended to continue harassing the girl. She warned him off, but he just laughed in her face. Sidonie had no husband, no father or brother to defend her honor, so Dorothy challenged him to a duel, which he, of course, refused. Really that was foolish of her, but she considers herself quite a gentleman, you know. And a good thing it was that he refused, too, for very likely he would have killed Dorothy, and then where would Sidonie have been? He called her—Dorothy—a silly bitch; she called him a cur. She was livid with rage. 'Distempered dogs ought to be put down,' she said to me when she told me of her visit, 'and Simard is a cur.' I agreed. We discussed his shameful treatment of Bertie as well.

"She took a bottle of arsenic and went to call on him again the afternoon he was murdered, again warning him away from Sidonie. When she got the same response as before, she tipped a bit of arsenic into the brandy decanter. Did it when he was out of the room for a minute, flirting with Mary. She had tethered her mount in the spinney and went on foot to the house, went in by the study door and left the same way so no one would know she had been there. She planned to kill him, but remorse began gnawing at her and halfway home she turned around and went back to tell him what she'd done. In the meanwhile, I paid my visit to Simard and was there when he was shot.

"He was dead by the time Dorothy got back. She saw him

slumped over his desk and thought he'd already drunk the brandy. She saw me there, and feared I would either take a sip of the poison drink or be accused of having killed him, for our friends knew I was at daggers drawn with him over the shameful way he treated Bertie. That is why she shot the brandy bottle, to save my life, and also why she said she had seen Simard alive after I left, so that I would not be blamed for having killed him. When she heard in the village that he had been shot, she thought I had done it because of Bertie, you see, and felt I was justified."

Her story done, she passed her wineglass for a refill. For a long moment the room was silent as her audience absorbed the bizarre tale.

After a moment Coffen said, "She didn't see anyone else when she went back the second time?"

"No, she didn't, she was too preoccupied, as you may imagine. I am not sure she could have seen the cedar hedge from where she was standing, there by the trellis, and in any case, Malton had already left."

"Where was Sidonie while this was going on?" Coffen asked.

"At home. Dorothy did not tell her what she planned to do. She wanted Sidonie kept out of it."

Prance daubed at his eyes. "A moving story," he said. "One is always touched by these tales of fierce maternal love. It is quite Grecian. I have never enjoyed Grecian drama, I am ashamed to say. It does not speak to me, but I shall look into it again. A Sophocles or Euripides would have spilled more blood, offstage, of course. Dorothy, Sidonie, and the rest of them would all end in a bloodbath. William learned that trick of wholesale slaughter from the Greeks, but went them one better by enacting it for the audience."

"Hush up, Reg. You're making my flesh crawl," Phoebe said.

Coffen shook his head. "Tahrsome fellow."

"Sorry," Prance said, "but I felt a change of topic was required to wash the taste of blood from our palates before dessert. I made a singularly poor choice. I apologize."

"I find wine does the trick, even if it is red," Coffen said, and filled his glass.

Prance said, "If all this is true, then what ought we to do

186

about it? It seems to me Malton has gotten away with murder. Thrice." He looked to Luten. "Surely the Berkeley Brigade will not sit still for that?"

"It seems to me we have proved Malton might have done it," Corinne said. "We have not proved he did. I, for one, would not undertake any step to entrap him without more proof."

"Me, too, neither," Coffen added. "It don't explain the little brass button."

Luten's smile stiffened to annoyance. He wondered if Corinne would have leapt to Malton's defense if he were not a handsome fellow. "Malton won't be trapped if he is innocent," he said.

"That sounds as if you have a plan, Luten." Prance said.

"I have been thinking about all this," Luten admitted. "It seems to me a man who has killed three times to inherit money would not stick at killing again—if he feared someone stood in his way." He looked at Corinne and added, "If he is innocent, he won't fall into the trap." Four curious pairs of eyes studied him. "I am thinking of what Phoebe told us, that she thought Simard might have married Cybill by proxy, in which case Bertie would be the heir. I wonder what Malton would do if he thought Phoebe had found the marriage license."

He waited a moment.

It was Prance who said in a fearful whisper, "He'd kill her! You mustn't let him think such a thing, Luten. It would be a death sentence for Aunt Phoebe."

Phoebe said, "No, not for me, Reg. For Bertie. I trust your plan does not actually put Bertie at risk, Luten?"

"Not at all, Miss Dauntry. I am not an amateur after all."

"Yes, you are," Coffen said. "That's exactly what you are. We all are. Nobody's paying us. We do it for fun."

"He has some reason, Luten," Prance said with a laughing eye. "We are amateurs in the true sense, doing it for love of the sport."

"Speak for yourself, Prance," Luten said in his most toplofty tone. "I do it for love of justice."

"That, too," Coffen agreed. "So let us hear your scheme."

Chapter Twenty-seven

When the ladies refused to leave the table while the gentlemen took their port, Prance had to lay down the law.

"Bootees in lieu of proper slippers, even Luten's blue jacket with a whiff of the stable, I can tolerate, but I will not allow ladies to sully the dining room by joining the gentlemen for the taking of port. That ritual is sacrosanct. Next thing we know, they will be wanting a seat in Parliament."

"Then bring your port to the saloon," Phoebe said. "I for one don't plan to be left out of it while you gossoons decide Malton's fate."

Corinne rapped on the table and said, "Here, here."

Faced with a petticoat rebellion, Prance did the gentlemanly thing and asked the footman to carry the port to the saloon.

"Well, what's the scheme?" Coffen asked Luten, when they were all comfortably disposed before the grate and the port poured. The ladies were served Madeira as a punishment for their intransigence.

"Before we begin," he said, turning to Phoebe, "I trust Malton is aware that your sister's marriage to Puitt was a sham?"

"Yes, it was known within a small circle," Phoebe told him. "It was for the neighborhood at large that the story was cooked up, to save the family from disgrace, you know. Simard, the Fairchilds, Malton, McAlbie, and a few others knew the truth."

"Good. Then the first item is to let Malton know of the imaginary proxy marriage to Simard in a manner that will not arouse his suspicions," Luten said.

"No, the first item is to discuss it with Bertie," Phoebe countered, with a martial light in her eye.

"That was remiss of me," Luten agreed at once. "Let us send for him now."

Prance dispatched a footman to invite Bertie to join them. Until he arrived, they discussed again the various doings of that eventful day.

"I had a word with McAlbie," Coffen said. "That nag of Simard's that Malton was riding today ain't the one that was out of the stable last night. 'Twas the black Arabian. The groom says Malton is afraid to mount it. Of course, Malton might be lying. He's a pretty good rider."

"We had decided Tom took the mount and sent it back on its own," Luten reminded him.

"I doubt Tom could manage the Arabian," Prance said.

"No doubt that is why he sent it back," Luten retorted.

"There is no proof Malton was at the gazebo last night," Corinne said, with a cool glance at Luten. She felt he was being rash in trying to trap Malton without certain proof. When she remembered Malton's youth, and the hurt way he had looked at her that afternoon, she could not convince herself he was a murderer. "It would be a horrible thing to tell him he is not to inherit Atwood if he is actually innocent. There is no saying what he will do. Facing bankruptucy, he might kill himself."

Luten scowled. He was sure he was right, but he realized that what he was calling proof was circumstantial.

"There could be a second *kooey bono* lurking in the woodpile," Coffen said. "Who gets Atwood if Malton kills himself or is hung for killing Simard? If that is the plan, Malton will be another victim before it's over."

It was Prance who answered. "Joshua Hillerman, a cousin from Manchester. It was through Hillerman that Warner met Simard. Hillerman and the Warners were friends."

"Will he be a good neighbor?" Phoebe asked.

"I don't know much of the man," Prance replied. "He has some smallish estate near Manchester. Simard, in one of his rare moments of confidence, called him a scoundrel and said he would sooner see Atwood burned to the ground than in the

189

fellow's hands. Called him a Captain Sharp and a few epithets I shan't repeat in mixed company—but then, Simard was apt to exaggerate. It is hard to see how Hillerman can be worse than Simard."

"Is he a married man?" Phoebe asked, thinking of Sidonie.

"Engaged, I believe."

While the others were talking, Corinne spoke to Luten in a quiet aside. "How did you get Miss Dauntry to confide in you, Luten? She never told Reg any of those secrets you weaseled out of her."

He gave her a perfectly charming smile. "You know my way with ladies," he said. When this failed to get a rise out of her, he explained. "It was a bluff. I knew she was hiding something. I told her with a great air of confidence that I knew all about it, without saying what 'it' was, of course, and that we should discuss it to see what could be done to minimize the damage. She was actually eager to confide in someone. Once she began, the story came pouring out in torrents. She couldn't seem to stop. A pity she hadn't found a marriage certificate. Bertie would make a better Lord Simard than Hillerman, from what Prance says."

"Perhaps Malton will be Simard yet."

Luten stiffened. "Why are you so sure he is innocent?"

"I am not sure he is. My doubts are caused by his association with Mrs. Warner. I could swear he is afraid of her. I know, she had him by the nose, but if he has the courage to murder all those other people—and it would take courage, along with a total lack of morals—would he really let a milliner lead him by the nose?"

"He would, if he loved her."

She directed a cool glance at him. "Then he is a good deal more biddable than *some* gentlemen, who claim to be in love but pay no heed to their lady."

"Ah, but we were speaking of weak-minded gentlemen. Would you really have me a reed, bending to your every whim? I think not. You are Irish, and we know your race prefer an argument to anything, except perhaps poteen." He waited, hoping for a bantering reply.

190

When she leveled a haughty glance at him, he changed tack. "Once she provided him with an alibi, he hadn't much choice but to dance to her tune."

"Yes, but she is an accessory. She would have to admit her own part in the scheme if she reported him. I wonder . . ."

"What?"

"It was talking to Sidonie that put the notion in my mind. I wonder if Mrs. Warner is enceinte. That would account for the rush. What a pickle the poor woman is in if she is pregnant. And poor Malton, too."

"Perhaps that is why he has not murdered her as well," he snapped. "Your charity never ceases to amaze me, Countess. You can feel sorry for a brace of murderers, yet you have not shown a jot of pity for any of the victims."

When Luten called her Countess, Corinne knew he was unhappy with her. "Simard got what was coming to him!" she shot back angrily. "He was asking to be murdered. I do feel sorry for Mary and Tom, although if they were protecting the murderer from the law and gouging money out of him for their silence, then they were not entirely innocent either."

Luten's eyes turned as cold as ice. When he spoke, his words came in an angry rush. "Tom didn't deserve to be shot in the back, to die in a ditch like a dog. If Malton commits suicide, it is the best thing that could happen to him. It will save him the disgrace of a trial and save the government the expense of a public hanging."

"But is that entirely fair? No one checked the Fairchild stables, to see if Lady Fairchild's nag was out last night. She tried to murder Simard, so don't tell me she is not capable of it. Perhaps it was the Fairchilds that Mary was meeting last night. That little brass button might very well have been from a lady's riding habit."

Corinne had spoken almost at random, latching on to the only other suspect she could think of. But as she considered Lady Fairchild, other things occurred to her to substantiate the notion.

"In fact, it is possible she was the one lurking behind the cedars, the one who shot Simard. She has a blue riding habit and rides that big bay gelding. She has even been known to wear a man's curled beaver."

"Phoebe explained why Lady Fairchild was there."

"Phoebe told us what Lady Fairchild told her. Who is to say it is true?"

"You are forgetting Malton's prevarications about where he spent that afternoon. He lied."

"He was embarrassed at having to try to borrow money. The fact that Mrs. Warner's horse was at her back door doesn't mean that Malton rode it to Atwood. Your evidence is all circumstantial."

"Circumstantial evidence can be enough. When one sees a fox leaving the chicken coop with feathers in his jaw, one does not assume the fox has been pulling feathers for a new bonnet. Would you be so eager to defend Malton if he were old and ugly?"

"Would you be so determined to convict him if he weren't young and handsome?"

Luten's eyes flashed, his nostrils flared, but when he spoke, he voice was a bored drawl. "As we have sunk to ad hominem arguments, we may as well discontinue this discussion." He turned aside and talked to the others until Bertie arrived.

Bertie had changed into evening clothes and looked quite like a gentleman, although not much like his papa. He had not inherited the dark Simard coloring and good looks. His air of deference robbed him of dignity.

He bowed to the ladies, then said to Prance, "You wanted to see me?"

Prance patted a seat beside him. "Sit down, Puitt, and prepare to hear a strange tale. We are devising a scheme to entrap Malton. You are a strategic part of the plan."

"You figure 'twas Malton who killed Simard?" he asked.

"It looks that way."

"Don't see who else it could be. No one else stood to gain anything."

When Corinne saw the others were in unanimous agreement, she reluctantly accepted that they were probably right. And Luten was probably right, too. She had allowed her feelings for Malton to influence her judgment. She had seen what she imagined was a sweet look of innocence in his face. Perhaps it was a disguise he could don at will to con the ladies. His having had an affair with the dashing Mrs. Warner in the first place did not argue innocence.

Luten outlined what he had learned at Lewes that afternoon. Phoebe explained to Bertie about pretending his mama had been married by proxy to Simard. "Malton knows that the marriage to Puitt was a sham, of course," she said. She made it perfectly clear that the marriage to Simard was also a sham, to prevent his hopes from soaring. She need not have feared. Being a lord was the last thing Puitt wanted.

"I'm glad it ain't so, or Sidonie would make me marry her. Dashed odd girl. I believe she's trying to court me. She sent me a billy doo this evening. Asked me to meet her in her apple orchard tomorrow. I let on I was ailing. Her mama would have my head on a pike if she heard of secret trysts. Holds herself very high, Lady Fairchild."

Corinne felt some vague renewal of her suspicions of Lady Fairchild, and a sense of hopelessness for Sidonie. The lady was incorrigible. What gentleman would not run when he was chased?

"The question is, how do we get the information to Malton without making him suspicious?" Luten said. "I believe the lawyer is the proper vehicle. We shall tell Sinclair a marriage certificate has been found."

"Yes, but where?" Bertie asked. "I have nothing from Simard. He did not leave me a thing except that batch of useless shares in a company that went bankrupt a decade ago."

"But surely it is obvious," Prance said. "The marriage certificate was in the case holding the shares. It is just the devious sort of thing Simard would do, to cause posthumous mischief when he is no longer here to do it in person."

"Pity I burned it," Bertie said. "It wasn't an actual case, you see, just an old yellowed folder."

"You need not take anything to Sinclair when you visit him," Luten said. "Just drop in and tell him—" He stopped. Bertie was too innocent for the job. He would stutter and stammer and end up revealing the fraud. "Write him a note," he said. "I wager he will dart straight off to Malton to tell him."

"Wouldn't he be more likely to dart straight to me?" Bertie asked.

"Not if you are ill," Phoebe said. "You have already told Sidonie you are ailing. She might have broadcast it. That makes an excellent excuse for not going in person on such an important errand."

"Well done, Miss Dauntry!" Luten said.

"I may be a tad slow—well, I know I am," Bertie said, "but how is Malton to get at me to try to kill me if I am sick in my bed?"

"He will find a way," Luten said, with total confidence.

Phoebe stared. "I trust you will find a way to prevent it!"

"No," Luten said blandly. "I have been summoned to London on urgent business at Whitehall." Phoebe opened her lips to object. Before she could speak, Luten continued, "That will account for my absence here while I take Puitt's place in his sickbed at the gatehouse."

"I don't like the sound of this!" Corinne exclaimed. "It is you who will end up dead from a shot through the window or some such thing."

Luten turned a satirical eye on her. "By the innocent Malton?" he asked.

"By whoever the murderer is."

"But only Malton would have any reason to kill Puitt," he said triumphantly.

"Where will Puitt be in the meanwhile?" Coffen asked.

"Why not here, where he will be safe?" Luten said. "Your servants will have to be in on the scheme, Puitt. Are they trustworthy?"

"Oh, aye, I have only a married couple to look after me. The Foleys have been with me for donkey's years."

"Do you agree to this plan?" Luten asked, really as a formality as Puitt seemed eager.

"I feel it my duty to catch whoever killed my papa, even if the old slice never acknowledged me as his son. And your plan is clever as can stare. You are up to all the rigs, Lord Luten. When do I write the note to Sinclair?"

"Now," Luten replied, as he wanted to give Puitt a hand with the wording, "to be delivered immediately."

They went to Prance's study and were gone half an hour. When they returned, the tea tray had arrived. The note, written in Bertie's round, unformed hand, was passed around. When she read it, Corinne assumed Luten had allowed Bertie to use his own words, to lend an air of authenticity. It said:

Dear Mr. Sinclair:

While I was going through the mining stocks Lord Simard left me, I found a marriage certificate. It was dated May 18, 1787, in Gorey, Ireland. The names on it are Simard's and Cybill Dauntry's. It was done by something called proxy. It is certainly a hoax, rigged up by Lord Simard to sully my mama's and my own good name. She was already married to Herbert Puitt. I would appreciate your advice. I trust you will use discretion in this matter. I am abed with a cold, so I am sending you a note instead.

Sincerely,
Herbert Puitt.

"That will put a rocket under Malton. See if it don't," Phoebe declared.

Luten turned to Bertie. "I'll slip into the gatehouse while the others are at the funeral. You come with me and speak to the Foleys. Gather up whatever you'll need and bring it back here. I'll pack a few things and join you in a moment."

When he went abovestairs to make his arrangements, Corinne followed him. They stopped outside his door.

"I don't like this scheme, Luten," she said. "It is perfectly ridiculous. Make sure you don't eat anything. Malton might send you some poisoned food. And for God's sake, stay away from the window. That is the likelier way to get at you, I expect. He'll be lurking outside with a gun. And he is an excellent shot, too. He killed Simard from that cedar hedge, miles away."

195

"Hardly miles."

"You know what I mean."

A smile softened his haughty face. "I hope I do. This sounds remarkably like concern for my safety."

"Of course I am concerned! A new murder every day. How do you think he'll attempt it?"

"Then you do accept that Malton is the culprit?"

"Everyone seems to think so. I daresay he is the most likely one, in any case."

Luten didn't insist on complete capitulation. "I don't think he'll try to kill Puitt. All he needs is the marriage certificate, which is why Puitt asked for discretion. Malton feels sure no one else has seen it. He believes it is at the gatehouse. My hope is that he'll come after it tonight while Puitt is sick in bed."

"That is why you had Bertie write such a strange note. You have an exceedingly devious mind, Luten."

"What options does he have? He's murdered three times. He's not likely to stop at breaking into a house when he believes it will give him what he wants. He can't afford to wait. His creditors are nipping at his heels. He'll come. And then we shall have proof that convinces even you."

He drew her into his arms. "I am convinced," she admitted in a trembling voice. "I'm also frightened. He's sure to carry a gun. When he sees you, he'll shoot."

Gazing into his eyes, she saw the unhappiness there. Luten spoke as if it were a game, but beneath the facade, he felt sorry for all the actors in this ghoulish drama. Perhaps even a little sorrow for Malton. Luten had never known the sting of poverty, of having to wait long years for an uncertain inheritance. His life had been one of privilege, and righting wrongs was his way of repaying society. His major effort was in Parliament, but when such egregious sins as murder occurred within his orbit, he tried to bring some justice about. The dead could not be brought back to life, but the wrongdoer could be made to pay. She felt a panic rising in her. If anything happened to Luten—

"I'll be careful. Best to finish it as quickly as possible, love," he said gently. "There has been too much blood spilt already."

"Yes, you're right."

"And besides," he added, trying for an air of lightness, "we must get busy on our wedding plans."

"It seems the ceremony won't have to occur in a cold garden at least."

"I'm beginning to think we should have gone along with it. We'd be married now."

His head came down to hers. His lips were warm, then hot with desire as he crushed her against him.

Then he went into his room, and Corinne returned belowstairs.

Chapter Twenty-eight

The hired guardians swore an affidavit that the late Lord Simard's corpse did not draw a breath, move a finger, nor display any other signs of life during the length of their vigil. This being the case, his mortal remains were borne to the family vault that evening in a torchlit ceremony with all the pomp and pageantry befitting his station. The full panoply of plumed horses, crape, palls, pinkings, and coats of arms was in sufficient supply to impress the local population, who turned out in numbers to gape at the spectacle. It even impressed the few noble Londoners who wended their way beneath the charcoal sky, past black weeping willows and yews.

The final resting place of the Simards was as grand as their accommodations while living. Even in death, they wallowed in pride and wealth. The family vault was a miniature palace, protected from the common man by an iron fence twelve feet high, with spiked railings. When a raven chose the moment of interment to light on one of the spokes and croak angrily at the mourners, the locals gasped and felt they were observing a miracle. The croak sounded very much like his late lordship in a pelter.

Prance and Coffen attended, "as a mark of respect to the new Lord Simard, whoever he might turn out to be," Prance said. "It is really the position, not the man, one honors in such a case as this. Simard is dead; long live Simard."

They mentioned to Malton that Lord Luten had been summoned to London and had asked them to relay his regrets at not being able to attend.

Ladies were excused from the trial of burial. While it was

going forth, Miss Dauntry sat abovestairs playing a game of spillikins with her nephew to pass the time, and Lady deCoventry had an entirely unexpected visitor. She was sitting alone in the saloon awaiting the gentlemen's return when Blakeney announced, "Mrs. Warner to see you, milady. Are you at home?" His disapproving face suggested he was ready and willing to inform the caller otherwise.

It was the outside of enough for the hussy to call uninvited, but after a moment's hesitation, curiosity overcame reluctance. "Show her in, Blakeney," she said.

Mrs. Warner strode in with her chin high and her shoulders squared. She was not precisely in mourning, but her subdued toilette suggested half mourning. She wore a stylish dove-gray pelisse, and her bonnet had black plumes. The flirtatious tricks she employed around gentlemen were noticeably lacking. She peered around the saloon to ascertain they were alone. Then she rushed forward and sat facing Corinne without waiting to be asked to sit down.

"Lady deCoventry," she said, "you will think it encroaching of me to call on you, but time is short, and with all the gentlemen at the burial, I was sure of finding you alone. I wanted most particularly to ask your opinion on a few matters."

"I will be happy to help, if I can," Corinne replied.

Mrs. Warner made a business of pulling off her fine kid gloves. On the third finger of her left hand rested a large diamond ring, about the size of the one Luten had given Corinne, but a different cut. Corinne's practiced eye noted that all her trappings—bonnet, gloves, reticule, and shoes—were of the best quality and latest fashion.

Mrs. Warner took a deep breath and plunged into her story. "The thing is, Simard and I want to get married. You are a lady of the world, a widow like myself. The provincials hereabouts would be shocked if we married right away, but we do not want to wait. My thinking is that if we go straight up to London after the wedding, they will soon forget it."

"Is there a special reason for this undue haste?" Corinne asked. A quick glance at her caller's slender figure did not confirm the obvious reason that had already occurred to her.

Mrs. Warner's sharp eyes noticed. She gave a knowing chuckle. "Indeed there is, but not the one you think, naughty puss. Simard will be going up to London to open the house and take his seat in the House of Lords. I have, quite frankly, no intention of being left behind. He is an exceedingly handsome, eligible gentleman. Out of sight, out of mind, you know." She wafted her hand, as if swatting away a gnat. The diamond caught a light from the lamp, causing little miniature rainbows to sparkle.

She noticed Corinne looking at it. "Unlike yourself, milady, I do not find ten carats too large to wear. The ring belonged to the late Simard's wife, Lady Anne Havergal. She was the daughter of a duke."

"Very handsome. As your mind appears to be made up, why do you consult me, Mrs. Warner?"

"You move in the first circles. Would it be considered too farouche of us? Malton is also very eager, but he fears the ton would disapprove. I say we should do it and present Society with a fait accompli. The aristocracy always throws a protective mantle over its own. Why, look what went on at Devonshire House for years, practically a ménage à trois. The Tories won't snub us, surely? Simard could be a handsome addition to their cause."

Corinne noticed that Mrs. Warner wasted no time in assigning Malton his title. That was obviously what she was after. The second thing she noticed was that her caller had called Malton a Tory. "Does he mean to join the Tories?" she asked.

Mrs. Warner looked surprised. "The Simards have always been Tories. The late Lord Simard was home secretary in Addington's ministry in 1803. His papa before him was in Lord North's cabinet in the seventies. Without portfolio, but he would certainly have been promoted had he stayed with it. We come from a long succession of prominent politicians and statesmen."

We! It seemed Mrs. Warner already considered herself a Simard. She spoke knowledgeably and proudly and possessively of the family's honors—but she did not appear to know that Malton meant to break with the family tradition. He had said he planned to join the Whig party. Malton was but the means to an end for the hussy.

Her real interest was obviously to secure her place in Society, and she immediately reverted to her original subject. "Of course, we would do the wedding up quietly. May I count on you to befriend us?" She adopted a playful, lady-of-the-world attitude. "I know you and Malton hit it off admirably. I approve of your Luten as well."

Corinne's back stiffened at this piece of impertinence. The milliner "approved"! "My friends are mostly in the other party, Mrs. Warner. It is the Tory hostesses you should speak to," she said coolly.

"But socially the Whigs are top drawer," she replied, again with that galling air of condescension. She appeared to think Lady deCoventry had agreed to support her. "I shall ask Sir Reg to advise me on the wedding. Something quiet and discreet but elegant. It will be Malton's first wedding, and men are such romantics, don't you find?"

"I have not noticed Luten being particularly romantic."

"That is the way when a gentleman takes a lady for granted. Where is he, by the by?" She peered around the room as if he might be hiding behind a chair. "I did not see him in the funeral procession. I peeked from an upstairs window. The Tories sent down a few worthies to butter Malton up."

"Luten has returned to London on business."

"Ah, and the rest of you will be following him after the funeral, I daresay? Will you be leaving tomorrow?" A pair of brightly inquisitive eyes examined her.

"Soon," she said evasively.

"We shall miss you. Society is so thin hereabouts. Only the Fairchilds, and Sidonie, you must know, is hopeless. You knew she had been running after Simard—the late Simard, I mean?"

Now, how on earth did she know that? Malton must have told her. "I am not up on the local gossip, I fear," she said.

"My dear, the place is a seething cauldron of impropriety!

201

We shall get together in London. You can tell me all the fashionable Whig *on dits*, and I shall let you in on the filthy little Tory secrets."

"Would you care for some wine, Mrs. Warner?" Corinne asked. She was eager to be rid of the woman, but felt some offer of refreshment should be made and did not want to wait for tea.

"No, I must be getting back to Atwood. Malton will be expecting me. I am to play the role of hostess. We are serving some light refreshments to the gentlemen who came from London. It should be a proper funeral feast. I think it shabby, Malton's calling that horrid tea party the funeral feast. He ought to have honored the late Lord Simard properly. It was ill done of him."

This speech was accompanied by what appeared a genuine note of anger, perhaps because of the poor impression they would be making on Lord Eldon. She rose and began pulling on her gloves—with some difficulty due to the large diamond.

"It was nice, having a private chat with you. I shall speak to Sir Reg soon about the wedding. One hears he likes to dabble in such things. What an Original he is. I quite adore him."

She adjusted her bonnet, said, "Don't bother seeing me to the door," and left, as if she were an old friend. Encroaching creature!

Corinne sat on alone, mulling over that visit. The woman had the brass of a canal horse. She would bullock poor Malton into marrying her and taking her to London, where she would either ostracize the pair of them with her pushing manner or rule supreme. It was difficult to say what Society would make of her. She was lively and would have a title and fortune behind her. But it was all academic if Malton was guilty. If.

Was the visit for the purpose of instituting a friendship with Corinne? Mrs. Warner must feel she would be out of her depth, mingling with lords and even princes. Very likely that was it. She would require someone to recommend her to the patronesses of the redoubtable Almack's Club, for instance. A mere title was no guarantee of entry into that elite society. No doubt Malton would want to join Brooke's or White's, as well. Luten could be of help there.

Corinne decided to go abovestairs to tell Puitt and Miss Dauntry of the visit. As she went into the hall, she noticed Bertie Puitt's hat and gloves sat on a table. Had Mrs. Warner seen them? One curled beaver was much like another, but the gloves were of inferior quality, not the immaculate York tans Luten or Prance would wear, but perhaps they could be mistaken for Coffen's. Except that both Coffen and Pattle were at Atwood. She shook the vague worry away.

Puitt and Phoebe sat together in Phoebe's room, their heads bent over the table where the spillikin sticks were heaped in a jumble. Bertie looked up.

"What did she want?" he asked. "I saw her from the window."

"Let us hope she didn't see you," Phoebe said, and lifted a stick from the pile.

"I shouldn't think so," Bertie murmured.

Corinne said, "She plans to marry Malton right away and go up to London with him. I believe she wanted me to sponsor her."

"A rare treat for you," Phoebe scoffed.

They chatted a few moments, then Corinne returned belowstairs. The house seemed strangely silent, almost menacing, with no one about but Blakeney, who moved like a ghost through the saloon. He was just drawing the curtains. Beyond the windows, the world looked pitch-black. She asked him to remove Puitt's hat and gloves from the hall table.

It seemed a long time she sat alone in front of the leaping flames thinking about that visit and worrying about Luten. The familiar sense of foreboding was back with her. It was not really a sixth sense or a gift of prophecy. She reminded herself that her worries did not always or even usually materialize. By the time Prance and Coffen returned from the burial, her nerves were frayed.

"What kept you?" she demanded, with an air of pique.

"Malton invited us back to the house for sherry and biscuits,"

Coffen said. "Lord Eldon and a few Tory worthies was there, trying to collar Malton for the party."

Corinne told them of Mrs. Warner's visit.

"I wager Malton sent her," Coffen said. "He wanted to confirm that Luten had left. He don't want Luten to find out about that marriage certificate. He'd know how to authenticate it."

"Yes, she had noticed he wasn't in the funeral party."

"I mentioned it to Malton as well," Prance said.

"Then he'll strike tonight!" Corinne said. "We can't be sure Malton only wants the letter. He might try to kill Luten—er, Puitt. You know what I mean. Much safer for him, in case the secret marriage is discovered. Mrs. Warner asked when the rest of us were leaving. He wants a clear field, you see."

"What did you say?" Coffen asked her.

"I didn't specify a time. Let us go and tell Luten they were sniffing about."

"Best wait," Coffen said. "Malton said he would be calling on Puitt when the Tories left. They were planning to leave soon after us."

"I'm surprised Mrs. Warner did not invite them to stay overnight," Corinne said. "She was eager to get back to meet them."

Coffen's head jerked up. "Warner wasn't there," he said.

"She would be abovestairs, making a grand toilette to impress them," Corinne sniffed, and mentioned the diamond ring.

"She will have missed them if she don't put a wiggle on," Coffen said. "They had some important business in London. They planned to leave soon. About visiting Luten—we don't want to bump into Malton. It would look odd, your being there, Corinne. A lady. Mean to say, you scarcely know Puitt. Malton looked pretty worried at the burial. The solicitor has certainly told him about that marriage certificate."

"Did you not tell him Bertie is sick?"

"The housekeeper has her instructions. She's to say Puitt has just taken a dose of laudanum and might be asleep, but she'll nip upstairs and have a look. Whenever anyone calls, that's what she is to say. Luten figures Malton will have a quick look for the marriage certificate while he has the downstairs to himself. Foley will slip up the servants' stairs, tell Luten. Luten will slip down and catch him dead to rights."

Prance poured wine and handed it around. He had directed Blakeney to put the earthenware cups and teapot away. The sight of them brought back memories too dreadful to entertain. "Rather odd that Malton would announce he means to call on Puitt, *n'est-ce pas*?" he said. "They are hardly bosom bows, and now that Malton is lord of the manor . . . I mean, why display his curiosity to us? I should have thought a polite disinterest would be feigned, to show his lack of concern in Puitt."

"He thinks we don't know about Puitt's letter," Coffen said. "Puitt asked the solicitor to be discreet. Malton plans to get hold of the marriage certificate, burn it, and the thing's done. No one is going to go to Ireland rummaging through church records a quarter of a century old. He'd feel he was safe as a church."

"We don't know he'll do that. He might climb in the bedroom window and shoot Luten!" Corinne said.

Coffen corrugated his brow and peered at her closely. "Are you having one of your premonitions?"

"I don't know," she said. But she knew her anxiety was fast mounting to panic. Fear sat like a giant vulture on her shoulders, flapping its dark, evil wings. "I'm going to see Luten now."

As she rose, there was a knock at the front door.

"Who can that be?" Prance asked. Corinne's fear had permeated them all. He sounded as if it might be Death at the door, summoning one of them.

Blakeney appeared at the doorway. "Lord Simard to see you, Sir Reginald," he said.

Corinne turned bone-white. "Oh my God! He's going to tell us Luten is dead!"

Chapter Twenty-nine

Lord Malton entered tentatively, as if uncertain of his welcome. He glanced all around, bowed to Corinne, and nodded to the others, without smiling. They all stared at him as if he were some wild animal never before seen in a polite saloon. Corinne sat with bated breath waiting for the announcement, yet not really wanting to hear it.

Prance invited him to sit down. "Or did you wish to see me in private?"

"It is no matter," Malton said. "It will hardly be a secret for long." He sat nervously on the edge of a chair, not actually wringing his hands, but somehow giving that impression. Corinne waited on nettles.

"You will be surprised to see me again so soon," he continued into the echoing silence created by the magic word *secret.* "I come on a matter too delicate to discuss in a public place. I walked from Atwood, to give myself time to think. Sorry, I'm afraid I'm messing your carpet."

Prance looked down at his feet, where earth had crumbled onto the carpet. "Don't give it a thought," he said.

The tension began to ease out of Corinne's paralyzed limbs. A man carrying a death message did not apologize for dirt on the carpet. He had come directly from Atwood, his call had nothing to do with Luten. She listened and watched as Malton drew a troubled sigh.

"I'm sorry Luten is not here," he said. "He would know what I should do. The fact is, I had the most extraordinary visit this evening from Simard's solicitor. He had had a note from Puitt mentioning a marriage certificate from Ireland. Decades old. The names on it were Cybill Dauntry and Lord Simard. It was in with those shares Simard left him. Well, the upshot of it is, Bertie Puitt might just possibly be Simard's legal son and heir. Perhaps it's Miss Dauntry I ought to speak to. I hardly know what to do."

Prance frequently performed in amateur theatrical productions. He considered himself quite a seasoned actor, but his reply needed no acting. "But this is astonishing!" he cried. The astonishing thing was that Malton was sharing his secret with them, for, of course, Prance knew about the letter.

"It is!" Malton agreed. "I could scarcely believe my eyes when I read it, but the thing is just possible. Simard's wife did die before Miss Cybill gave birth to Bertie Puitt. The letter mentioned the marriage was done by proxy. I called on Puitt on my way here, hoping to see the certificate for myself, but he is ill, poor fellow. Mrs. Foley has dosed him with laudanum. Have you seen the certificate? Sinclair has not seen it."

"Er, no," Prance said. Malton caught the tone of uncertainty and lifted an eyebrow in question. Prance rushed on to elaborate. "I have heard rumors, Malton. I never paid them any heed. A mare's nest, I always thought. And now you think— just what do you think?"

"I cannot believe Puitt is trying to bam the solicitor, or me, or anyone. He is incapable of such a thing. Naturally I am eager to learn the truth of the matter. If there was a marriage, I am ruined." Then he uttered a bewildered, mirthless laugh. "Ruined!" he said again. "I have been living for years on borrowed money, thinking one day I would inherit Atwood. Oh, it was always possible Simard would sire a legal heir, but frankly, there was not much chance of it. Too much drinking and riotous living. And he was such a mean old buzzard, what mama in her right mind would allow a match with her daughter? Though Lady Fairchild would not have said no, I think, at one time. Something happened to cool that romance. Sidonie is a fool. What do you think, Prance?"

Corinne noticed that Malton was aware of the romance between Simard and Sidonie, though not, she thought, the false pregnancy.

"I hardly know what to say," Prance said, quite truthfully. "Why don't I call Phoebe?"

"Aye," Malton agreed at once. "If anyone knows, she must. She was in Ireland with her sister. But why did she not come forward sooner? Surely it is all a hoax." He looked around the group for encouragement and saw only confusion. A grim expression seized his youthful face. "Just like Simard, to give my tail one last twist from the grave."

Prance darted from the room, his mind reeling. What should he say? What should he do? The plan was not proceeding as it ought. Malton should not be here, asking these unanswerable questions. He should be at the gatehouse, stealing the marriage certificate. It almost sounded as if he were innocent.

Coffen Pattle's mind was not of that quicksilver sort that flashed at once onto a thing, often the wrong thing. He gnawed at a problem like a dog at a bone, but he never lost sight of the main point. Like Prance, he had concluded that Malton must be innocent. Therefore, someone else was guilty. Surely Simard had been murdered to secure the estate. Yet if Malton had not done it, who had? It could only be that fellow who was the next heir after Malton. This line of questioning led him to conclude that Malton was the next victim on the murderer's list.

When Malton rose and began to pace to and fro along the length of the saloon, Coffen turned to Corinne. "That fellow from Manchester," he said in a low voice, "what was his name, the one who stood second in line to Atwood?"

"Joshua Hillerman. Why? What does all this mean, Coffen? Do you think Malton is innocent?"

"It looks like it. Hillerman's our man. No one else stands to gain."

"Mrs. Warner stands to gain," Corinne said. Then she turned quite pale. "Coffen, she was not at Atwood to greet the guests from London. She told me she had to leave early to meet them. Where is she? She must be at the gatehouse!"

"Her and Hillerman, you mean?"

"Or her alone. I don't know. She wants to be Lady Simard. Good God, and Luten might decide to talk to her, to try to convince her to give evidence against Malton. She is his alibi.

208

Luten would never suspect her of murder." She leapt up from the sofa.

Malton turned and looked at her. "I have just remembered something I have to do. For Miss Dauntry," she added, and fled the room.

Coffen was at her heels. "We must warn Luten!" she said.

"If we ain't too late. Mind you, he might just be after the marriage certificate," he said, as they headed to the front door. In Coffen's mind, the unknown Hillerman was their man.

"She'll know this is all a trick when she sees Luten there. I told her he had gone to London. She won't hesitate a moment to shoot him." Blakeney came darting to hold the door for them.

"Tell Prance we've gone to the gatehouse," Coffen said over his shoulder. "Tell him to follow us, and bring a gun." As he and Corinne pelted through the park, he said, "Tahrsome how a fellow never has a gun when he needs one."

She stopped. "We had best go back and get one."

"Puitt will have guns," he said, seizing her hand to hasten her through the park, down to the gatehouse.

A gibbous moon floated in the pewter sky, casting an eerie light on swaying oaks and elms. The dry leaves whispered menacing secrets. When a branch of holly reached out and caught Coffen's sleeve, he gave a whoop of alarm.

"A dashed holly," he said, pulling free. "There's bound to be an owl about somewhere. There's always an owl when you're already frightened to death."

No owl came to frighten him, however. As they ran across the park, the gatehouse came into view. It stood out against the skyline, a squat, dark, unlovely thing that even Prance with all his artistic skills could not beautify. No lights were visible in the upper story, but belowstairs one room was lit.

"What room is that?" Corinne asked, as they drew nearer.

"I was only in the saloon. It faces the road. You'd not see it from here. Thing to do, take a peek in."

"We'll circle the house first."

"Why?"

"So no one sneaks up on us," she said vaguely.

"Keep an ear out for a whinney as well. Atwood is a longish

walk from here, but I doubt you'll find any mount in the stable except Puitt's. Hillerman would have his hidden a bit farther away."

They circled the old stone building, peering in vain behind trees for a mount.

"That's the saloon," Coffen whispered, as they passed two darkened windows facing the road. The window above it threw a patch of pale light on the ground. "That must be the room Luten's in," he added.

They continued the circuit around to the back. The lit window on the ground floor was low enough that Coffen could see in by standing on his tiptoes. He put his nose to the glass.

"Kitchen," he whispered.

"Who's there?"

"No one. Where the deuce are the Foleys? They'd hardly be in bed yet."

"Would they be upstairs with Luten?"

"Both of them?" Coffen asked, frowning. "Foley might be in the stable tending the horses. I'll have a look. Funny there ain't a dog barking. There was last time I was here."

He darted off toward a pitched-roof outbuilding. Corinne stood alone, waiting, listening, straining her eyes and ears for anything that might speak of danger. After a few minutes she decided to have a look in the window for herself. She found a woodpile, chose the biggest block of wood, and carried it to the window. She used the window ledge to steady herself as she climbed on it.

The kitchen looked a cheery place. A fire glowed in the grate, casting leaping lights and shadows over the room. Steam rose from the kettle on the stove. The stove also held pots and pans that gleamed from regular polishing. A small square table sat in the center of the room. It held a few dishes, a teapot, and what looked like another teapot in a white tea cozy. That was odd—two teapots? She looked again, more closely, and saw the wisps of hair protruding from the tea cozy. Then she saw the shoulders attached to it. A strangled gasp caught in her throat.

At that moment she heard footsteps running softly behind her and turned, fully expecting to see the murderer. But it was only Coffen. He reached out and steadied her as she slipped from the block of wood.

"In there," she said, struggling to recover her wits and her breath as she pointed to the window.

"Never mind that," he said. "I've just found Foley. He's in the stable, dead to the world."

"His wife is in the kitchen. Coffen, I think she's . . ."

He peered in the window. "I don't see nothing."

"On the table—a head."

"Good God! He's got her, too."

"You think Hillerman—"

"Or Malton. He could have been here, handled this job, then gone dashing up to Prance's place to act out his Cheltenham tragedy for us, trying to sound innocent. Since he's brought the will into the open, he must know Puitt's already dead."

"We've got to find Luten! He's murdered them all, Coffen! I knew this was a wretched plan."

"Nay, Foley ain't dead. Just drugged, and his missus the same, I fancy. He did it to get at Puitt. Daresay he shot him, then went darting up to Granmaison, letting on he knew nothing of what was afoot here."

"But it wasn't Puitt who was in that bedroom. It was Luten."

"I know that," he said grimly. He lifted his hand. It was holding a fowling piece. "This was beside Foley. He must have taken it with him in case of trouble, when he went to tend the horses. Odd they're both drugged, and the dog as well. They had orders not to touch anything sent from Atwood."

"Come," she said, walking uncertainly toward the back door. "We must find Luten."

Coffen patted her hand. When she looked at him, she saw the pity and sorrow in his eyes. "Best let me go alone, Corrie."

She swallowed down a large lump in her throat and said, "I'm going with you."

The back door opened at a touch of the knob. They stepped cautiously into the cheery kitchen.

Chapter Thirty

They stood a moment, listening. The only sound in the house was the soft hissing of the kettle. As they stood, the water boiled dry and the kettle began to make snapping sounds as it danced on the metal ring. Cofften tiptoed forward and lifted it from the stove to the stone apron of the fireplace.

He bent down and pulled off his boots. Corinne decided her kid slippers were quiet enough. She followed him as he headed from the well-lit kitchen into the hallway beyond. The gatehouse had only a root cellar. The dining room and parlor were on the same floor as the kitchen. They were soon in the saloon. Pale rays of moonlight slanting through the open curtains showed them the outline of sofas, chairs, and tables, and gave enough light to lead them to the staircase. They stood a moment at the bottom with their ears cocked, listening. No sound came from above.

"The stairs are bound to squawk," Coffen whispered.

They were carpeted, however, and as no other means of ascent suggested itself, they began cautiously to mount the stairs. Only three steps squawked, and the noise was muted enough that it would not have reached the bedrooms. At the top of the staircase, they discerned a soft glow of light from an open doorway. A murmur of voices came from the same room. Almost a seductive murmur.

It was the last thing Corinne expected to hear. A moan or a scream would have been less astonishing. And to add to her shock, one of the voices was Luten's. She soon recognized the other as Mrs. Warner's. She stood a moment, so shaken she could not think. When she absorbed what was going on, her heart seemed to stop beating in her chest, then it began a tumultuous pounding that reverberated in her ears like the ocean on a stormy day. As she stood, wondering if she was imagining it all, she heard a light trill of laughter.

Meanwhile, Coffen was creeping along the hallway toward the open door. Corinne, with her head reeling, followed him on stiff legs. Was it possible Luten's insistence on coming here was nothing else but a ruse to meet secretly with Mrs. Warner? No, it couldn't be! Not at a time like this, with a murderer on the loose.

As she drew close to the door, she could distinguish words. Mrs. Warner was speaking in the dulcet tones of a lover.

"What a delightful surprise it was to find you here, Luten," she said. "When you lifted the door of the dark lantern, I fully expected to see Puitt. It's true, Malton asked me to look for the marriage certificate. All a hoax, of course, but he was—shall we say, concerned?"

"You shouldn't allow him to make use of you in that way," he said protectively.

Corinne leaned forward and peered around the edge of the doorjamb.

She saw Mrs. Warner cozily sitting on the side of the bed. Luten sat beside her, with his arm around her shoulders. He was wearing a shirt and trousers, his jacket cast off. Mrs. Warner's fingers began playing with the buttons of his shirt, opening them. She was fully dressed, which was all that saved her from having her hair torn out by Lady deCoventry. That, and the fact that Coffen put his hand on her shoulder and gave it a warning squeeze.

"I know," Mrs. Warner crooned, smiling up at him. "The man is an oaf, but what is a lady to do? We cannot all be as fortunate as Lady deCoventry. And once I get to London, you know, I hope to meet more—*interesting* gentlemen. A married lady has a certain latitude, I believe, or so your fiancée was telling me. We have been laying schemes to fool our husbands once we are settled in Town."

Corinne felt a hot spurt of venom shoot through her. The woman was a witch! How dare she say such things! How dare she try to seduce Luten? And why was he allowing it? Coffen drew her back from the doorway, with his finger to his lips.

"Naughty of you," Luten said approvingly.

"Oh, I can be very naughty, Luten. I can also be nice," she added enticingly. "To begin, you may call me Chloe, as my more *intimate* friends do."

"I am flattered. How did you get past the servants, Chloe?"

"Malton gave me some laudanum to put in their tea. I slipped in the back door and did it while the housekeeper was upstairs with you, and her husband was out in the garden. She had just made a fresh pot. I gave them time to drink it and for the laudanum to take effect. We have an hour without interruption. How shall we pass the time?" The honied tone of her voice suggested the answer.

"Where is Malton? Is he likely to interrupt us?"

"He's waiting for me at Atwood. Don't worry, he'll not want to be seen near the gatehouse."

"Aren't you frightened at the prospect of marrying a murderer? He did murder Simard, I take it?"

"I don't ask questions," she said archly. "You should be less inquisitive and just enjoy the moment."

"What an obliging lady you are!"

Her soft voice, when she answered, was dripping with innuendo. "And how may I oblige *you*, milord?"

Coffen frowned heavily, trying to figure what was going on. Mrs. Warner was lying about Malton. Coffen figured she had come to look for the marriage certificate and been caught red-handed by Luten. She was trying to talk her way out of an embarrassing and dangerous situation. Or act her way out of it by this lovemaking. Luten, of course, was trying to learn what he could from her. The question puzzling Pattle was what he ought to do about it. It seemed a good idea to get Corinne away from the bedroom, yet there was the possibility that Mrs. Warner might turn violent at any moment. She might have a gun or poison the wine. No, he'd have to stay. And meanwhile, what was Hillerman up to?

He drew Corinne away and whispered his fears to her.

"She's going to kill him!" Corinne whispered back. "She's

the one behind it all. And when Luten figures that out, she'll have to kill him."

"That's why he's going along with her. That, and to quiz her, hoping to catch her up in lies."

"What should we do?"

"Keep an eye on them," he said, and tiptoed back to the doorway, holding Corinne behind him to prevent her from seeing things she shouldn't.

As what he saw was Mrs. Warner with both her arms wrapped around Luten's neck, plying him with kisses, he was glad he'd taken the precaution. He still didn't know what to do about it. But when Mrs. Warner removed one arm and slid her hand into her skirt pocket, he made his decision quickly. The hand came out holding a small lady's pistol.

He stepped into the room then, brandishing the cumbersome fowling piece. In the heat of the moment, the words that issued from his lips were, "Stand and deliver!" They were words often heard by him during his various encounters with highwaymen.

Luten's eyes flew to Corinne. For a split second he stared at her like a baited animal, then his face hardened to some wary expression she could not read. Warning, perhaps, or anger, or even fear.

Mrs. Warner released Luten and cast a wary look at Coffen. The lady was made of stern stuff. She soon recovered. When she saw Corinne peering out from behind his shoulder, she gave a cynical smile.

"Lady deCoventry, what a delightful surprise—for all of us," she said. As she spoke, she rose, concealing the pistol in the folds of her gown. Her eyes studied Coffen and the fowling piece.

"Murderess!" Corinne cried. "You killed Simard—and Tom and Mary. I knew it all along."

Mrs. Warner smiled at Luten. "Is she always so excitable, Luten?" she asked, and laughed.

"Leave us, Corinne," Luten said in a voice of deadly calm. "Go and tell Prance to fetch McAlbie."

"She's planning to kill you," Corinne said.

"She has a gun," Coffen added. "Hand it over, Mrs. Warner."

"Come and get it," Mrs. Warner replied. She raised the dainty piece and pointed it at Corinne. "It is small but effective," she boasted. "One of Manton's tube-lock pistols. Simard got it for me at Manton's, and taught me how to shoot it."

Luten pulled his pistol from under his pillow. "You're outnumbered, Mrs. Warner," he said. "Best hand it over."

She just shook her head. "I think not, Luten. It is my trump card. If I go, one of you goes with me. Lady deCoventry, I think. Ladies before gentlemen, you know."

"Let her go and we'll let you leave unharmed," Luten said. "We'll give you an hour to get out of the county."

"To go where?" she asked. "Atwood is my home! I belong there, more than Malton or Hillerman. Simard blood runs in my veins. I would even have settled for Puitt, if he were the heir, and if he were not my half brother."

Luten stared in disbelief. "Are you saying you're Simard's daughter?"

Corinne had less trouble believing it. She had noticed some resemblance to Simard before in the proud beauty. Mrs. Warner had always had some traces of nobility, beneath her bold manner.

"Of course I'm his daughter! He loved my mama. He would have married her, except that she was already married to that ne'er-do-well actor. Why should a Simard have to beg and scrape for a living and kowtow to every ugly old dowager who wants a bonnet? He told me himself that if I were a man, he would have arranged things so that I inherited Atwood. And he could have done it, too. I am the only one of his children he loved. The only with the gumption to do what had to be done."

"To kill him, you mean?" Corinne asked.

Mrs. Warner's face froze. A silence grew and stretched for some seconds, which seemed longer. Then she said in a sad, weary voice, "Ah no, that came later. Much later. I arranged matters so that we could be close. I deeply regretted his death, but what choice did I have? He would have married that milksop Sidonie if I hadn't, and lumbered Atwood with her brat. Atwood belongs to me, and I mean to have it."

"What about Malton?" Coffen asked.

She gave a cold, sneering laugh. "Malton, he's another spineless one. I told him to handle Simard, but all he'd do was wring his hands and whine. He will not be Lord Simard for long," she boasted. "As soon as he is executed for murder, the other heir will assume the title."

"Hillerman?" Coffen asked.

"Who else?"

Corinne, watching her, began to doubt the lady's sanity. There was a maniacal gleam in her eye. Nothing was to be allowed to stand in her way. Not even her own father. She had killed him to prevent his siring another heir, and arranged to lay the blame on Malton. And if he escaped the gallows, he would not last long. He would have a hunting accident, or eat poisoned mushrooms or oysters, to leave the way clear for Hillerman to inherit.

"Do you know Hillerman at all?" Coffen asked.

"Know him? My friendship with him is the reason Warner left Manchester. He wanted to go to London, but I talked him into coming to Lewes instead, so I could be close to Simard. Papa was delighted with my ingenuity. He would have done the same. Papa threw a little business our way. It was enough inducement. My husband was easily led. But when folks began to gossip, Papa felt it time we stop seeing each other on a regular basis. We met less frequently, in private. That is when he spoke to Malton, and suggested to him that he marry me. We were to live at Atwood, but Malton resisted. He knew Simard could not keep Atwood from him. When Simard began speaking of marrying again and producing another heir, Malton proposed marriage to me. But he kept shilly-shallying on the wedding. I feared it was giving Simard a disgust of him. Or perhaps Papa was truly becoming fond of the stupid Sidonie. He was flattered at her interest. Something had to be done."

She looked around, as if she were in command of the situation. "Now, what shall I do with the lot of you?" she asked. "Lady deCoventry, you will escort me belowstairs." She turned to Luten and added, "If I hear the sound of footsteps following us, I shan't hesitate to shoot her."

217

"A bit late for that, Mrs. Warner," Luten pointed out. "You have just confessed to murder in front of three witnesses."

She gave a bland, condescending smile. "Who says so? I have spent the evening at Lewes. My servants will verify it. It is only Malton who stood to gain from Simard's murder." As she spoke, she kept her gun rammed into Corinne's back. She directed her words at Luten, watching him like a hawk, which made it hard for him to outmaneuver her.

He glanced at Corinne, and saw her face was dead white with fear. Coffen stood immobile. The fowling piece would be difficult to aim and fire. And with Coffen, there was no guarantee it was even charged. He had obviously just picked it up in a hurry belowstairs.

Mrs. Warner spoke on. "I was also in Lewes when Mary and Tom were killed. Malton, however, was much closer to hand, and a horse from Atwood stables was used, as an added precaution. It can hardly be proved beyond a reasonable doubt that I killed anyone. The word of a jilted lover and a jealous female"—she smiled snidely from Luten to Corinne—"will not carry much weight in court. You may have Lady deCoventry back when you are ready to hand over to me three billets-doux declaring your undying love and imploring me to marry you, Luten. Do not try to contact me. I shall be in touch with you. Adieu." She pushed the gun harder into Corinne's back. "Walk to the staircase, and no tricks, milady."

Corinne cast one last imploring look at Luten, then stepped into the dark hallway.

Chapter Thirty-one

The instant Mrs. Warner pushed Corinne out the door, Luten stuck his pistol in the waist of his trousers, darted to the window, lifted it, and began to crawl out.

"Follow me," he said to Coffen. "I'll take the back door, you go to the front. They've got to leave one way or the other. Don't let her out of your sight. Shoot if you have to, but for God's sake, don't shoot Corinne."

"You'll bust your leg," Coffen said. "Let me tie up some sheets."

Luten was already dangling by his fingertips. "No time," he said. He peered below, to what looked like miles of air between his feet and the ground. It was no such soft falling as a flower bed or a bush below, but hard-packed earth. He closed his eyes, released his fingers, and dropped. As he hit the ground, a sharp pain exploded in his ankle. It shot up through his leg to settle as a hot lump in the pit of his stomach. Good God, he'd busted his ankle!

While he was writhing in agony, Coffen's head appeared at the window. "Catch this," he called, and dropped the fowling piece. It struck Luten on the arm, not breaking either arm or gun, but causing more pain. Luten rolled aside when he saw a pair of stockinged feet dangle from the window.

"Be careful!" he whispered up, but it was too late.

Within a second, Coffen landed in a lump beside him. He muttered a soft "Ouch!" but rose immediately to his feet. "Get a move on, Luten!" he said irritably.

"I've hurt my leg." Coffen helped him up, but it was obvious Luten couldn't walk. "I'll get you a cane," Coffen said.

Luten looked to the back door. "No, go round to the front. They'd be out the door by now if they were coming this way. Follow them—do—whatever you think best."

"I will. Don't worry. Take care of yourself."

"Take this," Luten said, and handed Coffen his pistol.

Coffen darted around to the front, and Luten, with fear and frustration gnawing at his vitals, looked around for something he could use as a crutch. He kept listening for a shot, a shout, something to tell him what was going on. If anything happened to Corinne . . . And she, with her woman's instinct and Irish insight, had been right all along. Malton was innocent; he did loathe and fear his fiancée, the murderess, Mrs. Warner.

Finding nothing within grasp to help him, Luten crawled on his hands and knees to the gardener's hut, where he snatched up a short-handled shovel and an ax that allowed him to limp, most painfully, toward the front of the house. His ankle was swelling so badly he could feel his boot pressing tightly around it, compressing the swelling.

He had lost track of time. It seemed an eternity of heart-pounding fear and recrimination as he struggled around the house, but his saner self told him it must be only a matter of minutes. If Corinne was killed, her last thought of him would be that he wasn't there to save her. What an ineffectual protector! Her last memory would be of him with Mrs. Warner in his arms. He had seen Corinne and Coffen at the door, but could not acknowledge it without alerting Mrs. Warner. Surely Corinne knew it was only playacting?

In his haste, he struck his left foot against a vegetable marrow that must have tumbled out of the gardener's wheelbarrow, giving his ankle another soul-destroying wrench. He bit his lip to hold in the scream of pain, and tasted blood on his tongue. A wave of nausea rose up inside him, then mercifully the shadows darkened to blackness as he fell to the ground, unconscious. When he opened his eyes, the pain had decreased. How long had he been unconscious? Curses and imprecations were bitten back between clenched teeth. He felt around for his "crutches," picked himself up, took a deep breath, and limped forward, with the shovel handle cutting into his soft underarm, and the ax blade slipping on the earth at every step.

He was just at the corner of the house that would lead him to the front when he heard the shot. He gave a convulsive leap as if the shot had entered his own heart. Then he dropped his makeshift crutches and ran to hold Corinne in his arms one last time before she expired. After one sharp, shooting pain, he didn't even feel his busted ankle.

In the saloon at Atwood, Malton waited impatiently for the return of Sir Reginald to tell him what Miss Dauntry had to say about the marriage certificate. After a hurried colloquy with Bertie and Phoebe abovestairs, Prance returned below, to find Blakeney waiting for his master. The butler's chest was big with news.

"What is it, Blakeney?" he asked.

"Lady deCoventry and Mr. Pattle went flying off to the gatehouse, sir. They requested that you join them as soon as possible—with a gun," he added portentously.

"What! What happened?"

"They did not inform me, sir. They seemed most excited, frightened, I would say."

Prance glanced to the saloon, where Malton was still pacing and running his fingers through his hair.

"Fetch my pistol." As he spoke, he opened the coat cupboard door and took from a peg a cape of black worsted wool with a red lining and a banded neck in lieu of lapels. It was a leftover from a gothic drama two years ago. He had had it fetched down from the attic during his Oriental phase. It seemed the proper attire for a hero, dashing off to save lives.

Blakeney had already taken care of the pistol. He handed Prance the gun he kept in his study desk. "Use your caution, Sir Reginald. The pistol is already charged."

"Excellent fellow. Tell Malton—tell him anything you like, but best not tell him where I have gone. I think he is innocent, but it might be a trick. Ply him with brandy."

"Yes, sir."

"Pray ask André to prepare coffee and something to eat,

Blakeney. I sense the moment of truth is at hand. With luck, we shall soon all be home and ready to celebrate. A bottle—no, two—of the Chambertin."

Blakeney opened the door and Sir Reginald swept out with a flourish of cape, to dart through the night. He enjoyed a frisson of fear as the shadows closed around him and the cool autumn wind blew through his hair. He had forgotten his hat, but no matter. A curled beaver had no place in this romance.

What could have caused Corinne and Pattle to run off so unceremoniously? Obviously they had received some word from Luten. Was he under seige? The request for a gun sounded like it. He would enter the house quietly. He regretted the lack of an audience as he pelted through the night like a hero in a play, his mind working furiously. He winced in dissatisfaction when he beheld in the distance the ugly outline of his gatehouse, which had defied improvement over the years. What he ought to do was tear the thing down and create a new building. Yet its very ugliness seemed appropriate tonight. A fitting place for murder.

As he drew near, he noticed the house was in nearly total darkness. Only the kitchen was lit. Foley should be able to tell him something. When he reached the house, he saw Puitt's old fowling piece on the ground. How did that get there? Had Coffen borrowed it, and been disarmed? This alarming notion disturbed him deeply. Was he going to have to attempt to rescue Coffen, and possibly Corinne as well, from a murderer?

He went to the kitchen window and peered in. His sharp eyes quickly recognized Puitt's housekeeper, with her head sprawled on the table. Dead? Was the murderer in the house even now, slaughtering all in his path? Perhaps the thing to do was to get a ladder, climb up to Luten's room, and peer in the window without entering the house. If Luten was alive and well and unaware of events, they would work together to sort out this lethal muddle. That was when he saw Luten's open window. He went to it and called twice. When he got no answer, he feared the worst.

Really it was an extraordinary situation. What ought he to do? His instinct told him to run home as fast as his legs could carry him—but then if his friends were still alive, he could never look them in the face again. He returned to the kitchen door, opened it, and entered quietly. Peering all about, he saw Pattle's boots on the stone apron of the fireplace. The thing went from bizarre to mad. Why had Coffen removed his boots? The answer came in a flash. Pattle was in the house, hiding somewhere. He had removed his boots to lessen the sound of his footfalls. The fowling piece had nothing to do with it. It had been left there by accident.

Prance was wearing evening slippers. With his light tread, there was no need to remove them. He drew his pistol from his waistband. When his hand stopped trembling, he tiptoed cautiously to the doorway, sweating at every pore, but determined to behave like a man. After all, he was a Prance! In his veins ran the blood of ancestors who had stalked the wild boar with Alfred the Great. Though at times he wondered if it was not, in fact, the blood of his mama's dancing master that flowed within him.

As he approached the parlor, he heard a woman's voice. His surprise was hardly less than Corinne's when she heard Mrs. Warner and Luten flirting abovestairs. It was Mrs. Warner's voice that he heard, speaking in her usual polite way, but with a new cynical edge.

"Oh no, we shall not leave yet, milady. They will be waiting for us outside, one at the front door, one at the back. We shall give them time to think we have escaped. When they are halfway to Atwood, then I shall take you away."

So Luten and Coffen were near at hand. Excellent!

Corinne's voice, when she answered, was tense with strain. She said only, "Where?" but Prance's sensitive heart picked up her agitation. Whatever of manly virtue he possessed was moved at the sound.

"Where you won't be found until I am good and ready."

He stood silent, listening, thinking, scheming. Obviously the hussy had managed to detach Corinne from Luten and Pattle and planned to hold her hostage. The men were out looking for her. He could dart out and try to find Luten. On the other hand, it seemed there were only the two ladies in the house. Surely

223

he was not afraid of Mrs. Warner? It was absurd. Yet if Corinne was not trying to effect her own escape, then the woman must have a weapon.

"I believe it is safe to leave now," Mrs. Warner said. "Stand up. Walk in front of me, and don't try anything. One peep out of you and you will regret it."

He watched as the silhouettes of the two ladies were outlined against the window. They looked elegant, dainty, harmless. But as he looked more closely, he noticed Mrs. Warner held something in her right hand. A pistol, obviously, but a very small one. She probably didn't even know how to shoot it. Under cover of their departure, Prance slipped quietly forward, rather enjoying the drama of the moment. What a shock it would be for Mrs. Warner, his voice coming like a ghost out of the darkness. But no, best not to shock her, or she might accidentally shoot Corinne. A simple knock on the head was the thing. He turned his pistol around in his hand so that he was holding it by the barrel and took the last two steps that put him close enough to strike.

At the last moment, some gentlemanly scruple at striking a lady stayed his hand. He stood with his arm outstretched, vacillating, like Hamlet. He heard a strangled sob, or sigh, issue from Corinne's throat, and overcame his reluctance. He lifted his hand and struck with sufficient force to knock Mrs. Warner unconscious. She fell forward, sending Corinne staggering to the ground. Corinne screamed, thinking she was going to be killed. A strong hand grabbed her wrist. She thought it was Mrs. Warner. When she realized the gun was no longer at her back, she raised the hand holding her wrist and sank her teeth into it. Prance howled. She recognized his voice at once, even in its anguish.

"Prance!" she gasped, and threw herself into his arms. "Be careful! She has a gun!"

Prance spotted it, reached down and picked it up.

"She had a gun," he said. "You must tell me all the wretched details later. But first we must summon Luten and Coffen, who have gone haring off after you. You watch her."

He handed her Mrs. Warner's pistol, then he went to the

front door and strutted out into the night, feeling like the cock of the walk. He raised his own gun and fired off a shot. "That should bring them," he said.

"Prance, what the hell are you doing here?" Luten exclaimed. He had dashed to the front door, expecting to see Corinne dead on the ground.

"Saving your fiancée's life. I have Mrs. Warner unconscious inside. Stubbed your toe, did you? Can you hobble inside? Corinne will want to see you."

"She's alive? She's safe?"

"Safe and sound."

Luten felt as if a lead weight had just fallen from his heart. A golden glow of joy suffused him. In this exalted state, he declared, "Sir Reginald, I love you."

"In a purely platonic spirit, I trust?" Prance said archly. "I am overwhelmed at your enthusiasm, dear boy. All in a night's work. When one's friends call, Prance comes running. I fear I had to disable Mrs. Warner, but then, one begins to sense she is no better than she should be."

"She murdered Simard and the others."

"Good God!" It came to Prance in a flash that it was not merely a woman he had been dealing with, but a murderess. His voice was less cocky when he spoke again. "That explains Malton's visit. Can I give you a hand?" he added, as Luten limped forward, grimacing in pain.

Luten put his arm over Prance's shoulder, and with the shovel under his other arm, he limped into the saloon, to see the outline of his fiancée standing with a gun trembling in her fingers, staring at the floor. Corinne looked up and ran to pitch herself into his arms. He crushed her against him as if he would never let her go.

"My dear!" he said in a hoarse voice. "My darling dear. I feared she would—"

"She would have without blinking. Reggie saved me."

Luten was so overcome with joy that he swallowed this galling speech in good humor and even thanked Prance.

The accidental hero wafted a dainty hand. "*On fait ce qu'on peut.* Should we secure the murderess in some fashion? I would dislike to have to incapacitate her again. I have no taste for violence against women."

He lit a few lamps and looked about for some bindings. The satin cords used to hold back the brocade curtains proved suitable. He tied Mrs. Warner's hands behind her back and left her on the floor. It seemed the best place for her. He noticed from the corner of his eyes that Corinne was fluttering like a moth about Luten, arranging him on the sofa with his injured ankle propped on a footstool. He had not seen this maternal side of her before. Rather touching. Luten was enjoying it, too, to judge by the way his eyes were eating her up.

Prance was just finishing his job when Coffen came limping in, still in his stockinged feet. Burrs, nettles, dead leaves, earth, and what looked like blood covered his stockings. The big toe of his right foot protruded from a hole in the stocking. A shard of green glass was lodged in the toe.

He looked all around and said, "I heard a shot. Anybody else murdered?"

"Nothing so dramatic," Prance replied. "I have captured Mrs. Warner and incapacitated her." He pointed to the body on the floor.

"Ah. I see I've missed the excitement. You got our message, Prance. Good lad. One of us ought to go for McAlbie, eh?"

"And the doctor," Corinne added.

Coffen said, "Aye, I've got a piece of glass in my toe. He'll want to have a look at the Foleys as well. I think they're only drugged, not poisoned. My toe—"

"My wrist!" Prance added, glancing to see whether the skin was broken. It wasn't, but the teeth marks would leave bruises. Rather dashing, really, and not so very painful.

"Luten's ankle is broken!" Corinne announced, as if it were a contest to see who wore more bruises.

"Sorry to hear it," Coffen said. "I daresay this'll delay the wedding another month or two."

"Not on your life!" Luten said firmly.

Coffen sat down and pulled the shard of glass from his toe. A little spurt of blood followed it.

Prance, who was uncomfortable at the sight of blood, turned away. "It looks as if I am elected to go for McAlbie and the sawbones," he said, and drew a dramatic sigh. "No rest for the wicked."

Mrs. Warner was slowly gaining consciousness, but when she realized the game was over, she kept her eyes closed, planning her legal defense. Insanity might do it. She would roll her eyes and let her mouth hang open and answer any questions with witless inanities.

"Don't discuss it until I am back," Prance said. "I don't want to miss a word." Then he left, smiling.

Chapter Thirty-two

Prance's French chef, André, did his master proud. A veritable feast awaited them when they returned to Granmaison. They had all waited at the gatehouse until McAlbie had arrived to take Mrs. Warner into custody, and the doctor to patch up their various wounds. Luten's boot had to be cut from his foot, revealing an angry swelling. His fracture was set in splints. It would require long rest. A massive dose of headache powder had been administered to ease the pain. It left him feeling woozy.

For the nonce, Prance had secured a proper pair of crutches from his attic, and the servants were working on his late uncle's old Bath chair, refurbishing it as a surprise for the invalid. Malton had been sent for to give testimony and returned to Granmaison with them to celebrate. Coffen was back in his comfortable felt bootees. Phoebe and Bertie also came downstairs to share in the revels. Two bottles of Chambertin were not enough. Prance, in a euphoric mood, ordered another three bottles.

They sat about on sofas and chairs, each with a tray on the lap. Luten's ankle was supported by a footstool.

"The dining room is cold, and with so many *invalides*, it would be an unnecessary barbarity to leave the grate," Prance explained. Besides, he wanted to show off the set of carved mahogany picnic trays he had had constructed to his own design, with a pattern of Oriental dragons and lotus blossoms inlaid in lighter wood.

They feasted on oysters and Chambertin, shrimp, Westphalian ham, and three cheeses, followed by a hastily concocted *crème française à l'ananas* and *petits soufflés de pêches*.

"I would never have agreed to marry Chloe had Simard not been ravaging the estate to set monies aside for her," Malton said. "When I agreed, he left the money to me. And there never was any marriage between Simard and your sister, Miss Dauntry?"

"No," Phoebe admitted, with a rueful look at Bertie, who cared not a whit. "It was a ruse to trap the murderer."

Coffen leaned toward Puitt and said in a quiet aside, "You needn't take credit for the blame. Some of the best people are bas—er, illegible, in London. The wrong side of the blanket is all right, as long as your papa's a nobleman. Duke of Clarence has ten of them with Mrs. Jordan. Fact." Bertie nodded.

"The ruse worked," Malton said ruefully. "I showed Mrs. Warner the letter I received from the solicitor. Had it not been for my debts, I would have been happy not to be Simard. It would have rid me of *her*. I liked Chloe at first. She is a handsome woman, but in time I came to loathe her. She was a horrible grasping, climbing creature. And with her papa's streak of cruelty and lasciviousness, but with a feminine guile that could conceal it if she wished."

"Who was her mama?" Coffen asked.

"An actress, a married woman Simard was carrying on with before his wife died. Had a fairly lengthy liaison with her. Initially he took some interest in the child. I think he admired Chloe's brass in contacting him when she was all grown-up."

"Did you never suspect her of the murders?" Luten asked.

"It never entered my head. Simard was her father. She adored him. How could she murder her own papa?"

"They have a name for it," Coffen informed him. "Pattercide, I believe it's called. Isn't that right, Prance?"

"Patricide, actually. Very similar to Pattlecide, is it not? Stop interrupting. Malton is telling us how it all came about."

Malton resumed his speech. Between relief and liberal potations of Prance's Chambertin, he had relaxed from his usual shyness. "I am coming to realize what she really adored was the title. I ought to have suspected, when she was so eager to give me an alibi. I realize now that what she was really after was an alibi for herself. I was not eager to admit I had been trying to get a loan, you see. She said it would give me a good motive for the murder. She would say I had been with her. To tell the truth, I suspected Lady Fairchild—and I would not have lifted a finger to catch her either. If she were Lord Fairchild, Simard would have paid the price for Sidonie's seduction in the Court of Twelve Paces." He gave a conscious start. "That is—"

"We know about Sidonie's affair with Simard," Corinne said. "Why did you not break with Mrs. Warner after his death?"

He gave a shrug. "Gentlemanly scruples. I hoped to delay the wedding until she lost patience and gave me my congé."

"Then, too, she was your alibi," Coffen pointed out.

"That, too," he admitted sheepishly. "And I felt sorry for her. She made a great to-do over the death, you know. Crocodile tears and all the rest of it. I had given Simard my word. I considered it a marriage of convenience. She would make a good hostess in London, and we would find our pleasures elsewhere."

Corinne gave Luten a pointed look. "I was not party to that notion!"

Luten smiled. "That is when I knew for certain she was lying. I was half taken in by her claim that you, Malton, had sent her to look for the marriage certificate." He turned to Corinne. "Since she was there, I tried to discover what she knew."

"When I told her I was coming here to Granmaison this evening, she told me she was going home to Lewes," Malton said. "She could always make things sound plausible. She half convinced me I ought to turn Tory. The Simards have always been Tories—until now," he said, smiling.

"She said her servants would give her an alibi. What is the story with them?" Coffen asked.

"She pays them well, and threatens to turn them off without a character if they disoblige her. Her housekeeper has already been in prison for thieving, so threats of accusing her of theft would also carry weight."

Coffen was gnawing his way through the ham. He cared less for seafood. "So it was Mrs. Warner Mary saw hiding in the cedar bushes, then?"

"Yes." Malton nodded. "She made a dart to Atwood and shot Simard while I was with my man of business—and getting a haircut, which she suggested, to make sure I was gone for some time. She has a blue riding habit. I expect she wore her late husband's curled beaver in case she was seen—as she was. I'm not sure how Mary got in touch with her. A note, perhaps. It was Mary's death warrant. I don't know Tom's part in it, but I fancy he followed Mary to make sure she was safe. Chloe spotted him, followed him, and killed him. Something of the sort."

"It explains one thing that's been bothering me," Coffen said. "The little brass button. Don't tell me Mrs. Warner didn't have 'em on her riding habit."

"She did, Pattle. When I charged her with it, she told me it was a very common sort of button. She said Lady Fairchild had them on her riding habit. The inference was that Lady Fairchild was guilty, you see. She pretended to believe it, as I did myself. Chloe has bottles of buttons at the shop. She just replaced the one Mary tore off, I expect. She rode over from Lewes on her own mount that night, and took Simard's mount from the stable for the actual meeting at the gazebo. Got it out while the grooms were sleeping, and sent it back saddled and unbrushed, to hint that I had ridden it. She was always careful to make me look guilty, so I would need her for an alibi. Or to see me dancing at the end of a rope."

"What about Joshua Hillerman? Was he a part of the plan?" Corinne asked.

"No, no," Malton said. "He is courting an heiress from Manchester. He was carrying on with Mrs. Warner some years ago, but I'm sure he had no notion what she was up to. He's a carefree, spendthrift sort of fellow, but he's no murderer. That great romance was all in her mind. His name only came up when she realized I despised her. I was extremely loath to rush the wedding forward. So inappropriate!"

"Where did she plan to take me tonight, I wonder," Corinne said, shivering to consider her close escape.

"Probably to Lewes. Her female servant would have helped her keep you hidden," Malton replied. "McAlbie has sent a man over to arrest the servant."

Coffen had got the rest of the story from McAlbie. "When Mrs. Warner left Atwood tonight, letting on she was going home, she drove her gig into the bushes and sneaked into the gatehouse to look for the marriage certificate, and to kill Puitt if it looked real. She dumped a sleeping draft into the Foleys' tea, just as she said, except she didn't get it from Malton."

Puitt left early. He had to meet a Gentleman regarding his importing business. After an hour's discussion, Malton left and Phoebe said she was for the tick. The four old friends remained around the dying embers, reminiscing and making plans for the future.

"It's what comes of mixing with Hindoos," Coffen said, with a dark look at Prance. He had imbibed generously. He sat with his bandaged toe held to the grate. "If you hadn't made us come here to see your *china-yo-hoo*, Prance—"

"Chanoyu," Prance corrected, "but I believe you mean my *nina*." He was through with the *Sakuteiki, shibui, niwa, shu-misen*, and all the *ochis*. After his bravery in single-handedly confronting a murderess who had killed three people, he had decided it was, after all, the blood of warriors that flowed in his veins. He wanted to discover what other heroes dangled from the family tree. It should be a fascinating study.

"The only good thing that's come out of it is them felt bootees," Coffen said, wiggling his toes. "You really ought to follow up on that."

"Dare to be different, Pattle. Wear them in London. You might start a new style."

"I shouldn't think so," said Coffen, whose ambitions did not fly so high, nor in that particular direction. "Well, I'm ready for the feather tick," he said, stretching and yawning. "Can we give you a hand upstairs, Luten?"

"You run along. I'll manage," Luten replied.

Prance smirked suggestively. "I daresay it is safe to leave

232

these two lovebirds alone. Luten can't catch Corinne if she doesn't want to be caught, in any case. On the other side, Corrie, now is your chance to land Luten."

"There is no sport in catching a lame fox," she replied. "I always give my prey a fighting chance."

"Excellent! Then I have time to arrange the nuptials properly."

"Bath chair," Coffen said. Prance scowled him into silence. The Bath chair was to be a surprise. "We'll go trundling to church in Bath chairs, is what I meant. I'm not saying you're fixing up your uncle's—"

Prance said hastily, "*We* will go trundling in Bath chairs? Is this to be a *mariage à trois*?"

"No need to get French on us, tahrsome fellow." Coffen pointed at his toe. "I'm lame, too, is what I meant. I'm to be the best man."

Prance just stared. They would see about that! He turned to Luten and Corinne. "I feared this little contretemps would catapult the pair of you into a scrambling, hasty wedding."

"Marry in haste," Coffen said blearily, "resent at leisure."

"Well put," Prance said, and latched his arm through Pattle's to lead him off.

When they were alone, Luten turned to his fiancée. "Well, how about it?" he said. "I'll not be much good at the House for the next few weeks."

"You'll not be much good to me either," she pointed out. "You'll have to stay in bed." As Luten's lips stretched into a grin, she added, "Or rest, in any case. We wouldn't be able to do anything." He lifted his arched eyebrows playfully. "To go anywhere, I mean."

"Precisely. We'll just barricade the door and enjoy our honeymoon in the traditional fashion, in complete privacy."

"I would never live it down. Everyone would say exactly what Prance said, that I'd caught you when you weren't able to run away from me." She looked at him from the corner of her eyes, waiting for him to convince her.

"When have I ever tried to run away from you? Did I not forsake my duty and come scrambling to Granmaison when

233

you left London in a pique? When I thought, tonight, that Mrs. Warner had shot you—" A shudder seized him at the awful memory.

She gazed at him, smiling. "Is that what you thought?"

"Yes. And I was profoundly sorry that we had wasted so much time." His arms crept around her, drawing her against his chest. "Let us not waste any more time, darling."

He wasted not a moment in smothering her in smoldering kisses.

She ran her fingers over his cheeks, where incipient whiskers caused a pleasingly masculine prickle. "Well, I suppose we need not wait until you are completely cured," she allowed.

He seized her fingers and kissed them. "Of course not. It is not my left ankle that is required for the treacle moon. And the rest of me is more than ready, I promise you."

Blakeney caught Prance on the stairs and informed him the Bath chair had been brought down the servants' stairs, polished, the wheels oiled, and a new cover tucked in over the old cushion. Prance quietly tiptoed back downstairs, pushed the chair along toward the doorway into the saloon. When he saw his friends so amiably occupied, he decided to just leave it there.

Ah well, he understood. "Time goes on crutches till love has all its rites," as the omniscient William said. It looked as if the crutches would soon be abandoned. It was not crutches or a Bath chair Luten wanted at the moment, but a bed. Prance went, alone, upstairs, thinking sadly sentimental thoughts of his dear Comtesse Chamaude, until less sentimental ones of Coffen's having been chosen as best man behind his back intruded. Really it was too bad of them, after he had saved Corinne's life.

234

Now available!

ISLAND OF THE SWANS
by Ciji Ware

In this resplendent love story, a dazzling era comes vividly to life as one woman's passionate struggle to follow her heart takes her from the opulent cotillions of Edinburgh to the London court of half-mad King George III . . . from a famed salon teeming with politicians and poets to a picturesque castle on the lush, secluded Island of the Swans . . . an island that can make her dreams come true or break her heart . . .

Published by Fawcett Books.
Available wherever books are sold.